Judy Astley was frequently told off for day-dreaming at her drearily traditional school but has found it to be the ideal training for becoming a writer. There were several false starts to her career: secretary at an all-male Oxford college (sacked for undisclosable reasons), at an airline (decided, after a crash and a hijacking, that she was safer elsewhere) and as a dress designer (quit before anyone noticed she was adapting *Vogue* patterns). She spent some years as a parent and as a painter before sensing that the day was approaching when she'd have to go out and get a Proper Job. With a nagging certainty that she was temperamentally unemployable, and desperate to avoid office coffee, having to wear tights every day and missing out on sunny days on Cornish beaches with her daughters, she wrote her first novel, *Just For The Summer*. She has now had eight novels published by Black Swan.

Also by Judy Astley

JUST FOR THE SUMMER
PLEASANT VICES
SEVEN FOR A SECRET
EVERY GOOD GIRL
THE RIGHT THING
EXCESS BAGGAGE
NO PLACE FOR A MAN

and published by Black Swan

MUDDY WATERS

Judy Astley

BLACK SWAN

MUDDY WATERS
A BLACK SWAN BOOK : 0 552 99630 0

First publication in Great Britain

PRINTING HISTORY
Black Swan edition published 1997

5 7 9 10 8 6

Set in 11/12pt Melior by
Phoenix Typesetting, Ilkley, West Yorkshire.

Black Swan Books are published by Transworld Publishers
61–63 Uxbridge Road, London W5 5SA,
a division of The Random House Group Ltd,
in Australia by Random House Australia (Pty) Ltd,
20 Alfred Street, Milsons Point, Sydney, NSW 2061, Australia,
in New Zealand by Random House New Zealand Ltd,
18 Poland Road, Glenfield, Auckland 10, New Zealand
and in South Africa by Random House (Pty) Ltd,
Endulini, 5a Jubilee Road, Parktown 2193, South Africa.

Printed and bound in Great Britain by
Cox & Wyman Ltd, Reading, Berkshire.

Although the location and characters in this book are entirely fictional, I can't deny being locally inspired. This therefore comes with sympathy and good wishes to all those artists who lost their studios and workshops in the Eel Pie Island fire of November 1996.

Chapter One

'Martin has taken a *tart* to New *York*!'

Stella, holding the phone containing Abigail's shrill anger a little away from her ear immediately pictured a peach flan, neatly parcelled in one of Maison Blanc's pink and white patisserie boxes. She imagined Martin, tall, dark and thoughtful, hesitating before allowing the pretty package to be passed through the X-ray machine at the airport, afraid that it might later irradiate those who were to eat it. In her mind he was swinging it gently and indecisively from its silver ribbon bow, while co-travellers (the female ones anyway) wondered why so attractive a man should look so concerned. Her attention meandered back to Abigail, who could, she thought, at least have started the call with 'Hello Stella, how are you?' after what must have been at least a year (not counting the gilded-Virgin Christmas card) without communication.

'Stella, are you still there?' Stella looked at the phone as if expecting Abigail's skinny body to follow her sharp voice out of it. The Archers theme music, drifting through from the kitchen, sounded quite gently soothing by comparison.

'The tart's got *yellow hair*,' Abigail hissed.

Stella's sympathy was at last hooked and landed. 'Oh goodness, poor you. How completely dreadful.'

She sat down on the window seat and prepared to give Abigail her full attention.

'I don't care what they say about blondes having more fun, she won't be having much of it with *him*, I can tell you,' Abigail told her. 'He's forgotten what it is. At least I thought he had,' Abigail continued, and Stella heard her pause for a deep intake of breath and a Rothman's kingsize.

'Is it serious? Permanent? Do the children know?' Stella wondered if somewhere in a guidebook to modern etiquette there was a list of all the correct things she should be saying. She might be making things worse for all she knew. She could hear Abigail sniffing, which might mean tears, but it wasn't far off summer and she did get hay fever, Stella remembered.

'I don't know.' Abigail's voice sounded smaller, as if having psyched herself up to say the big thing, she'd now run out of energy. It must have taken a lot to admit she'd been *left*. Stella couldn't remember any of Abigail's previous men doing the leaving, that had always been her role. She'd always fancied herself as something of a bolter, like Fanny's mother in *The Pursuit of Love*. After her own mother had met Abigail, Stella remembered her saying, with wary admiration, 'She's a heartbreaker, that one,' as if it was some sort of dubious talent like being able to do the splits or hail cabs by whistling. Stella remembered at the time feeling quite grumpily envious that such a disreputable description was unlikely ever to be applied to her. 'Responsible' and 'conscientious' had been the most used words on all her school reports. 'Flighty' might have been fun occasionally, 'temperamental' even better, but only to be dreamed of.

'He hasn't taken much with him, just the usual business trip clothes and this slut called Fiona. You wouldn't think a "Fiona" would do a thing like this, would you? It's such a good-girl name. Though of course being blond . . . Oh Stella, could I come and stay for a little while? Please? Just till I know what's going on? It's so awful here all alone . . .'

Stella had said yes because that was what you said to your oldest friends when they asked you for help. You didn't stop to think about whether it was a good time to have a visitor to entertain, or how the rest of the family might feel. 'That's how they get to be your oldest friends,' she told her reflection in the driftwood mirror as she paused by the kitchen door on her way out to break the news to Adrian, working down in the summerhouse at the end of the garden. She hoped he'd be pleased. At college the three of them had been such close friends – she and Adrian the settled cosy couple while Abigail's boyfriends came and went from her room next door to Stella's and, Abigail liked to half-boast, were changed almost as often as her knickers. Back in those days, if life could have been compared to a box of chocolates, sex definitely resembled After Eights, with everyone secretly getting through as much as they thought they could get away with and later pretending it wasn't *them*. Sex didn't come, in those days, with government health warnings and the threat of a grizzly death. Stella, who had only enjoyed rampant promiscuity vicariously through the giggled-over Adventures of Abigail, nevertheless felt quite sad that her own teenage children, bombarded with warnings about everything from sexually dreadful diseases to the dangers that might lurk in eggs, beef, tap water and sunshine, didn't even have the option of wild and perilous living.

Stella had met Abigail on the first day of their first college term twenty-five or so years previously. They'd been a pair of awkward new girls, eighteen years old and trying to look nonchalant, waiting to be shown to their rooms in the once grand, but now gently decaying, Queen Anne premises by a volunteer band of mostly male second-year students. Other new students were accompanied by parents who wouldn't leave until they'd made sure their first-time-away-from-home babes had somewhere suitable to settle, somewhere they could picture them cosily making coffee, making friends. Abigail and Stella stood aloof and together linked by their sophisticated independence, scorning the embarrassingly fussing mothers and the tetchy fathers who looked at their watches.

'Bit bloody far from town,' Abigail had grumbled half under her breath, eying with hostility the once grand building's crumbling portico and peeling paint, and cursing the former protectors of young ladies' virtue for siting teacher training establishments just that bit too far from urban temptations.

The second years eyed the newcomers and took their time, loitering with cigarettes and insider gossip. Abigail had tapped her long slim foot and made complaining, what's-keeping-them faces at Stella. Then the two of them were joined by a third lone girl on whom the boys suddenly swooped like ravens on a carcass, bearing away girl and baggage with over-eager speed, leaving both Stella and Abigail open-mouthed and outraged.

'Are we so truly repulsive or something?' Abigail had asked the empty air.

'She's tall and gorgeous and blond,' Stella, small, and roundish had pointed out.

'*I'm* tall!' Abigail had fumed, leaving the 'and gorgeous' unsaid but implied and undeniable.

'That leaves the blond then. It's just because she's blond, that's all. That's all men *see*,' Stella said. She'd looked at Abigail whose shaggy-layered hair was a deep rich red, about the colour of a wet fox, she'd have guessed. Her own was conker-brown, shiny, short and straight and cut, as it still was, in a childlike bob.

'Idiot men fall over themselves for any old dog with yellow hair. They get *everything*. I hate them,' Abigail had stated with considerable venom. She meant blondes, not men. It had quickly become clear that she didn't hate men.

As she thought about what to tell Adrian, Stella noticed that her own hair was looking quite a lot lighter these days. It would never be a youthful, man-snaring yellow of course, not now, but it seemed to be well on its way from its original deep chestnut to an almost golden walnut. Most of this was thanks to Wayne the hairdresser who, just lately, had been tact-fully highlighting with ever-paler streaks.

Becoming more or less blond herself one day, she realized, was not now completely out of the question. Unfortunately I'll be far too old to get the benefit by then, she decided gloomily, not to mention all those women like me and Abigail who would distrust me on sight.

Adrian, in the octagonal summerhouse built onto the riverbank wall, was putting the finishing touches to his day's writing. He closed down the computer with enormous care, murmuring the small procedures out loud just to make sure he'd done them all. He barely trusted either himself or the computer to remember its password from one day to the next. Then he went outside, double-locking the door on the chaos of paper and reference books and abandoned crosswords. The computer was stuffed full of the highly erotic fiction that earned him a comfortable, though uneasy living. Sometimes when he'd written a particularly carnal passage, he wondered why the computer didn't explode, or why a message of indignant moral protest didn't appear on its screen, as if he had his Methodist

11

grandmother reading over his shoulder. The password and the double-locking were left over from when Ruth and Toby were young and inquisitive – now they'd probably not give his works a second glance, on the basis that, when it came to sex, what could an idiot *parent* possibly know? From what he remembered about being a teenager, they could get sexually frantic from just the thought of a word like 'nipple'. They didn't need whole novels full of titillation. Still, something that resembled a wary conscience kept Adrian securely locking the door as if the lustful shameless writings had a nightlife of their own like the undead in a horror movie. He couldn't help feeling the words just might slither out under the door and spread themselves into the sleeping psyches of the other Pansy Island residents, giving them dreams of unspeakable pornography that would haunt their horrified days and send them scurrying to counsellors and therapists. He could imagine Willow, the aging hippy, wondering which aromatherapy oil would be best for soothing away unbidden thoughts of dissipation and sweet young Charlotte, who painted naive street scenes, wondering why she felt a sudden urge to splash her canvases with lurid genital close-ups.

He put the keys in his pocket and sniffed at the air, identifying a roasting chicken wafting down the garden. From the path beyond the hedge he could hear the chatter of eager would-be artists on their way to Bernard's evening life-drawing class at the boathouse gallery. He'd always wondered why, when Bernard himself (quasi-famous artist-in-residence) specialized in nudes of teenage girls, he always gave his pupils a gnarled and shivering pensioner to paint. Probably something to do with light and texture, Adrian supposed charitably. Down below him on the river, a family of mallards had drifted across to the island from the opposite bank and was squawking urgently round old Peggy's houseboat, expecting to be fed that day's food scraps. I wonder if they have a sense of smell, he thought, closing his eyes and breathing in, along with the chicken from his own kitchen, the tempting aroma of Peggy's sausage and beans supper wafting up the barge chimney.

He looks like a badly groomed old gundog, scenting at the air like that, Stella thought affectionately, hesitating by the clump of agapanthus to see if they were intending to send up more than three flower stems that summer. Looking down the garden from the top of the terrace steps she watched him stretch his long limbs and yawn hard as if he'd just reluctantly climbed out of bed rather than finished a day's work. It crossed her mind that perhaps he had actually been sleeping, down there overlooking the river, in his big, cream leather all-ergonomic, pretend-executive chair, snug as a business-class passenger on a corporate freebie. No one would know, at least not until his royalty cheques stopped coming. Adrian liked to be left well alone when he was writing, so interrupting him had become, over the years, a matter of weighing up the urgency. Wandering in to ask whether he'd like plaice or halibut for supper wasn't really on, though Toby had found he was always welcome with the latest cricket scores.

'Adrian, supper's just about ready,' Stella called down to him. He stopped in mid-stretch and smiled up the garden at her.

'I'm starving!' he shouted back, rolling his shoulders to free the tension from them and ambling up to join her. 'I ran out of biscuits.'

'Oh, that's tragic!' she laughed. 'There're plenty in the house; you only have to come in and find them. Anyway, guess what, Abigail phoned. She needs to come and stay, so I said yes. You don't mind do you?'

She said this with the kind of voice that expected an acquiescent response, but to make sure followed up with, 'It'll be nice to see her again, won't it? It's been ages.' She didn't want to watch Adrian's face, just in case it registered '*Oh God, not her*', so she bent to examine the agapanthus more closely. The innermost leaves, deep in the plant waiting to be pushed up, bulged promisingly. There would be clouds of fat blue flower heads in August then, she thought with satisfaction, trying to recall where she'd read some know-it-all expert claiming with years of unobservant authority that they wouldn't grow anywhere north of Dorset.

Adrian, when she looked at him, was frowning thoughtfully. 'We haven't heard from Abigail in ages. Why does she *need* to come and stay? More man problems, I expect. I suppose she was bound to ask you to sort her out, occupational hazard. Got a problem? Ring up your friendly local Agony Aunt. Mind you, Abigail's never been known to admit to "needs". She's always been more inclined to have "wants",' he chuckled rather spitefully, adding, 'perhaps it's her age.'

'Hey, careful, she's the same age as me!'

'Yes, but . . .'

Stella laughed and prodded him none too gently in the ribs and marched on ahead of him into the house. 'Yes, but . . .' hung around, buzzing like a lazy wasp in her head. He obviously saw them as completely contrasting women – Abigail wild and sexy and still with a glamorously chaotic life, herself as tame and domestic and safe. A sleek predatory panther next to a plump, dozy pussycat. She would like to be thought of, just now and then, as being just as capable of unreliable and tumultuous passions as Abigail. She didn't yet feel too old for all that, not too old to surprise him. It was only when she looked in unexpected mirrors and saw someone undeniably *not* twenty-five that she felt reminded of the creeping years, and confusion as to what they were supposed to imply. Middle age was such a peculiar thing. Often she felt she just didn't fit the time properly – in terms of, say, footwear, she thought, as she went up the steps to the door, she felt too old for Doc Martens, and far too young for the Doc Scholls, but could rarely find anything really comfortable and stylish in between.

In the steamy kitchen she lifted the chicken out of the oven and vaguely wondered if the children would remember to come in and eat it. Adrian was opening a bottle of wine very slowly and distractedly, looking out of the window and not concentrating. Bits of the foil from round the cork were shredded on to the table as if peeled off nervously by someone waiting to see a dentist.

'Sorry,' Stella told him, 'maybe I should have said something to you before I said yes to Abigail. I should at least have put a time limit on it, said something like, "OK, come for the weekend."'

'God, you mean you *didn't*?' Adrian looked quite comically terrified and she felt like giggling at him.

'No of course not! I mean, you don't, do you, not when you're caught up in the moment. Perhaps you think I should have been even more coolly businesslike, saying, "I'll look in my diary and call you back."' Adrian grinned reluctantly, an admission that that was *exactly* how he'd have liked her to be. But that wouldn't have 'helped', Stella thought to herself. Where Abigail was concerned, in spite of her giving the impression of being invincible, somehow Stella had acquired a long, long habit of being helpful.

Stella assembled the vegetables and listened for signs of Toby and Ruth homing in for supper. She relied on them being like the ducks around Peggy's houseboat, drawn to meals by instinct and an acute sense of smell, too teenage-flaky to think about using a watch. Just as she was pouring port into the roasting tin she heard the distant creaking of the handle on the ferry raft that linked, by means of its platform of old wooden planks and a rusty chain, the island with the river's east bank. Well, someone's coming over anyway, she registered, listening hard to calculate whether the handle was being turned fast and furiously by starving youth or slowly and laboriously by some tired, work-worn resident.

'I could smell roasting chicken all the way from the garage,' Toby said, bringing in with him a less tantalizing whiff of engine oil and old car. 'Funny how I could tell it was yours and not, say, the MacIver's or Peggy's.' He slumped heavily but elegantly into the nearest chair, as if the effort of making his way a couple of hundred yards from the garage on the shore, across the ferry and along the path was all slightly too much for him. Stella wondered if that could be put down to *his* age too. 'Outgrowing his strength,' her mother had sniffed on her last foray from Yorkshire, unable to approve of her good-looking grandson beanpoling so fast past the six-foot mark and reminding her that great-grandmotherhood was not now out of the question. 'Catch the MacIvers using all that tarragon. They'd think it was horribly smelly and foreign! Anyway, on Thursdays they have what Ellen MacIver calls "high tea" or rather "*hay* tea" as she pronounces it, so they can go and sit at Bernard's feet and pick up artistic tips.'

Ruth came in behind him and stole a potato from the dish on the table. Her fingers, Stella noticed, were flaked red and green from painting her new batch of jewellery and neither she, nor Toby who was grimed with car-engine dirt, showed any signs of going to wash. They aren't babies anymore, she told herself,

16

they are their hands which makes it their dirt and their problem.

'We're getting a visitor.' Adrian had waited till everyone was actually sitting down and reasonably attentive, which gave his announcement, Stella thought, a suspicious air of foreboding. Ruth and Toby looked at him blankly, waiting to be impressed. 'Abigail's coming to stay,' he said, 'that old friend of your mother's,' he added.

'She always used to be *our* friend, not just mine,' Stella corrected him, then explained to Ruth and Toby, 'when we were students she always came out with *both* of us, especially when she was between boyfriends.'

There was a snorting laugh from Adrian. 'The only way Abigail was ever "between boyfriends" was when she got into bed with two at once!'

'Oh I remember *her*,' Ruth said, 'she liked to think she was glamorous. She's not particularly interesting. I thought you meant someone new, someone thrilling and dynamic. Antonio Banderas would be very welcome.'

'You used to find Abigail thrilling and dynamic,' Stella pointed out, pouring a large glass of wine for herself. 'You'd hardly leave her alone when you were little.'

Ruth pulled a face and with her paint-streaked fingers shoved her long curls out of the way of her food, leaving tiny shards of dried colour on the hennaed strands. 'When I was *little* I'd have thought anyone who brought twelve pairs of earrings when they came to stay was the next best thing to Santa and the Tooth Fairy.'

Stella remembered the twelve pairs of earrings. Those were just the ones Abigail, ten years previously, had brought for a one-week stay during a respite from builders and decorators. There was an implication of

17

at least thirty or forty more pairs left at home, rejected for that short trip, jumbled in a vast jewellery case, a safe-like cabinet with triple locks possibly. Or, more likely, filed neatly in miniature maple drawers labelled: Formal; Informal; Balls; Banquets and Adulterous Afternoons. Stella thought about the impossibility of owning so many, choosing them, deciding which ones were appropriate and for when. She herself had a pair of old pearl ones which she wore most of the time, just to keep the pierced holes from sealing themselves shut again, some gypsyish gold hoops for parties, several sad singles waiting for their long-lost partners to turn up from down the backs of car seats and sofas and three or four pairs of impossibly glittery ones, bought on impulse, that she had never felt she could quite live up to and had therefore never worn. She felt the same about wearing red. So often she'd come home from clothes shopping with something plain, tasteful, expensive and inevitably black only to have Adrian say, 'Hmm. It would look terrific in *red*.' Red, and even more, red with oversized dangling diamanté earrings, needed the kind of personality that shouted out 'Look at Me!' Stella's, and she often hated herself for it, was more along the lines of 'Don't stare, it's rude.' Abigail, by contrast, would probably burst into tears if people *didn't* stare.

'Well, I'm looking forward to seeing her anyway. It's been ages,' Stella asserted.

They all three stopped eating and looked at her and she realized she'd been dreaming away to herself about earrings and red while they'd moved on to talk of other things. Vaguely, she heard Toby finishing a sentence that, as usual, contained a veiled request for car renovation funds.

'What will you do with her?' Ruth asked, as if Abigail was a rare animal with exotic needs.

'Oh, I'm sure she won't be expecting any special

treatment, other than a one-to-one counselling service from me. She'll just have to fit in.'

It was easy enough to say, Stella thought later, as she sat in the lantern-lit garden with Adrian and the remains of the wine. Abigail wasn't best known for 'fitting in'. The baggage she brought on visits tended to be as much emotional as wearable.

'Last time she stayed it was the abortion, wasn't it? Or was it when she couldn't decide about marrying Martin?' Adrian asked.

'No, it was way after that. They've been married well over ten years now. Their children have been sent off to prep school. And of course I've met her for lunch in London several times. I think it must have been the court case, when she ran over that actor who changed his mind and decided not to sue.'

'Wonder why . . . You know, Ruth's got a point, what *are* you going to do with her?'

Stella thought about the contents of her own computer. She had just handed in the final chapters of her latest teenage romance so she could count on having a couple of weeks before having to deal with her editor's comments, but there was her weekly 'Go Ask Alice' advice column for the pubescent, hor-monally frantic, readers of *Get This!* magazine. Probably Adrian was right and that was why Abigail had turned to her for help, as if telling young girls (and many boys) that they didn't *have* to think French kissing was wonderful (yet), that the epithet 'blow-job' wasn't literally accurate, or that yes, they could get pregnant standing up, also meant she could iron out crumpled mid-life marriages. There would be enough time for in-depth God-What-A-Bastard sessions over the late-night gin, letting Abigail wail away the awful-ness of Martin. All that was really keeping her occupied was the Pansy Island Art Fair, of which she'd managed to end up as co-ordinator, simply because being neither a sculptor, potter or painter she was deemed to be impartial and could be relied on to organize the exhibitors with scrupulous fairness. It was almost psychically clever of Abigail to have picked *right now* to book herself in for help.

From the path came the sound of Bernard's art class returning and calling loud goodbyes to Ellen MacIver as she reached her own gate and left the group, hurrying in for her cocoa and the *Daily Express* crossword in bed. In a few minutes, Stella thought, she'd hear the ferry cranking its way across the cut. If it came and went twice, that would mean Bernard had had a good turnout that night, more than ten anyway, which would make him happy.

'I suppose she could help you with the art stuff – send out invitations or something,' Adrian suddenly suggested, reading her thoughts. 'I mean, if her mouth's busy licking envelopes, it can't be ranting on forever about the dreadfulness of men, can it?'

'Good idea. It'll keep her occupied, and then maybe I can slide off and do some work. She'll need *some* looking after though, Adrian. I mean do *try* to be a bit welcoming, won't you? We all used to be such good friends, way back then.' Even in the half-dark, Stella thought she could see him flinch slightly.

He smiled at her, though nervously. 'I'll try, I promise. But you know what they say, don't you? A friend in need is a complete and utter pain in the arse.'

Chapter Two

Stella lay awake early in the morning and watched Adrian as he slept. She'd always considered that sleeping with someone, in the literal sense, was far more intimate than sex. It certainly required more trust. The usual kinds of sex carried informed mutual consent, but to a sleeper you could do anything. You could photograph them ludicrously splayed and naked, cut off their hair, castrate them, murder them even. People did – it was in the papers all the time. Probably a sleeper was the easiest target for a murder, she thought now as she watched him. Apart from the obvious fact that they couldn't defend themselves, sleep could be seen as halfway to death. A well-placed knife or a swift blat with a hammer would simply tip the balance, with a tiny bit less input from the conscience than when faced with rabid terror or appealing, full-awake eyes. Adrian, whom Stella did not at all (at the moment) want to murder, looked as if he was very busily dreaming: twitching and snuffling slightly in the way that dogs did when they dozed on hearthrugs. She'd been seeing him sleep for more than twenty years, she thought. Somehow he looked very much the same as he had in their narrow and creaky college bed, though with a few more lines and folds on the skin that made his face seem as worn and

21

comfortable as an old handbag. Living with someone every day made the impact of increasing age so much more gentle than the rather startling sight of someone not seen for several years. Trying to look at him objectively, she could see that Abigail, who hadn't seen him for a couple of years, would notice his hair was still all there and still quite shaggy and long, but was now chalk-striped like an old-fashioned consultant surgeon's suit. His body also looked, in clothes, quite muscular and fit, though Stella knew that beneath the deceptively youthful T-shirts and jeans lurked a torso that had started to sag slightly as if ·it had a slow puncture. Abigail must have lain awake looking at no less than three husbands over the same years. Possibly she *had* felt like murdering them. Sooner or later all Abigail's men did something wrong, something terminally unforgivable. There were probably untold numbers of lovers too, but she didn't think Abigail would have let them sleep. She'd never been very good at being alone, Stella remembered, always wanting someone to write essays alongside her in the library, always emerging from her room with a spare cup of coffee, looking for someone, anyone, to share a work break with. She wondered about the three husbands, if, perhaps, Abigail ever struggled up from deep sleep with the third one (Martin) and felt a semi-conscious shock that she wasn't lying next to the second one (Noel) or the first one (Johnny).

Leaving Adrian still deep in his dreams, Stella decided to make an effort towards preventing her own body sagging by taking a brisk row round the island before breakfast. Abigail's body, long, lean and streamlined as a racehorse, had always made her feel comparatively dumpy and lumpy – a feeling she suffered from with no one else, so it was probably merely a habit of envy left over from vulnerable youth.

The day was already promisingly warm and steamy,

the new leaves on the trees gleaming like paint that wasn't quite dry. There was no sign of life yet from Peggy's barge – the last defiant one left after the council cancelled all houseboat moorings in preparation for the proposed building of a bridge and a general officious tidying up of the anarchic mess that surrounded the island. No resident of the island would admit to wanting a bridge across to the bank, seeing the proposal as a dodgy conspiracy that would end in higher house values and an immediate leap up three bands of council tax rating. Peggy, who had lived in her barge for at least ten years, simply had nowhere else to go. Rowing round the island was just far enough to make it feel like a good work-out, though Stella conceded that this was by the standards of a middle-aged woman with a sedentary occupation who hadn't participated in active sport since compulsory hockey at school. She tweaked at her fleshy hips guiltily as she walked down the garden, wondering how far up the scale of 'letting yourself *go*' Abigail would rate her. She cast off the rope from her skiff and set out at a steady pace, hoping she wouldn't come across one of the super-keen members of the rowing club on the shore, showing up her lack of technique and hollering that the club was ideal for beginners and the social life was *terrific*.

The island was quite large by usual Thames eyot standards, about half a mile long and banana-shaped with a scruffy scrub and woodland wilderness at its north end. It was only about fifty feet from the east bank, with the main river channel on the west side, but as access was only by boat or ferry and subject to the whims of tide and tempest, it attracted creative and adventurous personalities rather than those whose idea of 'waterfront' was a concrete seaside marina. Over the years, it had evolved into a predominantly artistic colony, partly because there was a subtly ruthless weeding-out system for potential house-seekers. Anyone who struggled off the ferry with an estate agent, a sheaf of house details and an air about them of having a nine-to-five job might find their would-be neighbours eager to discuss the disadvantages of an erratic refuse collection system and no milk delivery. The difficulties of hanging about during a high spring tide when the 7.33 to Waterloo might need to be caught would also be mentioned, quite casually, in passing. Stella sometimes felt that she and Adrian had only just slipped through the net, being mere writers. Charlotte, a painter with a red-headed toddler daughter, had once let it out that there had actually been a good deal of discussion about it three years previously when they'd been buying their house, making Stella imagine an official meeting and an unflatteringly close vote.

Stella and Adrian's house was probably the biggest on the island – one of four Edwardian houses on the side that faced out across the main stream and the flood meadows beyond. In summer, day trippers on pleasure boats cruised past and pointed, oohing and aahing enviously at the pretty roofs and balconies and the decoratively frilled wooden bargeboards and the cutouts patterned like broderie anglais, reminiscent of the days when a trip out to the river was, like in *Three Men in a Boat*, a very jolly and frivolous excursion. The rest of the island was dotted about with an odd mixture of weather-boarded bungalows and cabins that had probably originally been built as weekend retreats – some were little more than shacks (especially Willow's, whose flimsy tin-roofed dwelling was a hymn to primary colour and referred to as a *cabaña*). Most of these were perched ominously up on concrete piles facing the shore on the side closest to the ferry, with a less enviable view of the rowing club, a terrace of dilapidated boathouses converted into garages and some spare scrubland used by all as a carpark.

Stella's stately progress took her gliding past Fergus and Ellen MacIver's garden which was a thriving reminder that the island's resident-selection process occasionally slipped up. The MacIver's had moved in, installed a gleaming aluminium greenhouse, a B & Q plastic shed, built-in breeze-block barbecue and militarily straight rows of vividly clashing bedding plants before anyone realized their artistic taste ran to a liking for municipal park layouts. Everyone else, with casual and lazy artistry, went in for plants that rambled, tumbled and trailed in a deceptively dishevelled manner, in colours that blended and harmonized and gave the impression of spontaneous but sensitive disarray. Far more carping went on among the residents about the MacIver's prim planting schemes than about Enzo the sculptor's scrap metal collection strewn all over his scrubby patch.

Stella rowed on, feeling bad about being so snobbish. About *plants*, for heaven's sake, she thought. I mean, what's really so criminal about being fond of salmon pink geraniums alternated with soldier-stiff scarlet salvias? Bernard, whose home closest to the north tip of the island she was now rowing towards, would probably have some impressive colour-theory-based argument about that, she thought. He lived alone over a very large old boathouse, the lower part of which was supposed to be a gallery and had been opened with enormous enthusiasm and newspaper fuss a couple of years before, never again to see the number of visitors in total that had been there enjoying the free drink at the launch party. Bernard, a painter described in broadsheet culture sections for almost twenty years as up-and-coming, believed that art was a club exclusive to artists and art lovers, not for the casually cruising general public who'd run out of shops to browse round on a wet Sunday afternoon and so he did not encourage publicity. A poster advertising the gallery, tacked to the board beneath the 'Private, Keep Out' sign by the ferry, had been removed and 'lost' as soon as the council grant had been spent on renovating the boathouse and incidentally providing him with a large airy studio and living space. Outside and round about, as a decaying reminder of when the boathouse had been exactly that, rotting skeletons of abandoned cabin cruisers and a defunct ferry boat rusted in the undergrowth like the carcasses of elephants. As she rowed, feeling a rewarding muscular ache in her legs, Stella looked up at Bernard's enormous window opened on to the broad balcony and saw him standing there, block-shaped and solid, fingering his thick ginger beard and staring across at the trees and fields and distant tower blocks on the opposite bank, waiting for a fine-bodied female jogger to run along the towpath and inspire his day's painting.

'Morning Bernard!' Stella called. She could hear him sigh even at that distance, as if she'd interrupted the final savouring of his last night's dream. She wondered if he, like Adrian, twitched and fidgeted in his sleep. She didn't expect a reply, being way over twenty and therefore way outside Bernard's range of interest, but he did manage a gracious, sleepy wave.

Up in her room, high in the roof where gulls gathered and peered in through the skylight at her while she slept, Ruth woke up and tried to work out what time it was and whether she'd got many classes to go to that day. She wanted to go to the Art Fair meeting at the boathouse with her mother after lunch, just so she could hang around close to Bernard and show off that she knew her way around his kitchen. Willow the dippy hippy would be just furious, being quite convinced, though Ruth couldn't think why, that

Bernard was somehow *her* property. She got up and went straight to the mirror, as she did every morning, to see if spots had covered her chin in the night, springing up like mushrooms on a damp lawn. The ritual reminded her of when she was a small child on the coldest days of winter, reaching high up to pull aside her curtain in the daily joyful expectation of snow. Not that there'd be anything joyful about finding *spots*, she thought, inspecting her creamy skin carefully. 'You have skin like the top of Jersey milk,' Bernard had complimented her once, running a rough finger slowly down her cheek and making her feel like simply purring.

'What's Jersey milk, exactly?' she, a child of the semi-skimmed Nineties, had asked her mother later.

'Thick, yellowish stuff,' Stella had said, unknowingly demolishing several hours of delirious near-perfect happiness, 'rather out of fashion these days.'

Ruth checked through her timetable and found that although the morning (French and Media Studies) couldn't be missed, the afternoon art class could possibly take the form of research, perhaps a spot of photography towards her project on water life forms. It was a typical affectation, she thought, of Pansy Island, to hold the meeting in the afternoon instead of more conveniently in the evening, as if to show off that they were Artists, so they Could. This deliberately left out anyone dull enough to be holding down a proper job along with students with a conscience. She had every right to be at the meeting, being for the first time an exhibitor. Her second favourite fantasy was about having a major dealer browsing round the summer-house on art fair day and discovering her jewellery, commissioning work for a London gallery and making her instantly famous. She went happily into the shower, lathered her generous soft curves with Body

Shop vanilla gel and thought some more about Bernard. She squeezed her soapy hands hard into her skin, and thought about his shaggy lion-like head, imagining what it might feel like, bristling and chafing down between her thighs. It was such a pity he was called *Bernard*, she thought as she wrapped herself in a warm towel. For maximum charisma he really should be called something more bohemian like Pablo, or Lucien or, most blissfully perfect, Augustus. Bernard was hardly a name to fire the fantasies. She'd never come across a name like that among her contemporaries at the sixth form college – it just didn't fit in with Alex or Simon or Damien or Luke. It sounded so thoroughly middle-aged, but then, she reminded herself, that was exactly what he was.

Ted Kramer sat outside the rowing club in Philip Porter's dazzling white Nissan Micra, opened the window and wished miserably that he was at the evening end of the day and not the morning one. He breathed the cool, sharp early air and closed his eyes and blamed Philip Porter for being the cause of this fate-tempting sin of wishing away time. Never before had he met anyone whom he so hated to be in an enclosed space with, who was so obsessed with bad-odour obliteration. Philip Porter, who was in his bustling mid-career mid-thirties, carried a clashing reek of aftershave, deodorant and hair gel. His whole being and body screamed, it seemed to Ted, right into your face like a caricature sergeant-major: 'I am CLEAN! What am I? CLEAN!' His scrubbed car smelt of vinyl polish and was equipped with scented hand-wipes, dangling air fresheners and a pair of polyester covers for the headrests. Ted, who kept telling himself he was far too old to care that early retirement was only a blink away, had an irritating childish urge to flake dandruff from what was left of his own hair all over

28

the plush seats and tread dog muck into the meticulously vacuumed carpet.

'Got to be vigilant. Got to get it all down on here,' Philip Porter muttered, consulting his clipboard and then glancing across to where the island slept peacefully and the ferry sat rocking gently on top of the receding tide.

Ted sighed again and looked across at the brightly painted shack owned, according to the electoral register, by one Wilma Doreen Ellis. It reminded him of hot Caribbean nights and the rhythmic cackle of tree frogs. He'd paint the cottage walls this summer, he decided, perhaps a deep, campion pink. People appreciated a bit of original colour down in Cornwall. It went with the sea air and the special light that blessed St Ives.

'There's one,' Philip suddenly said, his head swivelling about excitedly like a train-spotter catching sight of a rare locomotive. Ted looked across without much interest and saw a woman rowing gently past, her face turned sunwards, looking, he thought enviously, as if she was savouring every perfect, private moment. He looked away quickly, feeling rudely intrusive as if he'd glanced over a garden wall and caught sight of a neighbour sunbathing naked. Philip Porter tapped the clipboard with his gold propelling pencil. 'Which category, do you think, arriving or leaving, visitor or resident?'

'Who cares?' Ted told him, 'I really hate this spying on people.'

Philip frowned, 'It isn't spying, it's *observation*, *feas-i-bil-ity*.' He droned the syllables out, as if their very length defined their importance. He clicked at the pencil impatiently. 'It's bona fide council business.'

Ted Kramer watched the woman smiling as she glided swiftly past a group of swans.

'Bona fide bollocks,' he said. 'It's nobody's business.'

'How was the river?' Adrian, pouring coffee and still looking half asleep, asked Stella as she staggered with exaggerated exhaustion into the kitchen.

'Wet, would you believe?' she replied, flopping into the nearest chair. He looked slightly pained and she realized that it was still too early in the day for him to deal with even the gentlest sarcasm. He woke slowly and reluctantly from the twitching dreams, claiming that thinking up devious twists of pornographic plot kept him awake long into the night. Perhaps in the early sleepless hours he lay watching *her*, and possibly planning her murder, she thought as she reached across the table and poured herself coffee.

'Sorry. No, it was lovely – flat and slow-moving and not quite woken up yet, rather like you.' She got up and kissed him lightly and delved into the bread bin (made by Willow) for a croissant.

'Those two men were there again, the ones the council sent to watch who uses the ferry,' she told him. 'A pretty boring job for them, sitting there measuring everyone's comings and goings.'

'And it really takes two of them?' Adrian commented in disgust. 'They'd be far more useful cleaning dog shit off the pavements,' he grumbled. 'Isn't it today that Abigail comes?'

'Yep. Lunch time. Or lunch*ish*, anyway. I expect she'll stop off somewhere on the way. I can't imagine her arriving here starving, just in case all we've got in the house is something she couldn't possibly force herself to eat, not even on a desert island, like a can of spaghetti hoops or whatever.' Stella laughed, remembering the awful things she and Abigail had lived on as poor and lazy students, long before affluence had over-refined Abigail's palate and given her selective amnesia. They'd particularly enjoyed toast spread with drinking chocolate powder and there had once been a supper of Angel Delight (butterscotch flavour) with nothing but Jacobs Cream Crackers to dunk into it.

'If she gets here in time I'll take her to the art fair meeting,' Stella told Adrian. 'I'll introduce her to everyone, then she'll feel more at home.'

'Perhaps she'll find herself a playmate,' Adrian suggested. 'Then she'll be out of your way a bit. How long did you say she was staying?'

'Er, actually I didn't.' Stella confessed, staring guiltily into her coffee. 'Though it can't be for long, can it? I mean, Martin can't be away for ever.'

'Ah, but he can, can't he?' Adrian pointed out. 'If he's really gone off and left her then presumably "ever" is exactly how long he's gone off for.'

He looked pale, Stella thought, as if the idea of Abigail permanently resident in their spare room was enough to make him quite ill. There'd been a time, she was pretty sure, when he hadn't felt at all like that about her.

Abigail remembered too late that she didn't need to get a cab all the way out from central London – there *were* local trains. But she just wasn't used to having to think about the simple mechanics of such a situation, and her bag was terribly heavy, full of clothes that just might be needed, like an all-purpose slinky black frock, large baggy sweaters to deal with the inevitably damp evenings, sensible shoes that would survive the high tide mud. And there was the cat-basket. She could hardly be expected to trail poor yowling Cleo all the way out to distant suburbia with no help at all. She dearly wished she'd brought her adored little Mercedes. Just one more day and its front offside wing would have been all replaced as good as shiny new and

31

the kind young boy who was thrilled to have been allowed to come and disentangle it from the gatepost would have delivered it back to the house again. She would have given him a ten pound tip and driven him at a splendidly crazy, dizzying speed through the narrow lanes back to his workshop and persuaded him, quite easily, not to tell Martin (if he ever came back) about this latest little mishap. It was typical of her that she simply couldn't allow herself to wait even that long. As she kicked her baggage slowly forward in the taxi queue she wondered if she should, instead, have simply booked herself a week in Venice, just to show Martin when (if) he trailed home that she could have little going away treats too. She wouldn't have had to admit that she'd gone alone, she could easily have spent enough money for two. She could have done a lot of secretive smiling, leaving him wondering and agonizing, picturing her perhaps being cosy in a gondola with the young, stallion-hung pool cleaner he'd caught her eying from her sun lounger in the garden the previous summer. Instead the 'Gone to stay with Stella and Adrian' message she'd recorded on the Ansaphone was almost as dreary as telling the world she'd run home to mother. He wasn't stupid – he'd identify it immediately as an admission of a need for comfort. She would have gladly changed her mind, phoned Mrs Wiggins to tell her, when she next came in to clean, to switch off the damn machine if it wasn't for a nagging superstition that if Martin suddenly decided to call and grovel for forgiveness but found her untraceable, he might just change his mind back again and plight a permanent troth to this Fiona person.

Abigail ran out of patience, pushed past three men in travel crumpled business suits and climbed into the next taxi as it pulled up. Like a spoilt child, she didn't even acknowledge, let alone thank, those who so kindly piled her baggage in after her. She lit a cigarette, glaring at the 'Thank you for Not Smoking' sign and waited, her face contorted with angry challenge, to be told off.

Toby lay on the damp greasy ground outside the garage and poked about with a spanner and a torch. His adored VW Beetle (1303S, metallic purple, 1972, sloping headlights, flat windscreen) had developed a stubborn little jolting noise from somewhere in the region of the back axle. He heard the rattling throb of a taxi and glanced out to see, stepping out of it, the lower end of pale slim shiny legs wearing long beige low-heeled shoes. This he identified immediately as a creature far removed from the usual sloppily-shod island visitor. From so frequently lying flat out under his car he had come to recognize most of the inhabitants by their legs and feet – Willow's star-painted boots, Bernard's odd socks, the tattooed daisy on Charlotte's ankle, the MacIvers' matching Hush Puppies, Enzo's battered Italian loafers. It was none of those, definitely no one local. Abigail's here then, he thought as he hauled himself out from beneath the car and wiped his oily hands down his oily jeans. Dressed entirely in something silky and cream and fumbling with money for the cab driver as if cash was something she, like the queen, wasn't quite used to handling, she looked completely and pitifully out of place, he thought, as if she'd just landed in coldest Alaska in a strapless ballgown. She was staring across the water at Willow's little house, at the scarlet and yellow oil drums planted with trailing nasturtiums, at the dancing black carnival figures painted in bold silhouette on the sky blue front door.

'Hello Abigail, how are you?' Toby greeted her politely. She continued staring at the house as if she hadn't heard him and then, pointing across the water, said, 'Is that *allowed*? Don't you have planning regulations on this island or what?'

Toby looked blankly at Willow's jolly paintwork and shrugged, 'I dunno. I thought you could just paint your own house any way you want. Aren't you allowed to down in Sussex?'

Abigail sighed, already losing interest in Willow's colour scheme. 'I suppose so. Who knows. Who cares?' she said with another, deeper sigh, her voice full of remembered woe.

Toby picked up her bag and the cat basket, wondering if his mother was actually expecting this extra little visitor. 'Come on,' he said to Abigail, 'I'll take you across on the ferry and show you the way. You look tired.'

Abigail tried a pathetic smile and looked up at him. 'You do realize,' she said, 'that at my age the words "you look tired" are almost always polite-speak for "you're looking about a hundred years old."'

Toby hauled the bag and the basket onto the ferry with a graceful ease that Abigail could only envy. She felt quite literally stiff with misery and the humiliation of Martin's rejection, and all her own suppleness and casual ease of movement had been tensed by awful uncertainties about what life could now be like. Toby took her hand and pulled her carefully from the bank to the raft. 'Sorry, I didn't know that and you don't actually look any different from last time I saw you. You just look, well, troubled, I suppose.'

He was being kind, Abigail thought, a boy of what? Nineteen or so? Last time she'd seen him he'd been spotty, blushing and silent, engrossed in his GCSE revision and firmly at the grunt-for-an-answer stage. He was taller than her now, spot-free, and with that flopping hair and an easy body that wouldn't look out of place in a jeans advert. His concern touched her. Were boys supposed to notice women being emotional at that age or just think about football and sex? Her eyes filled with tears and she was glad he was occupied with turning the handle that moved the peculiar ferry and sent it trundling noisily towards the island landing stage. This is a perfect example of what it could all be like from now on, she thought – unexpected people being *kind*. I'm an object of pity like a new widow adrift and brave at a dinner party. She didn't like the feeling one bit. And there would be far too many whose offered sympathy would hide a sneaking triumphant glee that she, *she* of all people, wasn't immune from vulnerability. Her role in life had been to be admired and desired by men and envied and emulated by women. As she stepped on to the island she felt she had left behind her all familiar civilization. She would have to find something distracting and amusing so her looks wouldn't deteriorate permanently through unhappiness. Control must be regained. Sadness (and boredom, she suspected) set lines deep into the face out of reach of even the choicest moisturizers – she'd read about that in *Harper's*. Toby swung the heavy bag off the ferry platform and looked back at her. His smile, she thought, was like a warm blessing. She noticed then the perfect teeth that would make such a perfect arcing mark on skin, the golden frosting of hair on his oil-streaked forearm, the way his muscles tightened as he picked up her luggage, and suddenly, with relief and gratitude, discovered that she wasn't yet too emotionally numb to feel desire.

Chapter Three

It's funny, Stella thought, how women who haven't seen each other for quite a long while automatically say 'You're looking *wonderful*' and then oh so politely avoid doing any real inspecting. It was probably only one's mother who could legitimately stand back and say 'Now, let me have a good look at you' before giving a candid appraisal, and only then if there was the trusting expectation of admiration. Some mothers, Stella guessed, probably relished that once-in-a-year or so chance to say 'You know, I've always thought that shade of green wasn't really you' or suggest, helpfully, of course, 'Perhaps longer skirts, these days, do you think?'

Between Abigail and Stella, good, loyal friends though they both would swear they were, it would be just too impertinent to do what they both really, deep down wanted to do which was to have a good greedy stare at each other, to estimate any extra pounds of bodily flesh, peer at hair partings for signs of greying roots and search out sagging eye-bags and loose necks. She and Abigail had done the hugs and the greetings, the showing of Abigail to her room in the roof next to Ruth and the settling in of the cat, and they were now skirting round each other in the kitchen, politely mentioning neither Martin nor signs of ageing while Stella organized lunch.

'Nothing for me, honestly, I hardly ever do,' Abigail protested while at the same time hungrily picking flakes of hot crust off the garlic bread that Stella had just pulled out of the oven.

'No wonder you're still so thin,' Stella told her, ignoring the protest and ladling Sainsbury's tomato and basil soup into two bowls.

'Just lucky metabolism, I think. I do rush about rather,' Abigail replied, looking down at her flat stomach and narrow thighs. Stella swooped a quick glance over her as she sat down. Abigail's flowing silk skirt was droopy at the waist as if she'd recently lost weight. That was probably something to do with the shock of Martin leaving. Her hair, the wet fox colour discreetly shaded with tawny lowlights, was also looking unusually lank as if it too was dispirited. It was tempting to ask whether she really was looking after herself and eating properly but Stella didn't want to sound motherly – some people's misery makes them too wound up to eat much, she thought, and others' makes them practically live with their heads in the fridge hoovering up the comfort food and chocolate. I'm probably one of the latter, she decided. She was pretty sure it would only take Adrian having a one-night fling and she'd put on at least a stone, entirely made up of toast and honey and dark, expensive, appropriately bitter chocolate.

'What happened to Toby? Isn't he having any lunch?' Abigail asked, looking out of the window.

'Oh, he's probably gone back under his car – I sometimes think he lives under it. I expect he'll grab some crisps or a burger. They all study proper nutrition in school, but it seems to end up as nothing more than an exam subject – about as relevant to their own real lives as the exports of Argentina. Adrian's down the garden working in the summerhouse – he just takes a

37

sandwich down there in the morning and doesn't come out till at least late afternoon, which is very rude of him when he knows someone's coming – and Ruth *should* be at the college.' Stella could hear footsteps outside, perhaps Adrian had found enough good manners to come and say hello. A door opened and in a rush of air and a slamming and thumping, Ruth hurtled past the doorway and up the stairs. 'Can't stop, see you later,' she yelled.

'Good grief, what's that?' Abigail asked, her spoon midway to her mouth.

'Just a teenager in a hurry,' Stella told her with a grin. 'Wait till yours are that big.'

'I probably won't see any more of them than I do now. Martin thinks boarding school is character building,' Abigail murmured glumly.

'So's prison and the French Foreign Legion,' Stella giggled. 'You don't put their names down at birth for those though.'

'Isn't Ruth eating either? She hasn't gone anorexic, has she?' Abigail asked.

'Er, no.' Stella couldn't help smiling at the thought of Ruth's curved and rounded body being suspected of self-starvation. 'Wait till later, you'll see her then. There is absolutely no way that she could be mistaken for anorexic.' Abigail was hardly eating anything herself, Stella saw. Her bread was crumbled into untidy pieces by the side of her plate and not much of the soup had gone. A glass of wine had been drained and refilled and Abigail was working her way steadily though that, holding tight to the stem of the glass as if she thought it might be stolen away from her. Stella felt a rush of sorrow for her. 'Look, I'm sorry about having to go to this meeting today,' she said. 'We can have a proper talk later. Do you just want to rest this afternoon or would you like to come with me and meet some of the neighbours? You might hate them of course.' Abigail frowned for a moment, staring at the table, then looked at Stella and summoned up a dazzling smile.

'I'm not *ill*, Stella, you know, just *angry*. I'll come with you and join in and see if there's fun to be had. Anything to stop thinking about that bastard.' Defiantly she slugged down the rest of the wine and stood up. 'I could have stayed at home and wallowed in fury about Martin but I thought it would be more interesting, more fun even, to be somewhere else, having a look at someone else's life for a change, you know?'

'The idea', Stella explained to Abigail as they walked along the path towards the meeting at Bernard's boathouse, 'is that everyone on the island involved in producing art, and that's most people actually, whether it's paintings or sculpture or textiles or whatever, everyone opens up their home – the workspace part of it – to the public and people come and look round.'

'So it's just a promotion thing?' Abigail, accustomed to Martin's language of commerce, asked.

'Well, not entirely. There's a charity donation at the door and it's for local interest as much as anything. It started a few years ago because people in the town thought the islanders were weird and way-out and there was a bit of hostility. Just before we moved in there were rumours of werewolves and witchcraft and really it was just because there are no token chartered accountants or stockbrokers. It's all very informal and friendly, that's all.'

'This art fair event,' Abigail looked puzzled, 'do people just show off how they work then and not *sell* anything? That sounds awfully *folksy*.'

Stella laughed. 'There's not that much charitable spirit over here! Of course people sell things. Actually it's not so easy to wander into someone's house, poke around and then just wander out again. It seems such terribly bad manners. If you don't buy, it's like admitting you've come in just to be nosy. And of course most people have – it's all the "Private" notices out by the ferry, everyone in the town thinks they'll be ensnared into a cult or a commune if they set foot over here. It's quite hard to get kids to deliver the papers, in case artists are a bit on the deviant side. And the ferry makes so much noise no one can hope to land here for a sneaky look round without anyone noticing.'

'So this open day thing is really just like having a fête in the grounds of an historic house. We do that in Sussex,' Abigail said, relieved that she'd caught up at last with something vaguely familiar. As they walked she kept slowing to look into the overgrown gardens, catching sight of a collapsing corrugated structure in one, a full-size tepee in another, and the MacIver's green and orange plastic shed. Her ears were troubled by the soft discordant jangling of wind chimes, not too far away, like someone who was just starting to practise campanology and hadn't at all got the hang of it. The island, which had looked like a sweet piece of offshore suburbia from the bank, seemed at close range to be all metals and nettles.

Stella looked at her watch and wished Abigail would walk a bit faster. The dainty beige feet were picking their way with exaggerated care along the path, a perfectly good tarmac path, as if it was root-strewn woodland. Perhaps not eating properly is making her weak, she wondered, or perhaps it was just lunchtime alcohol.

'You don't see any of this from the bank,' Abigail said, slowing even more and staring wide-eyed through a gap in an escallonia hedge at a square of scruffy land as neatly laid out with old chrome car bumpers, hub caps and bicycle wheels as the

MacIver's was with dwarf begonias. In the middle sat the wheel-less carcass of a Reliant Robin housing scrawny squawking chickens.

'Those are Enzo and Giuliana's hens. They're Italian – Enzo and Giuliana, not the hens. They give us delicious free-range eggs. Enzo's a sculptor and Giuliana paints silk – she's his sister by the way.' Stella felt the need to point out, in case Abigail (unlikely though it was) might find the information useful during her stay. Abigail shuddered slightly, though whether at the thought of eating anything that had originated in the filthy and rotting Reliant or at the possible implications of a man choosing to live with his sister, Stella couldn't tell. Enzo combined being the scruffiest man Abigail was likely to have seen with being one of the most easily elegant. Stella put that down to having grown up within commuting distance of Milan – only Italians could look so effortlessly stylish in ripped and rust-stained Armani jeans and wearing odd Gucci loafers.

Between the houses on each side of the path, glimpses of river could be seen and Stella wondered if Abigail was feeling quite literally isolated, stuck on the island as if she'd found herself suddenly on an ocean liner, cut off for weeks with people she couldn't quite see her way to liking. Well, this ship's going nowhere, Stella thought, increasing the pace. Abigail only has to make a few energetic turns of the ferry handle and she's safely back on the mainland, two streets away from an ordinary town high street and all the familiar comforts of Boots and the Body Shop.

In the gallery space below Bernard's living quarters, the unsold remnants of the last exhibition had been removed from the rough white walls and stacked face-inwards ready for collection. Once safely inside on level ground, Abigail perked up and started looking around with interest.

'Goodness, are these all rejects? Didn't whoever it was sell many then?' Abigail asked, peering round curiously as she and Stella clicked across the beech-plank floor towards the spiral iron staircase that led up to Bernard.

'Hardly any. Usual lack of publicity, I think. Poor chap will have to load them all up on a trolley and wheel them back the whole length of the island. It'll be quite embarrassing for him, I should think. He'll imagine everyone's looking but they won't be. They're used to it.'

'Perhaps they aren't any good.' Abigail tweaked one away from where it faced the wall like a punished schoolchild and peered over the top of it. 'Ugh! Dead babies – at least I think they are. Not one for the dining room!'

'Actually, I think you'll find it's allegorical.' Willow's slow voice came from somewhere above them. Each syllable of 'allegorical' was pronounced with careful separation as if it was the day's new word that she was determined to practise. She sounded like a small child but with far more carrying power. Deceptively fey, Stella always thought. Willow then appeared, clattering down the spiral stairs on her high round-toed lace-up boots, painted by herself in shades of purple with silver stars.

'Good grief,' Abigail murmured, taking in, above the boots, the drifty, high-waisted, many-layered, multi-ribboned chiffon dress in shades of pink and mauve. Then there was the long mousey mottled plait that was greying so brazenly unchecked from the roots that it looked like a pro-ageist policy statement. Here was someone close to fifty yet determinedly hanging on to toddlerhood.

'Hello Stella,' said the bizarre vision, reaching the last step, and then turning to Abigail, added with a voice of breathy welcome and a show of big creamy teeth, 'hello Friend-of-Stella, I'm Willow. Now you're Taurus, I can just *tell*.' She held out a heavily ringed hand and Abigail shook it carefully as if Willow might really turn out to be a fragile glass dolly.

'I'm Abigail, actually,' she announced, in a voice that strongly disdained belief in horoscopes.

'Oh. Oh, *right*,' Willow sighed, her smile faltering only slightly.

The three of them clanged up the iron stairs into Bernard's loft where several residents were already settling themselves on to the enormous ancient sofa whose ragged shabbiness was decently hidden by lustrous velvet cloths. Bernard's domestic arrangements could be described as how a romantic teenager might *imagine* an artist to exist. There was a strong smell of oil and turps, and the walls near his easel were flecked with drops of paint. The walls were white, hung here and there with blown-up black and white photos of the Artist at Work – action shots of Bernard when he was still young enough to be described as up-and-coming in upmarket colour supplements.

Among those already arrived, Charlotte chased her unsteady baby around, fending her away from the stairs and from Bernard's carelessly left out paints. Peggy swayed gently in a rocking chair, wrapped in crocheted shawls to protect her increasingly arthritic joints, and smoking a small cigar. Ruth was there at the kitchen end of the long room, busying herself importantly with coffee cups and a tray, opening and shutting drawers and the fridge and generally showing off with maximum clatter.

'Ruth, why aren't you at your afternoon classes?' Stella asked her daughter, anxious that independence and irresponsibility might have become confused since Ruth had been at the sixth form college and not school.

'It's OK, it's allowed. Time off for research,' Ruth

explained glibly, smiling past her mother to Abigail. 'Hi Abigail, haven't seen you for ages, it must be at least a year or two.' Her happy smile then disappeared, and her face took on an instant expression of sorrow as she remembered the reason for the visit. 'Are you *all right*?' she asked with intense concern, but looking as if she, being only seventeen and not equipped to help, dreaded any answer but 'Yes, fine.'

'Yes, fine,' Abigail replied reassuringly, looking her up and down and clearly dying to say 'Goodness you've grown'. 'Stella and I just had lunch – don't you students get time to eat?'

Ruth grinned. 'Oh, I had something here with Bernard,' she informed Abigail, her voice raised a good deal more than was necessary and aimed across the room in the direction of Willow. Stella, who was trying to stop Charlotte's baby chewing strands of wicker from the chairs immediately worried about the fact that she hadn't specified *what* it was she had had with Bernard. It might not be food. What a lot of girls of Ruth's age had with Bernard, she'd heard, was sex, which was rather a shame because it suddenly occurred to her that he, as a kind of runner-up to Enzo the sculptor, might, just for this visit, do for Abigail. It was a grown-up version of what her 'Go Ask Alice' column would have advised a dumped-by-the-boyfriend teenage girl – extend the social life, find new friends. On the problem-solving professional level, she knew it wouldn't help over Martin's disappearance, but it might do something about Abigail's self-esteem, and she could then perhaps cope with (or without) Martin.

Ellen and Fergus MacIver, dressed in identical Aran sweaters, hauled themselves up the iron staircase and looked around for the right place to sit. Stella, pulling Hob Nobs from their packet and wondering why Bernard thought himself too grand to do his own biscuit-arranging, watched the matched pair looking alarmed at the possibility that they might have to sit separately. The two of them had taken early retirement from an insurance company and installed themselves on the island, deaf to all possible off-putting and determined to join in. They spent their days gleefully making the most of OAP concession rates at adult education classes, at one of which they had learned, they thought, to paint, going about the process as methodically as they had at Beginner's Upholstery, Your Camcorder, and Yoga for Health. Ellen's speciality was indistinct boats at sunset, which she described as atmospheric, but Fergus preferred river fowl which he painted in meticulous detail. 'His coots,' Ellen had announced proudly at the last arts fair meeting, 'are close to perfection.'

Fergus looked around the room, approving of the turnout and studying the paintwork. He ran a finger over the wall behind the sofa. 'Very nice. You can't go wrong with Brilliant White, I always say,' he commented to Bernard, 'Brilliant White vinyl silk, clean and fresh, just the thing.'

'Just *white* actually, standard trade white,' Bernard replied archly, 'completely different wavelength, I think you'll find.'

'Oh, quite,' Fergus said, confused.

Bernard strode forward to the middle of the room and assumed his place as chairman of the meeting. His sweater, paint-streaked to the point where it was hard to see its original colour, was unravelling in places just like his cane chairs. He wasn't terribly appealing, but he did have a small amount of fame, which had to count for something. Stella sneaked a look at Abigail's face to see if she was registering any initial interest in him – her eyes had always been a complete giveaway when she'd fancied someone at the college, Stella remembered. They'd light up and focus beadily on the

45

object of desire who would have no possible doubt about her dishonourable intentions. Abigail made it easy for them, the lucky boys, putting out none of those 'will-she, won't-she, is she just a teaser' adolescent signals. But just now she was simply perched neatly on a canvas chair, looking placid and polite, waiting and watching without the slightest hint of sexual interest. That must be what happens when you're heartbroken, Stella thought with sympathy, watching, for contrast, the rapt face of Willow who sat on the floor cross-legged in front of Bernard, gazing upwards like an acolyte at the feet of a prophet.

Ruth sat back, a little apart from the others as if she didn't need to be part of the throng, she knew already all she needed to know. She leaned against the rail at the top of the stairs, arms behind her, linked round the cool metal uprights, and her magnificent breasts jutting forwards towards the focus of her own desires. She felt glorious and powerful with youth, but didn't forget to pray that the balustrade wouldn't give way beneath her considerable weight.

'Just a few loose ends to clear up,' Bernard was saying, 'to do with the route the punters, sorry, visitors, should take. We should decide whether they get off the ferry and immediately have something to go and see or whether they should be directed up to the far end, start, say here at the gallery and work their way back.'

'If they start at the ferry end they might not even bother to walk as far as here. Especially if they're loaded down with her great fat pots,' the speaker, Enzo, jerked his scarred thumb rudely towards Willow, who pouted crossly. Stella wondered if Abigail had noticed how wolf-like his face was, with cool defensive eyes just that bit too close together.

'Well, you would say that, you live down *this* end,' Willow replied curtly, adding for good measure, 'at

46

least they *buy* what you call my "fat pots". That's more than they do with your bits of twisted old car bonnets.'

Charlotte put her hands over her baby's ears to protect them from the discordant sounds of conflict. 'We need a proper route map,' she suggested quietly.

'Funny you should say that, I made one last night,' Ruth stated, standing up and handing over to Bernard a sheet of card. Her hand shook slightly, Stella noticed, as if this was something that really mattered to her. Her whole face, tilted up at him, was childishly demanding approval, willing him to like it and like her.

He smiled at her and Ruth's large blue eyes glistened happily. 'You are such a good girl,' he praised her, and her face went quite pink with delight. 'This is wonderful, much better than last year's plain old list of exhibitors.' He studied it for a few seconds more, showing no democratic urge to pass it round for general comment. 'Terrific. It shows where all the relevant people live, with an explanatory key. With a copy of this, our great public can just ferry themselves over and make up their own minds where to go to be parted from their cash.' He chuckled and beamed round, expecting agreement and, as it was his home and they were all good-mannered, he got it.

'Stella, I'll leave this one with you, shall I, to organize printing and mailing and such?'

'OK,' she agreed, 'no problem.' She made a note in her diary, adding it to the list of other things that she'd said would be no problem that week. One of the items on the list, the care of Abigail, seemed to be going smoothly so far as Abigail was now looking quite relaxed and amused. Another thing to be done was to persuade Adrian that Ruth should be allowed to use the summerhouse to display her jewellery for the Art Fair. He was so precious about his workspace, as if the slightest disturbance to his routine might destroy for ever the flow of his writing. Every now and then, for the pure wicked hell of watching him being thrown into panic, Stella reminded Adrian that the summer-house had been built for the whole family to enjoy and suggested that they took people down there for pre-dinner drinks. She herself had to write with her computer perched on top of a junk-shop desk squashed into an alcove on the first floor landing, with reference books lined up on a shelf above and paper-work and correspondence filed away beneath it in Habitat baskets. Adrian 'went out' to work, whereas she got on with it right there in the house's very centre, which meant she was constantly available to answer the phone, be told that they'd run out of bread or be pleaded with for lunch money.

'What about food?' Ellen MacIver asked. 'I thought I might rustle up a few batches of my famous saffron scones. I've still got some damson jam, I think, some-where.'

'Absolutely no catering, not this time,' Bernard decreed firmly. 'You're with me on that, aren't you Stella?'

He turned to her, appealing for support, but before she could answer, Abigail leaned forward and stared incredulously at him, eyes large and appealing. 'No wine and cheesy bits?' she pleaded sweetly. 'One always needs something to nibble at when one's looking at art,' she went on with a tinkly laugh, '*I* do anyway, it gives me something to do with my hands.'

Willow smirked at her. 'Well actually, you'll find some of the exhibits are really quite tactile,' she told her, sneaking a slidey-eyed look at Bernard to see if he reacted to the suggestion of touching. 'My pots just cry out for stroking.' There was a sceptical loud grunt of 'Huh!' from Enzo which Willow ignored and she continued, 'Though I do partly agree, it's so *sensual* to combine food and art. I was planning some lentil dips

48

and couscous and breadfruit.' The whole room groaned quietly.

'No, I'm with Bernard on this,' Stella said, 'Last year got ridiculously competitive on the food front, with everyone thinking they'd got to provide something to keep the visitors interested. I suggest we have nothing home-made and don't even bother with wine, then costs are cut down.'

'What? Do you mean just *bought cakes* or something?' Ellen looked outraged, as if Stella had suggested they greet the visitors clad only in their most revealing underwear.

'Biscuits, bulk bought and distributed among the exhibitors,' Stella explained, 'so there'll be no bickering afterwards about anyone unfairly luring the buyers by tempting them with a banquet.' There was some guilty sniggering.

'But still no wine?' Abigail persisted, as if on behalf of everyone present. Stella wished she'd keep quiet – on the day itself she'd probably be back home in Sussex giving hell to a penitent Martin. She was obviously just enjoying making her presence felt, throwing in the odd interfering spanner.

'I shall get a tea urn from the Scouts,' Ellen MacIver was muttering quietly, as if afraid someone else might get in first. Fergus nodded his head violently in agreement.

'*A tea urn from the scouts*?' Abigail snorted derisively, adding in a stage whisper to Ellen, 'You two, Pinky and Perky, you really know how to *live*.' The few nearby who had heard her comment either giggled disloyally or glared at Abigail, who looked blithely unconcerned. Stella missed what she'd said but sensed tension and a need to end the meeting.

'All right, wine then. Own expense,' Stella conceded. 'But don't go mad, we don't want any trouble like last year.'

　　　　*　　　*　　　*

'So tell me what happened last year?' Abigail asked Stella eagerly as soon as they'd got out of earshot on the path home. She seemed to have cheered up quite a bit, Stella thought, feeling glad she'd managed to find the afternoon at least a bit amusing.

'Well it got terribly competitive in the hospitality department – everyone outdoing each other as if it was Private View day at the Royal Academy. Willow laid on a calypso band and an oil-drum barbecue and Ellen and Fergus did a full-scale English tea, Enid Blyton style, with *lashings* and *lashings* of clotted cream. They both sold loads of their work and everyone else accused them of bribing all the buyers by force-feeding them.'

'Goodness, exciting stuff,' Abigail said, laughing, 'I hope I'm still here to see it.' She's too tough for suicide, Stella thought, so with the art fair still a few weeks away, it looked as if Abigail had moved in for quite a long visit.

Chapter Four

Adrian sat in the summerhouse playing Tetris on the computer and trying to recall what it had been like having sex with Abigail. *She* probably didn't remember that long-ago one-off occasion at all, lost as it must have been among so many others. At the time, she'd seemed to be glorious sexual liberation personified, a truly celebratory of-the-times representation of complex-free living – no hang-ups would have probably described it in the vocabulary of those days. You couldn't even have described her as a pushover – that would imply you had to make a bit of an effort – Abigail had been more of a fall-over. Now he was older and supposedly wiser and the words were different, he'd simply say she'd been rampantly promiscuous. He wasn't sure if it was times that were a-changing or himself – either way, the thought depressed him. That sultry, rustic evening, with Abigail and his old and smelly Afghan coat spread out beneath himself and the willow tree, was a very long time ago and he probably hadn't been very adept at sex then, quite literally groping in the dark. With gut-curling embarrassment he recalled how, elated and heady with sex, wine and the rare splendour of a hot summer night, he'd even, in post-coital idiocy, asked her to marry him. He'd never since heard anything as instantly detumescent as the harsh tease of her laughter. How mockingly kind her response had been. 'Not just now, thank you, but perhaps I could marry you later when Stella's had enough of you.' After the appalling risk he'd taken, sneaking off to make love, no, *lust*, to Stella's best friend, he'd selfishly expected to feel more special than some kind of toy that she'd played with in the shop but not quite wanted to buy. For him, sex then was still all about the thrill of coming across the unexpected. At that age, nineteen or so, around the age his son Toby was now, he had never failed to be completely astounded that if he made unchallenged progress under a skirt and past the complicated barrier of tights and underwear, he would always find the same warm, moist furry equipment inside a girl's knickers. They all had *parts*, soft, welcoming, wonderful parts, each and every one of them like finding a kitten in a bag. He remembered sitting on buses, walking down streets, looking round in lectures and thinking of absolutely every woman he saw: *she's got one.* He was permanently, sometimes almost cripplingly, horny, in that way only youth on the sexual look-out can be. He wondered if Toby felt the same, or if he sublimated it by constantly tinkering with his beloved Beetle's mechanical innards. He sighed, thinking of the confident grace of his son, who seemed to have none of the problems boys sometimes confided to Stella's 'Go Ask Alice' column (The perennial 'Is mine too small?' 'Can you forget about a condom when she's got a period?'). The readers of his own books, on the other hand, probably *did* have problems.

He abandoned Tetris and called up his latest oeuvre on to the screen. 'Sleazy little tale,' he muttered as the title *Maids of Dishonour* flashed up. So tabloid, he thought, so horribly tit and bum, romp and frolic like the *Daily Star*. Somewhere inside him, he was sure, there was an absolute heavyweight *Sunday*

Times of a novel battling to get out. He and the Apple Mac were ready. He'd created a folder for it, opened a document, named it Serious Book, organized the page layout and inserted Chapter One as a header. Then he'd closed it, opened another document titled Plot and Notes and the mouse had nudged that one into place beside Chapter One. After that he'd sat and daydreamed about having twenty-five completed chapters all lined up, a hundred and twenty thousand words of prize-winning fame-gathering profundity instead of these ten-chapter batches of pseudonymous profanity. His readers, his agent had crudely reckoned, were all wanked out by fifty thousand words, couldn't take any more, might go too blind to buy the next book. He felt he was too grown up, too old anyway which might not be the same thing, to whinge that it just wasn't *fair* but sometimes he sure as hell felt like it. In the sitting room was a shelf full of Stella's teen novels with her name out there proudly on the covers — people introduced her as 'Stella Hutchens, she's a *writer*, isn't that exciting?', whereas his own books were, quite literally, not allowed houseroom and his own name had never appeared on any of the lurid covers, not in any of the twenty-six countries that they sold to. If his readers could only see just who was the real 'Marcia Teal' or 'Cassandra Wiley'. He was the real day-to-day writer in the family, the hack who had traded his creative soul to earn the bread, butter and lavish dollop of jam that the family lived on. Ruth and Toby still thought, if they thought about it at all, that is, that he wrote English literature school textbooks. He had done a few of those, back in the days when O-levels still existed. They'd paid reasonably but not stupendously well, he recalled, wondering if he'd really, now, give up his gorgeous new Audi convertible for the satisfaction of putting together coursework on contemporary poets

53

and critical analysis of William Golding.

He tapped at the keyboard, wishing there were more words that meant 'fuck'. He'd used every one he could think of in the previous chapter, setting himself a target of at least twenty, just for the tedium-relieving challenge of it all. Playfully, he considered using them all again in exactly the same order, wondering if any of his bog-eyed readers would notice. He sighed once more and forced himself to tackle an unusual way for one of the Maids to be parted, yet again, from her underwear, what there was of it. That was another thing; he'd long ago stopped associating titillating knickers with real-life sex. His books were full of women who couldn't contemplate wearing anything more substantial than a silk G-string fronted by a lace butterfly and as a result he could now get deliriously aroused only by sensible Marks and Spencer hi-leg knickers, preferably in sober grey. He thought some more about Abigail as his typing revved up. He thought about her way back then, remembering her stealthily guiding his hand under her skirt in the cinema darkness, (Stella concentrating on popcorn and *The Italian Job* on the other side of him) and the heart-stopping shock of encountering no underwear at all. He couldn't imagine her, all designer-smart like an advert for Harvey Nichols, doing all that naughtiness with him now, but he tried, for the sake of the craft of fiction, he tried.

'Your bastard husband buggered off then?' was Adrian's cheery bravado-shot greeting to Abigail when he eventually let manners and hunger get the better of him and drive him into the house just before supper.

'Oh *Adrian*!' Abigail, to Stella's unsurprised amusement, went straight into a dramatic poor-me wail and flung her arms round him as if he was to be her saviour and shining knight. Stella hauled the heavy lasagne dish out of the oven and watched out of the corner of her eye as Adrian put tentative arms round Abigail's shoulders, rather as if he was hugging the kind of animal that might just turn nasty. Stella, flushed and limp-haired from the oven heat, put the lasagne on the table while Abigail continued to sob gently into Adrian's sweatshirt. Adrian glanced over the foxy head and mouthed 'Help!' which Stella grinned at but callously ignored. Serve him right for skulking in the summerhouse all afternoon, she thought as she tossed the salad and watched the touching little scene. Abigail's face was hidden against Adrian, but her hands were skilfully fondling his back, all the way down to the pockets on the back of his jeans at which point she lingered and pressed in a way that didn't look as if she was checking for loose change. 'Just keeping her hand in, I expect,' Stella murmured sympathetically to him with a smile as she went to call Toby and Ruth. When, as teenage feet clattered down the stairs, Abigail's face eventually emerged from the sweatshirt, Stella wasn't at all astounded to notice that it showed no trace of actual tears.

'Delicious food – but just the teeniest morsel for me, please,' Abigail said as she took Stella's usual seat next to Adrian. Stella sat down opposite and gave Ruth, who was about to comment, a look that told her it would be petty to suggest a swap-round.

'I hope you haven't gone to lots of extra trouble just because I'm here. I don't want to be any more than just one of the family,' Abigail smiled wanly and added, 'I've been rather missing that, you see.' Her smile ranged the room and settled on Toby, who beamed back at her. 'It's so lovely to see you two again as well – so much more grown up and . . .' she looked hard at Ruth and then at Stella, 'and so very much *bigger* than last time.' She laughed and put her hand on Adrian's leg, squeezing hard at his thigh, 'Not *you* of course, darling,' she said as he flinched and shuffled. 'You men are so lucky, aren't they, Stella? Their bodies stay just as hard and firm as always, unlike us.' She looked at Ruth, who was glaring, and gave a hard little laugh, 'Oh don't look so shocked, sweetie, Adrian and I, and Stella of course, go back to the dark ages. I'm sure *I'm* allowed to touch him, aren't I, Stella?'

'Goodness, I don't know.' Stella laughed, helping herself to more salad and wondering if she was imagining she'd been somewhat insulted. 'You'll have to ask him – he's a big boy now.'

It was time, Stella decided as she started clearing away the dishes after supper, for Abigail to do some proper talking – to tell her exactly what had happened so momentously between her and Martin that could make him take off suddenly with someone else. At least, she assumed it was suddenly. Perhaps Abigail hadn't spotted the signposts that would have told her he was going. Probably, given a complacent habit of vanity, it hadn't occurred to her that there might be any to look for. Ruth and Toby disappeared, one out to see friends and the other to the TV as soon as they could reasonably claim to have tidied the kitchen, and Adrian wandered off to the sitting-room to watch a European Cup match.

Abigail and Stella faced each other over the kitchen table with a newly opened bottle of wine and a box of Bittermints that Abigail had thoughtfully bought at the station on her way. This was the point at which Stella wished Abigail had simply written to her instead, she was far more used to giving advice at a distance, and, she thought, better at it. She could have looked up the relevant counselling services, carefully thought over possible arrangements for the children. Once people knew she worked as an agony aunt they sidled up quietly and asked her about all sorts of things – Ellen MacIver whispered to her about Fergus's haemor-

56

rhoids. Charlotte asked her about the Child Support Agency and her baby's ear infections. She did her best but felt she was much better at the job she actually did, advising on acne and abortions, bullies and boyfriends, failed exams and whether a pair of budding teenage breasts were supposed to be of identical size. She took a large sip of her wine and started carefully dissecting Abigail's misery.

'Didn't you have any idea he was having an affair? I'm sure I'd have found out, Adrian couldn't resist letting me know, one way or another.' Stella opened the discussion, trying to keep it light.

Abigail grinned, but without real humour. 'Well I did wonder, just a teeny bit. He'd started getting terribly vain, forever preening, coming home with cosmetics for men and special shampoo and all that. I put that down to him working round the corner from Selfridges – and his age, of course.'

'What, like the male menopause type of thing?' Stella said. 'You do hear about sensible VW Golf types suddenly rushing out to buy a scarlet Porsche, don't you, or accountants with an urge to go to work in snakeskin cowboy boots.'

'Exactly. And would you believe it, in Martin's case I thought it was just going to be skincare. How naive can you get . . .' Abigail drank some wine and looked around to see if any of the herb pots on the window ledge might be sitting in an ashtray.

'I'll get you one,' Stella offered, recognizing the panic-stricken expression that smokers adopt when suddenly realizing they might have accidentally trapped themselves in a smokeless zone.

'He's always worked late at the office, that old cliché, ever since I've known him. He wouldn't get paid so deliciously much otherwise. I can't think where he found the time for an affair,' Abigail told Stella, with an involuntary satisfied smile at the thought of the earnings. She sighed, 'He was such an improvement on Johnny who was around all the time, always getting in the way.'

Stella smiled, thinking of Adrian. 'I suppose working from home does have a sort of tricky intimacy about it,' she agreed. Abigail's first husband had been a successful pioneer in home-based desk-top publishing, rigging up computers all over the house (more of a tele-mansion than tele-cottage) and being constantly smug about strike-bound commuters and the wrong sort of snow disrupting Network South-East.

Abigail grimaced and chuckled, 'Sorry, I mean it obviously works for you and Adrian, it was just that with Johnny, he couldn't stop checking up on what I was up to all the time, as if I was . . .' She hesitated and her glance wavered away from Stella's and she watched her cigarette ash scattering over the ashtray. 'Well, for a trial run at marriage I suppose he wasn't a bad effort.'

'And what about your second one, Noel, wasn't it? I never met him,' Stella prompted, feeling like a doctor trying to get to the origins of an awkward patient's problems.

Abigail shrugged, as if dismissing the entire marriage. 'Ah well, he was American and we were only married just a teensy short while, so I hardly count him. No Martin was *the* one. The forever one.' She smiled, her grey eyes full of the dream-like past. 'Do you remember at college we used to wonder how we'd know, out of all the boyfriends, which would be Mr Perfect, Mr Rest-of-your-life? Goodness, and we were supposed to be intelligent, not to believe all that magazine romance shit.'

'I'm pretty sure *I* didn't believe it,' Stella laughed. 'I just wondered if there was such a thing, or if you just ended up marrying whoever you happened to be going out with at the age when it seemed the thing to do. Or if the family pressure got too much, like when your mother started shopping for elaborate hats and dropping awful hints like, "There's some *lovely* Wedgewood in the Debenhams sale".'

'Yeah, I thought you were being cynical, I remember,' Abigail laughed.

'I thought *you* were,' Stella countered, 'You said you'd only marry someone rich enough to afford a huge house with no mortgage. And then you actually did! Three times!'

'Yes, I know. Silly me, but that's the way I am. I have this need for comfort, an absolute craving. All that love-in-a-starving-garret stuff would never have suited me. And of course way back *then*, it never occurred to me you could maybe have love *and* money.' She looked wistful, gazing round the kitchen. Stella looked round with her, noticing that the pink paint was cracking over the sink (where no one had yet got round to choosing tiles) and that Mrs Morris had still, after several casual remindings, never managed to reach the cobwebby corner of the ceiling by the window. The dresser was permanently cluttered with loose change, homework, bits cut out from newspapers, bunches of keys and gardening magazines. It was a big enough house, comfortable, colourful and haphazardly furnished with a mixture of Heal's best, combined with car boot and junk shop bargains and mis-matched arty pieces that suited them all. Stella remembered Abigail's Sussex rectory, on the other hand, as being a meticulous work of tasteful splendour in shades of cream with gleaming antiques. It had the kind of highly polished grown-up grandeur that could only be maintained by sending, as Abigail and Martin had, their pair of boisterous children to boarding school and then whisking them safely away from the pristine premises for skiing, pony club camps and

Corsican beaches during the holidays. She wondered suddenly, if those children, only aged about ten and eight, ever thought of the house as a proper home.

Abigail must have been reading Stella's train of thought. She sighed, her eyes fixed on the ceiling cobwebs. 'I'm sure I got everything wrong. If only I'd been able to settle for what you and Adrian have got. Perhaps it isn't too late to settle for it *now* – I'm sure I'm owed some kind of *contentment*, don't you think?'

Stella frowned. 'What do you mean, "settle for"?' she demanded defensively, ignoring Abigail's rhetorical question. 'It's hardly impoverished inner-city misery we're living in. We do OK. A lot more than OK, actually.' She's shameless, Stella thought, half-admiring Abigail's lack of tact. Generally relatively polite as she was to chosen friends, she was just the kind of woman who'd come swanning up to those less favoured at a party and say, 'Goodness, darling, have you still got that ghastly jacket?' without her brain connecting fast enough with what her mouth was saying. Stella used to find this rather enviable, and had done ever since Abigail had queried a low essay mark she'd been given by bluntly challenging her male tutor with, 'Are you quite sure you aren't marking me down because you're shorter than me and feel inadequate?' It must be bliss, Stella imagined, to come straight out with whatever daft thing was in your mind without having the thought of possible consequences hopping in first and slamming the emergency good-manners brakes on. She tried a practice attempt at being blunt, 'So why did he want to go and have an affair in the first place? What was going wrong? Was it sex?' Abigail's eyes widened and she fiddled with her cigarette lighter, turning it over and over, watching the gold catching the light. If she'd been a child, Stella thought, that might be construed as guilty fidgeting. For once, she really was choosing carefully what to say.

'Everyone all right? Not finished the wine? Good.' Adrian came bustling in, reached across the table and picked up the bottle to top up his own glass. 'Sorry, am I interrupting?' he asked cautiously, wary of their silence.

'We weren't talking about you, if that's what you were thinking.' Abigail beamed a sweet smile at him, reaching out a hand to caress his fondly as if she was reassuring her cat. Sweet of her, Stella thought, to be as pleased to see Adrian as to see her – men could be so nervous of women *ganging up*.

'Never crossed my mind,' he assured her, scuttling nervously backwards to the door, suddenly eager to return to the TV and the second half of the match.

'You didn't answer my question,' Stella reminded Abigail. There was more to this than she'd been told, she decided. Martin's defection might not be so completely out of the blue as she'd been encouraged to think. At college, though she'd probably now deny it could possibly have happened. Abigail had once set herself a personal target of sleeping with a different man every night for a week. Stella remembered her joking about having knickers with days of the week embroidered on them, peering under her skirt and joking with something like, 'If I'm wearing Wednesday it must be Paul.' One of the men, a brawny rugby player with far less sexual experience than bar-room bragging would have the rest of the team believe, had even left a grateful £20 on the pillow which Abigail had been so thrilled about she'd taken Stella out and treated them both to extravagant steak and chips at the pub. It had been there that she'd confessed with a lot of drunken giggling just how ill-gotten was her sudden windfall. Perhaps, Stella thought, she still liked a spot of casual, anonymous sex now and then, in the same way that Ellen MacIver had joined a local sports club because she still

61

nostalgically enjoyed the occasional schoolgirlish game of lacrosse.

Abigail was again saved from being trapped into an honest reply by a sudden urgent rapping on the door. Peggy came in without waiting for an answer, bringing with her the cool spring night air. Abigail sprang to grab her cat before it escaped into the night. 'Council man just came round again. Sneaked round in a rowing boat in the dark, the bugger. They usually come in two's, nice and nasty like on police programmes, but this time it was Nasty on his own,' Peggy said to Stella glumly, eying what was left of the wine. She sat down heavily next to Abigail who clutched Cleo on her lap.

'At this time?' Stella said, fetching her a glass. 'Whatever was he doing harassing you this late?'

'Harassing's the word,' Peggy complained. She coughed and shifted her arthritic legs till the least painful position was achieved. 'He said I couldn't pretend to be out if the light was on. He brought another reminder that they want me off the mooring. It's not as if I'm going to be in the way of their precious sodding bridge.' She looked depressed and defeated, Stella thought, angry at council bureaucrats.

'They're obsessed with suburban tidiness,' Stella said angrily and then explained to Abigail who was looking bewildered but politely interested, 'Peggy's got the last houseboat left here, just by the end of our garden. There used to be about ten of them. She's lived here for fifteen years, all wired up and more or less plumbed in. It's absolutely no harm to anyone.' The 'plumbed in' was definitely less rather than more, Stella remembered. Peggy had a fresh water supply but had long ago dispensed with the heavy and complicated chemical toilet, preferring to cut out the middle man, as she put it, and dump bucket contents over the side. 'If ducks and rats can put shit in the river, I don't see why I shouldn't,' she'd declared, leaving Adrian

62

and Stella wishing she simply hadn't mentioned it.

'The bridge is supposed to be much further round the other side, nearer to the ferry, so it's not as if Peggy's in the way. But they can't build it till she's gone because she's keeping open the rights to ten other moorings that in theory could be claimed and then occupied.'

Abigail looked puzzled, 'And does no one really want the bridge? I'd have thought it would be a godsend, loads easier than turning that awkward great handle on the ghastly raft-thingy.'

'Well, if even I can still do it . . .' Peggy interrupted scornfully.

'Perhaps what you really need is two bridges,' Abigail suggested casually, lighting another cigarette. 'One to connect the other bank as well. Wouldn't that be rather nice? Especially for you older folks?'

'Over my dead and buried body. And I mean that. Do you know, he said I should be in sheltered accommodation. I told him I was, I was sheltered by friends.' Peggy glared at Abigail and thumped her fist on the table before levering herself up and shuffling as fast as she could out of the door and back to the barge.

'You've upset her now,' Stella accused Abigail. 'She's too old for fuss and bother and she doesn't need any help to start imagining the worst.'

'Sorry.' Abigail looked contrite. 'Putting both feet straight in it seems to be a speciality of mine. I just can't seem to help it.'

Toby sat in a quiet corner of the pub with four of his friends and together they flicked through magazines salivating over the glossy photos. Girl students from the sixth form college perched cutely on bar stools with their tiny skirts stretched high across their thighs, swinging their legs and eying the boys, waiting in vain to be noticed and bought drinks.

'God, just look at the bodywork on that will you,' Nick, a tall broad boy with a black ponytail was saying, 'and check the bumpers.' He passed the magazine across to Toby who groaned longingly, 'What I'd give . . .' he said.

'Not sure about the colour though. A bit washed out for me,' he then decided after a few moments close inspection.

'Yeah, maybe,' Nick agreed, 'pale blue's all right for polishing up and showing on the concourse, but a bit poncey for daily driving.' He turned the page and found another VW Beetle. 'What about a nice little 1302 in British Racing Green? Classic. You can't go wrong with that.'

Toby had seen the girls looking. He was used to that. One of them wasn't bad in a gawky-legged sort of way, but he was a methodical boy, handling his bank account with a responsible maturity that would be the envy of any middle-aged man. He had a job at a car showroom from which he was saving diligently to take the Beetle round Europe before university. All girls always proved to be expensive, a serious threat to the cash flow, however much they'd been brought up on caring, sharing and independence. Older women were better, not just better about money but not so silly and clinging and wanting reassurance. He suddenly thought of Abigail and her long slim legs the way he'd seen them from ground level. She'd arrived by taxi but he was willing to bet she flashed around Sussex in something like a BMW convertible or possibly a Discovery and hadn't the first clue about how to open the bonnet. She'd probably never needed to. There wouldn't be much point discussing the progress of the Beetle with her: if he mentioned a flywheel gland nut she might think he was talking dirty and start avoiding him in the house. Lucky, he thought, as he gave the girls at the bar another idle looking over, the spare

64

room she was occupying in the attic had its own bathroom, shared only with Ruth, otherwise the scope for embarrassing clashings outside the door might just be too much. He'd have to go and crash at Nick's. There was something about her, that just-been-shot-at look probably, that made him want her to like him. He felt like being kind to her, in the way he had been to a terrified squirrel the previous autumn when the MacIver's Corgi had chewed off half its tail. It would be interesting to try and get her to smile properly, not just in that hard glassy way he'd seen so far, he thought cautiously, flicking unseeingly through *Volksworld*.

Abigail paced the bedroom floor and wondered how she was to be expected to manage for money if Martin never came back. After generous settlements from both Johnny and Noel she could reasonably claim to own most of the house – the children would need somewhere to live during the holidays and Martin and the blond bimbette wouldn't want to have to entertain them. But the bills for running the house were huge, so Martin might manage to force her into selling it by simply being mean about paying them. She didn't really have much to do with that side of things. He'd always made such a point of finding her 'adorable' that she'd played along with it by handing him any envelope that came through the door looking as if it might be a bill. He paid for her astronomical health club membership, her hairdressing, Harvey Nichols account, American Express charges, car expenses, blissful holidays, the Colefax and Fowler fabrics, National Trust paints and the teams of designers and artisans who came in to apply them, the garden landscapers, pool maintenance, children's school fees – everything that made her luscious lazy life the comfortably privileged way it was. The room she now fretted and paced in was pretty in a home-spun sort of way, she thought – though if it was hers she'd have chosen a shade of yellow closer to unsalted butter than to lemon. The bed on which Cleo was curled up and purring was brass, but not the new luscious sort, rather the aged and tarnished type as if it might conceivably have been Adrian's grandmother's. Perhaps she'd died in it, Abigail thought, recognizing that she was getting morbidly fanciful. Abigail preferred her antiques to be scrupulously anonymous, polished and restored (authentically, of course) till no trace of undesirable age-stain was left. She liked history to be a simple matter of which century, which king and which auction room. She could not bear the fact that a linen press might actually once have contained less than perfectly Persil-laundered sheets; that mice three centuries ago might have been trapped and suffocated in her Tudor chest. Beside the window overlooking Stella and Adrian's waterside garden stood an old pine chest of drawers that someone, perhaps Ruth as a ten-year-old by the look of it, had had a go at painting in two shades of sludgy blue. It looked like jolly poster paint, whereas in her house only the sleekest, most authentic Dead Flat Oil was permitted. Cleo was dozing on a patchwork quilt that Stella must have made – Abigail recognized Liberty prints and bits of Laura Ashley from dresses she remembered her wearing years and years ago. Stella's whole house was put together with bits and pieces of happy memories. Paintings on the yellow walls were of flowers and boats, and there was a jolly one of the rowing club she'd seen as she stood with Toby by the ferry, perhaps also done by Ruth or Toby. She thought of the smart prep school where teachers who were paid to get results had the brief chance to admire but then throw away her children's artistic efforts, keeping only the ones suitable for showing off on open days. And she thought of her own Picasso etchings, an investment but not a treasure it seemed to her now, carefully grouped in her golden drawing-room where she'd never allowed her small son and daughter to blemish the cream silk cushions with their sticky fingers and uncontrolled feet, and she shivered with lonely misery.

Chapter Five

Stella sat in the kitchen in the early morning sorting through her mail and waiting for Abigail to come downstairs. It was almost ten, and Abigail's non-appearance suggested either that she'd lain in anxious misery till sleep had finally caught up with her in the early hours of the morning or that she could manage the effortless rest of the innocent. Her cat had already got up, pattering downstairs as soon as it heard kitchen noises and Stella had fed it. She'd then accompanied it into the garden where it had nervously, on this unfamiliar territory, scratched several experimental holes, dislodging Stella's young foxgloves before daring at last to pee, closing its slightly crossed blue eyes in blissful relief. Stella had also felt relief that the cat hadn't taken the chance to run away or been chased off towards the fox-inhabited wilderness by Willow's cats prowling in from up the lane. Imagine, she thought, having to tell Abigail that she'd been abandoned by her cat as well as her husband. Back in the house, the little cat snaked itself up onto a kitchen chair and purred loudly, settled on the cushion and started washing its back left leg. Stella watched it as she made herself some tea, admiring its obvious contentment. Cats are just like small children, she thought, only really happy with what's completely familiar and undemanding. The trouble with grown-ups, she decided as she sat at the table next to the cat, was that they thought they couldn't be happy unless they were forever searching out new, stimulating novelties.

She turned her attention back to the post and to her work. The weekly Jiffy bag had arrived from *Get This!*, well stuffed with the multi-coloured envelopes that all adolescent girls seemed to collect, containing another batch of teenage anguish. Now this was one group of people who were *supposed* to go out and look for the novelty value in life, she thought, wishing she couldn't accurately predict what would be bugging them all this week. In terms of teenage magazines, it was a truth universally acknowledged that a fourteen-year-old girl in possession of her right mind must be in want of a boyfriend. If it wasn't for that 'truth', she thought as she risked her nails tugging the staples from the envelope, there wouldn't *be* problem pages, which would be a very good thing if it didn't involve biting off one of the hands that fed her. She tipped the contents of the padded bag all over the table, chose a bright pink envelope addressed in urgent purple pen and opened it carefully. 'Dear Alice, I got drunk at a party and did something really stupid . . .' Stella would put £50 on the chances of there being at least five more letters in the pile that started with exactly the same words.

'Some time today,' Adrian said as he walked into the kitchen, 'is there any chance of you collecting a couple of reams of paper from the stationer's? And is it today my grey jacket's ready at the cleaner's?'

Stella looked at him across the heap of mail he hadn't noticed and then closed her eyes, pleading with the heavens for patience. What's the phrase, she thought? Could it be 'too busy?' She should have taken it all up to her desk – it was her own fault for opening work mail in the kitchen where she was easily confused with a domestic item.

'I've got all this,' she told him, waving her hand vaguely across the table. 'Perhaps Ruth could go on the way back from college, or maybe Abigail – don't forget I've got her to take out and entertain as well. I've got to go to the printers too with the art fair map.'

Adrian latched on to the last statement and looked pleased. 'Oh good, well while you're there, perhaps you could pick up the paper at the same time, it's only down the road.' He leaned across the table and kissed her forehead. 'Thanks, darling. I'm nearly at book-end, and while it's on a roll, you know . . . Ruth and Toby still upstairs?' He glanced rather furtively at the door, opened a drawer in the dresser and pulled out a copy of *Mayfair*. 'Popped it in here last night,' he said, flicking through to the readers' letters page from where many of his ideas for books, over the years, had come. 'Didn't want to leave it lying around.'

Stella stopped opening letters and looked at him intently. She felt suddenly curious. 'Do you ever really get off on reading that stuff?'

He looked at her over the top of the magazine, like a professor expressing scholarly outrage. 'Of course not!' he declared with a hoot of laughter. 'Do you imagine I sit out in the hut all day in a state of horny frustration? Good grief, it would have dropped off by now! You know this is just *research*.' He was munching a piece of cold toast and reading with as much calm detachment as if it was a leader in *The Times*.

'Do you think they make it all up?' she asked, 'or do people really get up to all that odd stuff like doing it while they're driving up the M4 and under the table at weddings and such.'

Adrian shrugged, 'I don't know, never thought about it. I just find it occasionally useful when I'm stuck for a chapter. Do *yours* make it up, do you think?' He looked at the pile of letters.

'Probably, but all these problems are universal what-ifs, really. A sixteen-year-old girl dating a man of her father's age, parents who won't let their precious only child out after nine p.m., and she's seventeen, that sort of thing.'

'Well, there you are then. It's much the same with this, though most of it's showing off, not grumbling. Could be anyone's sex life in here.' He went back to his reading.

Stella though was still searching for something, 'But what *really* turns you on, you know, in that instant . . .' she waved a hand vaguely over her colourful heap of letters, 'in that *teenage* sort of way?' She felt somehow she shouldn't be asking this, she should already know the answers, be fully *using* her knowledge of the answers. She was sure she used to know – they'd never have had any kind of relationship otherwise. Now, thinking about it, it seemed an awful long time since they'd had one of those delicious, spontaneous bouts of sex, say in the open air on a thundery summer night, or fast and frantic, rummaging away among the piled-up coats while a terribly sedate party went on downstairs. 'Sex is a bit like cooking, isn't it,' she said, mostly to herself as Adrian seemed to be absorbed in his reading, 'you know, after some keen experimenting you tend to stick to the things you're familiar with and that you know you like and are easy.'

'Hmm,' Adrian agreed vaguely, adding rather oddly, 'can't beat a good risotto.'

She couldn't imagine Abigail wondering about the secret sexual fantasies of any of her husbands. She'd simply assume (till now) that they were all based on her, make *sure* they were, in fact. She'd wheedle out all their deepest naughtiest secrets and serve them up with positively cordon bleu panache. Adrian had put

71

down his magazine and was looking out of the window, far across the river. He thought for a long moment, tapping his ear with his pen. 'You look so studious,' she said, 'just like when we sat together in bed at the college revising war poets together. Do you remember? And Abigail used to join us sometimes. She always sat on my feet. I got cramp.'

Adrian looked up and laughed, 'About the only time she was ever on a bed with her clothes on. I can't imagine her wasting time in bed with a man on Eng. Lit. revision.'

Stella suddenly felt a tweak of anguish, 'Was that all we were doing? Wasting time?' But Adrian had returned to being absorbed in his magazine, leaving her alone to decide whether she'd been unfavourably compared or not. Sometimes, Stella remembered that in those revision sessions, Abigail had entertained them with tales of what she'd just been up to, telling them about having sex in the church tower and being trapped by the campanology club coming in for bell ringing practice, or doing it on a roundabout on the A40, or fellating a visiting lecturer under a restaurant table. Her stories, rather than the 'Happy Hooker' column, could easily, Stella suddenly thought, have been the original inspirations for Adrian's career.

'Oddbins,' Adrian suddenly announced, making Stella jump, 'that's always got me going. I get really horny going in there knowing I'm in for some serious wine shopping. In fact, I'm really quite promiscuous about it, any good wine store will do.'

'What are you wearing?' Abigail's foxy head appeared round the door of Stella's bedroom, followed by her body in a cream silk kimono.

'Oh, just usual day-to-day stuff,' Stella told her, looking down at herself in her jeans and old blue linen shirt and wondering if, compared with long, lean

Abigail, she slightly resembled a beach ball. Work would have to wait till she'd taken Abigail round the town and helped her do a bit of therapeutic shopping. She could at least show her properly how the ferry worked so that she was then free to come and go from the island as she pleased.

'We could have lunch at the Italian deli, or the wine bar or something if you like, but we don't have to dress up for that.'

'Oh, OK.' Abigail sounded disappointed, as if she'd secretly been expecting a surprise trip to Knightsbridge and a chance to wear something chic from Agnés B. Stella noticed she had bitten both her thumbnails right down to raw red flesh, ruining what must have been an expensive French manicure. Perhaps she really was terribly unhappy, truly bereft without Martin. As a student, Abigail had seemed to discard boyfriends as thoughtlessly as other people might chuck out holey socks. Someone at a party had once said, 'If all the men in the county were laid end to end . . .' only to be interrupted by Adrian with 'They have been, mostly by Abigail.'

Stella went to the mirror, flicked a token touch of mascara lightly over her lashes and tried to remember Abigail being dumped by someone, but couldn't recall it happening. She'd growled and complained when one of them, like Martin, had turned to a vibrant blond for comfort rather insensitively soon after she'd abandoned him, but that was more to do with the fact that he'd so quickly sought and found solace than any regrets about her decision.

Abigail (having decided on black Levis and a long, honey-coloured cashmere cardigan) cheered up noticeably the moment she stepped off the ferry and onto the bank from where she could admire the island safely.

'The island's really awfully pretty,' she said, looking

across the water at the abundant trees, the pretty pastel-painted (apart from Willow's) houses. 'No wonder you decided to live here. I remember your last house – it was OK but it was *exactly* the same as the one next door to it,' she said, as if this, in suburban London, was a highly unusual arrangement.

Stella grinned at her. 'We like it here. There's a kind of outlaw quality about being cut off from the land. Adrian says we're just fifty drunkards clinging to a mudbank, which makes it all sound a bit mad, but really we're just getting by, like anywhere else.'

'Not a lot like anywhere else. You don't get cut off by high tides in the middle of Petworth.' She shuddered at the thought. They reached the High Street and Abigail, enchanted to see traffic and bustle, was almost at sprinting point.

'There's no rush,' Stella laughed, 'it's only a small town.'

'I know but it's got *normal people*,' Abigail said, 'not just a collection of artsy-folksy types. You and Adrian excepted, of course. You know . . .' her voice softened and became tremulous, 'I can't tell you how grateful I am, you putting up with me like this. I want to buy you something, just a little thank you present.' They slowed down as Abigail peered round, looking for a suitable shop. 'You'd look really good in red, you know,' she said, turning and looking Stella up and down. Stella immediately got the fat feeling again, hating to be inspected.

'Adrian's always saying that too, which reminds me I've got to pick up his bloody paper from the stationers. We'll do that last, it's too heavy to carry far.'

'You shouldn't be running round after him like that,' Abigail scolded, 'you've got your own work to deal with. Would he expect to be sent out like the office gofer and pick up paper clips and staples for you when *you* needed them?'

Stella thought for a moment before replying, wondering when the last time was she'd actually asked him. 'Well I suppose he would, of course he would if he was going that way. Why wouldn't he?'

'Because he's a man and by nature they think they're just too big-time, that's why. You should have told him to ring the office supply people, put the stuff on account and have them bike it round. That's what I'd have done. He takes you too much for granted, you know. If I was Auntie Alice or whatever your professional name is, I'd suggest you give him a teeny bit of a shock to perk him up,' she declared, hauling Stella into the doorway of Whistles. 'Look at that dress, isn't it just to kill for? Let's go in and try things on, just for fun.'

Stella giggled. 'I haven't done that for years. I remember when it used to be a kind of hobby. The spare time I must have had . . . Do you remember when we bought those white Minnie Mouse platform shoes that we could only just totter about in? I only clothes-shop when I desperately need something these days. Sad really.'

'Well, I think you desperately *need* that dress, so come on,' Abigail said, opening the shop door.

Ruth ran lightly down the path towards the boathouse, hoping that this would be the day she did more than just modelling for Bernard. She'd planned a whole afternoon college skive, missing double English so she hoped it would be well worth it. She loved posing for him, adored preparing her body before she went, making sure it was oiled and creamed and smelling luscious in case he wanted to savour its abundant delights. He hadn't yet, but she knew he soon would. It was what he did with all his young models, first the painting, then the sex. Bernard's reputation contributed enormously to the town's wariness of the island.

'Don't you think it would be better the other way round? Sex first, then the painting after?' Ruth had speculated with her friend Melissa while they'd been inattentive at a French class. 'Surely he'd paint me better if he'd sort of felt his way round as well as just *looked* at me.'

'You're probably right,' Melissa had agreed solemnly, adding with commercial common sense, 'After all, I know he thinks he's really big-time, and I suppose he is in a *local* sort of way, but as artists go, he's not exactly a household name, is he? Perhaps that's his big mistake. He needs a more hands-on approach.'

Ruth could feel her breasts and belly undulating as she ran. On modelling days she wore no underwear so as not to make distracting marks on her skin and she loved the primitive, free feeling this gave her as she moved. She was big, what grandmothers of old would have approvingly called 'well-covered', and she was unusually comfortable with that, revelling in her expanses of flesh, defying the hysterical anti-fat propaganda that shrieked at her from every fashion magazine, every shop that stopped at size 14. She pitied the many, many sad girls who were always writing to her mother, wailing that no one would ever fancy them till they weighed less than seven stone, as if being size eight would be a bigger achievement than A-levels. She was blessed with a face of what Bernard had described so thrillingly as 'glorious beauty' – a large, deep-red mouth with slightly buck teeth, enormous blue eyes and a cloud of dark hennaed curls that he wouldn't describe as pre-Raphaelite (too obvious) but hadn't yet thought up anything more original to say that would impress her.

'You're in a hurry, going to see the rabbits?' Willow was standing by the small gate that led to the neglected couple of wilderness acres beyond Bernard's boat-house. She was holding a bunch of buttercups in front of her with both hands like a conscientious brides-maid and looking ridiculous, Ruth thought, in a too-short pink and white dress that resembled a little girl's party frock.

'No, Willow, I'm not going to see the ickle bunnies, I'm going to see Bernard.' Ruth couldn't resist crowing at her, just to see the winsomeness fade into controlled fury.

'Oh, I don't think he's in,' Willow told her. 'I just rang the bell and there was no reply – though I suppose he might have been down in the gallery or some-thing . . .'

Ruth smiled at her, taunting with youth's casual cruelty, 'He'll be in for *me. I'm* expected.'

She felt rather ashamed as she climbed the outside staircase to Bernard's balcony. Hurting Willow was so easy it was like stamping on a butterfly. Willow hadn't been to see the rabbits in the wilderness either, she was pretty sure, unless she'd been loitering in there on purpose, frolicking among the wild flowers and hoping to be spotted from afar and likened to a wood nymph by Bernard. She had probably picked the buttercups with a view to dropping in on him and hanging around in his studio, getting him to notice how domestic and creative she could be, leaving the flowers scattily arranged in a jug (one that she'd made herself and given to him previously) on his big table by the window where he could look at them and think of her. She's definitely a witch, Ruth decided, imagining her humming a small but potent love-spell over the buttercups.

The dress looked stunning, a soft scarlet linen wrapover number that followed Stella's curves and flared out from the hips to swirl just above her knees.

'I don't wear things like this,' Stella told Abigail as they stood together in the shop, staring at their reflections in the long mirror.

'Well, you should. You're still thin enough for a bit of cling and your legs are great. You shouldn't hide them away all the time. It's so *apologetic.* I can't *bear* apologetic. Just because you won't see thirty again . . .' The young shop assistant, hovering on the scent of a sale, looked as if she expected lightning to strike.

'Thirty!' Stella spluttered, 'You and I both know we're losing sight of forty!'

'You might have. I've not quite given in to it yet,' Abigail sniffed.

'Listen, Martin is going to buy this dress for you, I insist, just to thank you for having me to stay and cheering me up.' She pulled out a wallet bulging with credit cards, selected a platinum one and handed it to the assistant.

Stella reached out and snatched it back. 'Don't be silly, I can buy my own dresses,' she said, hauling out her Visa card and stuffing it into the assistant's hand before Abigail could argue.

'In that case, I'm buying lunch, no arguments,' Abigail told her, 'you know how I sulk if I don't get my own way.'

Stella wondered disloyally if it was ten years of Abigail's bossiness that had helped Martin out of the palatial house and on his way to New York with golden-haired Fiona. Perhaps Fiona was restfully adoring, flatteringly submissive – all those things that tired, care-worn men of a certain age seemed to choose in a mistress. It wasn't that different from what the younger ones seemed to want either. Analyzing the letters she got from boys, she would say their ideal girl adored football, was willing to hang around patiently while they joshed with their mates and would allow them to put their hands in her knickers from time to time. Not much change over the years there, she thought. As they walked along the crowded lunchtime street she thought about the heap of problems that waited on the kitchen table to be dealt with – all those adolescents who were confidently expecting her to put in a full day's work on their anguish and give them the priority the young demanded as a right. Instead, she was swanning around town in the middle of the day, carrying, in a stiff black and white carrier, the tissue-wrapped, scarlet dress that she neither needed, nor, probably, would normally have bothered to try on, let alone buy. She couldn't, on the other hand, remember the last time she'd bought something that made her feel so utterly terrific – and that really was entirely thanks to Abigail. Spending money, even by proxy, seemed to have made Abigail positively jaunty – she was now bouncing along the pavement, Stella noticed. Perhaps it was true, like the old Joan Rivers joke, that some women really do only have orgasms when they catch sight of a credit card slip being signed. Just as Stella was considering whether the sexual thrill could be the same with a humble old jolly striped Access card as for a double-titanium, moonrock studded Coutts number, Abigail stopped abruptly outside a wine bar.

'Oh look! In there, isn't that your Toby?' she asked, pointing into the chic art nouveau gloom.

'Shouldn't think so, he can't afford places like this, he's saving up for some serious travel. Besides, he's more a Crown and Anchor sort,' Stella said, peering in towards where the pointing finger indicated and seeing only a row of gleaming legs of office girls shining from the bar stools.

'Well, we'll *have* to go in now,' Abigail decided, shoving the door further open, 'the barman's grinning at me and it would be too unkind just to walk off. He'd feel rejected.'

'Considerate of you,' Stella murmured with suspicion as she followed her inside.

Toby was sitting by himself at a table laid for four and studying the menu intently as if he really couldn't choose between the leek pie and lasagne. An empty beer glass sat beside him, so he'd obviously been there for some time.

'How did you know he was here? You couldn't possibly have seen him in the dark and round this corner.' Stella accused Abigail, who simply shrugged and smiled with a mysterious 'who knows?' kind of look.

'Hi Mum, I hear you're buying lunch,' Toby greeted her.

Stella sat down. 'Actually Abigail is,' she told him. She looked round to see Abigail's honey-coloured jacket weaving its way towards the loo at the back of the bar. What on earth was she up to, Stella wondered. 'She arranged to meet you here then? Why didn't she tell me, and when did you fix it up?'

'I don't know why she didn't say anything. Probably thought I wouldn't come. You know how it is with us *young* people.' He shrugged with a distinct lack of interest and ran a finger down the menu, obviously far more concerned that he should be fed. 'This morning on the stairs she just asked me where would be good for food and I said this place and she said if I was here about one-ish I'd be OK for a free lunch.'

'Haven't you heard, there's no such thing,' Stella warned quietly as Abigail returned.

'Now, isn't this nice?' Abigail said, sitting down and bringing with her a fresh cloud of expensive scent. She looked admiringly at Toby as he studied his empty glass with the one eye that wasn't obscured by his hair. 'I do envy you, Stella,' she sighed, 'I'm so looking forward to my boy being old enough to have grown-up lunch out with his ageing mummy. If he'd want to, that is. At the moment James and Venetia are still at the awful burger-and-chips stage.'

'So's Toby, usually,' Stella told her truthfully.

'In that case, it's all the more sweet of him to turn up here and indulge us,' said Abigail, reaching forward and patting his oil-streaked arm, at which he did not, Stella noticed with amazement, flinch. 'I'm not your godmother or anything, am I?' Abigail suddenly asked him, 'I mean if I am, I expect it'll take more than a portion of moussaka to make up for not taking you to *Peter Pan* or the circus and all that.'

'We don't have godparents. Mum and Dad were going through their pagan phase when they had us,' Toby told her, putting on a mock spaniel-sad face. 'We've been deprived.'

'Oh, you poor boy! Stella, how dreadfully remiss of you!'

Stella had an uncomfortable feeling she was being ganged up on in a joke she wasn't quite seeing. 'He does OK,' she said, 'he's never gone short of the usual treats. And he was never that keen on circuses.'

'Sorry for the animals?' Abigail asked Toby with an expression of tender sympathy. Stella felt irritated by Toby's look of lazy satisfaction at being the centre of attention.

'No he was, and is, absolutely terrified of clowns,' she answered for him. 'Now, shall we eat?'

Stella trudged home alone carrying the new dress and Adrian's boxes of paper which she delivered to the summerhouse. 'Abigail's picking up your jacket from the cleaners – I left her cruising the High Street.'

'Really? I wonder what else she'll pick up. Thanks for the paper,' he said vaguely, refusing to be distracted. Stella plugged in his kettle and clattered around making tea, also refusing to defer to his intense concentration. She felt aggrieved, somehow, done out of the chance to do her own work while everyone else around her went about fulfilling exactly what they wanted to do as if nothing else could possibly be expected of them. She'd worked herself into such a state of resentment that she'd decided she didn't even like the fact that Abigail had volunteered to collect Adrian's jacket. She didn't want her handling his clothes, even securely bagged in opaque polythene – it was all too intimate. Yesterday, any other day, she was sure she wouldn't have felt like that but then yesterday she hadn't seen Abigail pawing at Toby. Abigail had reminded her then of the sleek little Siamese cat which had sat on her lap that morning. It had purred ecstatically and kneaded lovingly at her leg, with its needle-sharp little possessive claws digging and hurting.

'Something wrong?' Adrian asked, suddenly sensing a cloud.

Stella looked at his face where an expression of dutiful concern was in place, but his hands were still over the keyboard, all ready poised to form the next sentence the moment he'd said the right thing. She squeezed his shoulder, 'Nothing I can quite put my finger on.'

Chapter Six

Perhaps next time, and if not, he could find himself another bloody model, Ruth thought glumly as she walked into college the next morning, already ten minutes late for the class at which she'd have to sit with Melissa and confess to failure. Melissa, waiting for her on the steps, stubbed out her cigarette on the scarred trunk of the sycamore tree and ran to join her as she saw her by the gate.

'Well? *Did* you?'

'No. He just painted away as bloody sodding usual,' Ruth sighed. 'I'd poured the geranium oil in the bath too. It's supposed to be irresistible. And I used my passionflower body lotion. What a waste. He did say I *glistened* and he seemed to like that but he still didn't touch me – not unless you count prodding my bum with the sharp end of the paintbrush and telling me to roll to the left a bit. He hardly even looked – it's so *insulting*. Christ, he's *old*, you'd think he'd be grateful.'

Melissa giggled, 'With all that oily stuff on your body, it's probably the best thing. You must have been like a skating rink. He'd have slid off.'

Ruth scowled at her. Into her highly visual imagination came a ridiculous and unwelcome cartoon of plump and naked Bernard skimming like a gold-medal

83

skater off her body and the velvet-strewn sofa, out through the balcony window and plummeting heavily into the river. 'It's not *funny*. I want to have sex with him *now*, not after the painting's all finished and done with and framed and hung up and it's too late for all the *passion* and the excitement.'

'Passion for you or the painting?'

'Both, I suppose. I want people to look at this picture and be able to *tell* that there's more to it than me sprawled on the sofa reading *Marie Claire* and hoping.'

'He might just be a lousy shag,' Melissa pointed out, 'and then there wouldn't be much use in that either, would there?'

Stella knew she was wasting precious working time. The rainbow pile of envelopes still waited in a basket next to the computer. She had just two more days to get next week's column done and faxed. Abigail had gone up to her room for a rest after lunch. 'I do occasionally have a little sleep in the afternoons. Or a little read,' she explained, waving a glossy magazine at Stella when she asked if she had a headache. Contrary woman, Stella thought, remembering Abigail protesting she wasn't *ill* the last time Stella had suggested she might want to rest. Imagine claiming a whole afternoon just for sleeping, claiming it as a *right*. She strolled idly along the path towards Willow's house, imagining having so little to do that time could be found in the middle of the day for a 'rest'. Surely it was only frantically busy people who needed one, not people like Abigail who could fill or empty their days as they chose. From when she was a small child, she remembered her mother having what she called 'a little lie-down' after lunch, dozing in her coffee-coloured nylon and lace petticoat under the pinky blue shot-satin eiderdown on her bed while her small daughter, far too big to need sleep in the afternoons and longing to get back to running around in the garden, lay bored on her own bed peeling tiny strips of rose patterned paper off the wall and dreading the smack she'd get for it later.

'It would do you good too, you know,' Abigail had recommended, 'it's so refreshing, you'll be ready for anything afterwards.' There'd been a suggestive gleam in her eyes that Stella recalled only too well from the days when the 'anything' Abigail had always been ready for had consisted of an over-excited fellow student eager to remove his trousers.

Willow's garden gate was of twisted, tortured iron work made as an experimental free sample by Enzo the sculptor who, when he and Giuliana first came to live on the island, had thought Willow might be useful, both as a source of bodily comfort and for the neighbourly borrowing of cups of brown rice. The gate, which was head-high with bent and lethal spikes and took a great deal of pushing to open, creaked and wobbled alarmingly but Willow refused to allow Enzo to rehang it on the grounds that its noise deterred burglars and the casually nosy. If he fancied a second go at romancing her, perhaps by sneaking in and surprising her in the night, his slapdash workmanship had scuppered his own chances. Willow, who despite her fey and fragile appearance, could whip up perfectly symmetrical pots the size of half-barrels with skill and ease, thought of Enzo as a flawed artisan, beneath notice – and besides, he was *terribly* fond of his sister. Willow and Giuliana kept a war-by-proxy going on, represented by Willow's cats and Giuliana's chickens, with Giuliana demanding that they wear warning bells on their collars and Willow arguing that the hens wouldn't hear them over the racket of Enzo's ludicrously giant wind chimes.

Stella shoved hard at the gate and its squeal was echoed by a chorus of interested miaowing from

Willow's three black cats. She was reminded of Ruth's opinion that Willow was a witch by the absence of the fourth cat, a mottled, kipper-coloured, long-haired stray, the shades of whose fur more than slightly resembled Willow's own peculiarly blotchy hair. 'You never see that cat and Willow at the same time,' Ruth had told them all during supper one night, 'so the cat must be her familiar. Willow *is* that cat.'

'Trans*moggy*fied, is she?' Toby had mocked.

'Over *here*! Stella!' Stella looked round the rampantly overgrown garden, half expecting to see the kipper-cat calling down to her, grinning from the branches of Willow's elder tree. Willow, in pink dungarees and a rainbow T-shirt was weeding her oil-drums where tobacco plants, outsize nasturtiums and marigolds already ran riot.

'They're surely not this season's, not at that size,' Stella commented admiringly.

'Well, they've hung on and reseeded themselves over the winter. No frost this side, you see, in the shelter of the bank. Almost tropical,' she sighed, looking dreamy as if she was seeing not the cottage garden flowers of England but banana trees and bougainvillaea. 'They grow like weeds. I've been thinking of filling the garden with herbs and having a stall to sell them. Perhaps for next year's open day I could make some herb pots too. Marjoram, rosemary, applemint — such romantic names, names for angels' children . . .' Her eyes gazed musingly into the distance as she spoke and Stella watched her closely, seeing for the first time the grubby black flecks of mascara lumped on to the rather stumpy eyelashes, grey eyeliner applied thickly as if it had been loaded on top of yesterday's make-up. She's quite a raddled old slut really, Stella thought, not without some fondness.

'I've come to buy a pot,' Stella prompted, 'I need something suitable for quite large salads, any colour as long as it's not purple or green. Have you got anything suitable, do you think?'

'Oh, you've come to *buy* something!' Willow's attention flew back at last. 'I thought perhaps there was a party going on or something jolly and fun like that.' She looked just like a little girl who'd been told the tooth fairy was fresh out of cash, Stella thought. It also crossed her mind that having a few people round, say the next night, would be something else she could do towards entertaining Abigail. She told Willow, instantly inventing, 'Not a party exactly, but tomorrow we're having a small supper gathering, seeing as we've got Abigail staying, just the islanders, so yes, do come at seven-ish. That's partly why I need the bowl.' She felt limp from lying and from the thought of the effort she'd just gone and landed herself with but Willow's face was lit up like a birthday child's.

'A party *and* a sale! Wow!'

'Is selling something so unusual?' Stella laughed.

'Only among the neighbours,' Willow told her as they went into the house. 'This island's supposed to be a close-knit artistic community, right? Support each other, right? *Wrong.* Enzo and Giuliana's place is full of their old grandmother's Italian antiques so they won't even *look* at anything under a hundred years old unless it's got a useful bit of bendable metal. The MacIver's don't trust anything that doesn't come in a flat-pack and most of the others think they should get a neighbours' discount so enormous it isn't worth selling. Of course, there's you and Adrian though,' she smiled as they walked through the cluttered and colourful kitchen to the studio. 'And there's Bernard.'

'He buys things from you then? That's good,' Stella said mischievously, bending to look at some unfinished pots waiting for their turn in the kiln. Bernard's loft contained many of Willow's best pieces, bowls for his fruit, jugs, mugs often carelessly piled into his sink or left out for days with mouldering dregs of coffee on the balcony ledges. No one imagined he'd had to pay for them.

'Er, now and then he does. What about this one? Or this?' Willow pulled from a shelf a scarlet bowl streaked at random with thread-like wisps of pale gold and put it on the table by the window where the sun beamed in on its soft gaze. 'It's exactly the colour of the inside of lips, don't you think?' she half-whispered to Stella as if suggesting something deeply secret – perhaps she didn't mean mouth-lips. Stella nodded uncertainly, though the idea did rather put her off using the bowl for salad. It would be like spooning leaves into someone else, at one end or another of them, which made the thought of spooning them out again slightly repulsive. She imagined cherry tomatoes falling through the layers of rocket and lettuce and never being seen again.

'I think perhaps that blue and cream one would be lovely,' she decided, pointing to a large, unevenly shaped bowl.

'Oh, all right then, but this one costs quite a lot more,' said Willow, fetching it down and looking pleased. 'How long is your friend who doesn't like me staying?' she asked as she wrapped the pot carefully in most of that day's *Independent*.

'Why do you think she doesn't like you?'

'Aura trouble, that's what *she's* got.' Willow twirled her silver-ringed fingers, dancer-like, over her own head as she explained, 'It's all yellow and smoky – like a *devil*. She'll be trouble and she should *never* be allowed to stay on an island.' She looked round nervously and came close to Stella's ear to whisper, 'Devil's spirits can't get past the water, so they've got nowhere else to go and spread their badness. Here it's all *contained*. It's *trapped* and has to make trouble wherever it finds itself.' Willow smiled suddenly and said kindly, 'Of course it's not *her* fault. She can't help it. I'll be nice to her tomorrow, I promise.'

Stella walked briskly, intending at last to tackle 'Oasis Fan, 15' who'd done something stupid at a party. Haven't we all, she thought, wishing, as she often did, that she could give the poor girl a glimpse of the future where she'd eventually understand that one night's foolishness was simply a drop in life's heaving ocean. The bluebells at the side of the path were starting to flower in the patches of sunlight under the trees, giving a purplish haze to the grass. Ferns were unrolling new leaves and stretching their baby fronds up to the warmth. Willow had sounded like a wise old woman giving a witch's warning. Stella knew she was just a silly old hippy who'd spent too many years bending her brain with skippy-trippy drugs and absorbing the mystical scribblings of fellow-trippers, but her words corresponded uncomfortably closely with Stella's own wariness. She felt, after Willow's warning, terribly eager to get home. She had a niggling feeling that disasters might have happened in her absence, as if she was a parent who'd risked going out and leaving a pair of too-young children hell-bent on trouble the moment her back was turned, rather than a pair of ordinary, responsible grown-ups.

Abigail could be trouble, they'd had plenty of it together in the past and it had been enormous fun. Usually. Brought up to be rather cautious, she'd always enjoyed being friends with someone who'd drag out the latent spirit of adventure in her. As she walked back, she remembered the time the two of them had skipped a lecture to accompany Abigail's current man, breaking into an empty mansion to see if it really was, as local rumour had it, a Regional Seat of Government, all equipped and ready for use in nuclear war. 'Wouldn't it have some sort of security guard?' Adrian had suggested sceptically, too conscientious to miss his seminar on the rise of the Third Reich. "Course not. That's the point, people would *know* if Securicor were all over it,' she'd told him excitedly, as she and Abigail had raided her wardrobe for dark, camouflaging scarves and sweaters.

'Bit of a soggy old sheep, sometimes, your Adrian. Where's his sense of adventure?' Abigail had commented and Stella hadn't felt like defending him, at least not until the police returned them to the college, lucky not to have been charged with breaking and entering, but exhilarated by the near-miss.

Adrian was, her mother had once told her with enormous approval, one of those men who were *born* sensible. 'He'll do you good,' she'd predicted, almost causing Stella to abandon him completely. She'd often thought since then that it must have been a true measure of how much she'd loved him that even her mother's damning approbation and assumption that she needed him to keep her under control hadn't put her off. Stella giggled quietly to herself as she reached her gate and looked across the garden to where, with inexplicable relief, she could see Adrian was all alone and safely occupied, tapping away at his keyboard in the summerhouse. If his mother-in-law only knew about the stuff he's writing these days, she thought.

Abigail, refreshed from her rest and with her make-up re-applied and her hair thoroughly brushed, was sitting demurely at the kitchen table when Stella came back in with the new bowl. She looked almost unnaturally neat, Stella thought, a bit like an old-fashioned child prepared by her nanny to meet her parents for tea, all dressed up in innocence. She'd probably looked just like that facing her various husbands straight after adulterous afternoons. Perhaps Martin had seen through it. Abigail watched Stella unwrap the pot's newspaper covering and took a slow critical look at it. 'Quite good. Did that clapped-out old hippy really make this?'

'Of course she did. Unless the fairies came in the night, like in *The Elves and the Shoemaker*,' Stella told her, thinking that where Willow was concerned, fairy help might not be so completely out of the question.

'It's just that I imagined her making pots with that ghastly lumpy, home-taught sort of texture like whole-meal porridge. She *looks* as if she would. This is really quite beautiful,' Abigail stroked a gentle finger across the glaze.

'Shows you shouldn't underestimate people. They never fail to surprise,' said Stella, looking into the fridge for some salad to put into it later. 'She actually sells quite well through galleries and a couple of London stores. Anyone who can live off their art work, I always think, can be said to be doing pretty much all right.'

Abigail lost interest in the pot and fumbled around in her bag beneath her chair for cigarettes. As she bent, Stella could see a tweedy hint of grey at the roots of the fox-coloured hair. That could either mean overdue tinting or that Martin's departure had been more of a shock than she had yet admitted.

'Tell me why Martin left you,' she demanded abruptly.

'We've had that one,' Abigail told her, lighting her cigarette.

'No we haven't, you've not actually said, not really. Only that he'd gone, not why.' Stella sat down opposite Abigail, the better to be able to look her straight in the eye and search out honesty. 'Did he have a good reason for going? Have you been having an affair?'

'Huh. An *affair*,' Abigail grinned wryly. 'When I met him, *he* was an affair I was having. He didn't seem to object to *that*. They have such double standards. God,

91

it was only sex,' Abigail lit her cigarette and inhaled deeply.

'That made him leave? Only sex with only whom?' Stella persisted.

Abigail wriggled slightly and picked at a loose splinter on the table. 'I'm easily bored. You know that,' she looked up, big brown tear-filled eyes appealing to Stella.

'Then you should have taken a job, not a lover.'

'I haven't had a lover. I've had sex. Martin was my lover. I told you, like we said at college: The One. Well, at least that's what I thought at the time. *At the time* is the only way anyone can think about lovers, isn't it? I'm sure he's only gone off with this Fiona for revenge.'

'Then he'll probably be back,' Stella said, wishing she could feel sympathetic enough to be more comforting. Abigail didn't seem to have changed one bit in over twenty years, as if the usual processes of maturity had passed her by. Surely there was something rather pathetic about a woman of her age still thinking that all of life's excitement lay in the unwrapping of an unfamiliar penis. Of course, there might be a certain amount of envy involved here, Stella admitted to herself reluctantly, Adrian's being the only one she'd ever actually had any dealings with.

'No. No I don't think he will – she's twenty-one, every middle-aged man's fantasy. He'd have to grow up to give her up and none of them want to do that, do they?'

'Oh, I don't know. Some of them do.'

Abigail frowned. 'Oh well, if you mean *Adrian*, well, who would know how grown up he is? I mean, he's got you in charge of everything, so he hasn't much choice but to toe the line. I expect he finds it comfortable. Not very *sexy* though, is it, all this mummied domesticity?'

'What?' Stella gasped. 'What the hell do you mean?'

'Oh nothing, really, only that here,' she waved her

92

cigarette round the room, 'here, you run the whole show, you're the one with the reins, aren't you? I noticed how you didn't like not knowing we were going to meet Toby for lunch – you'd lost control of everyone for a second or two there. Like with your job, all that telling people what to do, it's bound to spill over into running the family. Without you they'd either all collapse into a hopeless heap, or . . .' she hesitated, 'and don't take this the wrong way, or, they'd find their own liberated way quite merrily.' She stopped and grinned, 'Sorry. Who knows? Maybe I'm just jealous. You've got it all, always have.' She shrugged and went to flick ash into the sink. Stella, wary of being 'controlling', just stopped herself reaching over for an ashtray.

'You can't be jealous of me,' Stella stated, 'it's just not possible – I've always assumed I'm the one who's supposed to envy you.'

Abigail looked her up and down. 'Oh well, in the looks department, maybe,' she said bluntly, 'most people are. But otherwise, well, I think it's time I had a piece of what you've got, in terms of living.' She smiled, 'And I don't think any amount of "Dear Alice" advice is likely to help me there, is it? It'll be all down to me to organize.'

'. . . something really stupid with my boyfriend's best mate,' the pink letter still read the following morning. Stella sat at her computer trying to decide what to tell the girl. Three choices came to mind: a) stick with the boyfriend's best mate (if he'll have her) and make the best of it, b) apologize all round and take the grovel-and-promise option, c) forget them both and start again. And don't be such a sneaky little slapper next time, Stella added mentally as she started to type something along the lines of option b). She might reasonably suggest the same to Abigail when she came back from what she called having her hair 'perked up'. It had been quite easy to get rid of her for a few useful hours, simply by pointing her in the direction of the town's most expensive hairdresser. Working with Abigail in the house was like trying to sit down with a book in a room containing a cross moth. Perhaps an hour or two talking about holiday plans with a stylist might give her ideas about moving on, Stella thought, struggling to concentrate on teenage tribulations.

'Dear Alice – I've got in with some people who go shoplifting every Friday night and I'm scared we'll get caught but they're my only friends . . .'

'Dear Alice – I've told everyone at school my Mum's gone to star in a film in Hollywood, but really she's in prison for doing euthanasia to my Gran . . .'

'Dear Alice – I got caught having sex with my boyfriend in the school swimming pool . . .'

'Dear Alice – You think you know it all don't you, well I can tell you you know fucking nothing about people like us . . .'

Abigail's soft pale Clarins-protected hands were sore from turning the ferry handle. Her arms and legs were strong and well muscled from regular working out at the gym, her tight and toned bottom did not wobble and look dodgy from behind when she walked, but all the workouts in the world's most expensive and exclusive gyms could do nothing to prepare her for small, real-life physical tasks that were grimy and awkward and tinged her fingers with rust. 'Ugh!' she complained out loud, rubbing the chill coppery flakes from her hands and wishing she had a handy sachet of lotion or even a baby-wipe. On the shore, young men and women were shouting team-spirit banter to each other outside the rowing club. It occurred to Abigail that she'd never been much of a team-player, never known the support of any kind of group, or been asked to join in and provide it herself. Stella was a team captain, whereas she was third reserve, forever sitting on the bench and skiving the training sessions. Venetia and James would, no doubt, at their prep school, get a thorough overdose of all that, and she hoped it might be useful to them. The rowers looked happy enough anyway.

Over by the row of garages, the back wheels of Toby's Beetle were propped up on jacks. She wandered over and peered in past it at the oil stains and clutter. In the gloom she could make out the tools and rags and cans hanging from the walls and littered over a workbench at the far end. So *man*-like, she thought in vague admiration, sniffing at the oily air as if scenting pure testosterone. Even the shelves were uncompromisingly sharp, hard steel. There was also unlimited scope for getting filthy, she noticed, reluctant to go too far in. Toby wasn't around – he had told her about his job at a car showroom during the afternoons, polishing bonnets, shifting cars around, generally dogsbodying to save money for the tour of the warmer bits of Europe in the Beetle before medical school. He'd make a lovely gynaecologist, she thought. Female patients would hardly believe their luck – having his lovely hands (when clean) doing the more intimate examining was the stuff of wildest dreams – well, Abigail's dreams anyway. She felt disappointed that he wasn't around – such an attractive boy. It would have been cheering just to have him there in the garage trying to impress her, his grey eyes watching her face, eager to be admired the way boys needed to be, though she didn't want to be bored stiff by discussions of crank shafts or whatever such old cars had. That was the trouble with such very young men, she thought as she started walking towards the high street and the hairdresser, they were so terribly self-absorbed.

*   *   *

Willow coughed as dust clouded out of her wardrobe.
Her clothes, as she rifled through them, felt cold to the
touch and she wondered if damp might be creeping in
over everything. Some nights, especially during the
spring tides, she could feel the river's vapours, as if
they'd got left behind as the tide receded, slinking
under her door like a stealthy invasion of clammy
spirits. She picked up the sleeve of an ancient black
crêpe dress and sniffed at it experimentally. It seemed
just about all right, no greeny mould shone on the
fabric, perhaps it was just its age. She held up an old
green chenille skirt and wished Bernard was there to
admire it. Her clothes, she always felt, complemented
so perfectly the various antiquated fabrics of his home
– she was sure they must be meant to be together – his
crushed velvet bedcover, her silk patchwork cushions.
She felt a shimmer of pride that her clothes represented an enviable collection of antiques. There
were Victorian jackets beaded with jet, much-repaired
muslin skirts, full silk petticoats with black lace trim
that made her feel naughtily French, and georgette
blouses in over-blown rose prints. She frowned,
concentrating hard. For an outdoor party in early
summer, she couldn't think of a thing to wear.

Adrian finished his chapter and picked up *The Times*
crossword. For those like him who could complete it
by ten a.m. every day, he wished there was another,
harder one, a 'Here you are, clever bastard, now try
this' version. He thought of the crossword as work,
kick-starting the Thesaurus in his brain each morning
so that his writing flowed smoothly, his fluency with
his own language satisfyingly enhanced. 'Use it or lose
it' he'd read recently when flicking through the feature
pages coming across an article about the effective exer-
cising of brain cells. At this rate, he thought, by the

time he was ninety he'd still be able to come up with at least fifty-plus words that meant 'fuck' – now wouldn't that impress the great-grandchildren, he thought dourly as he reached across and pressed the 'ready' button on the printer.

'Well? What do you think?' Abigail demanded as she rushed excitedly into the sitting room where Stella was faxing her column to *Get This!*

'What? Oh *heavens*, you look so . . . so *different*!' Stella felt her mouth drop open with shock and closed it hurriedly, conscious of presenting a gawping and unpretty sight. Abigail's 'perking up' at the hairdresser had involved a quite drastically short fluffy haircut that was also a sexy and blatantly streaky blond.

'If you can't beat them . . .' Abigail explained with a broad grin, looking staggeringly pleased with herself.

'It is real, is it? It's not a wig or something?' Stella asked, wishing she didn't sound so dull and old-motherish.

'Course it's real,' Abigail said, running her fingers through it and tugging at the short ends. 'I just thought, well, if I don't do it now, I'll never know if they really do have more fun. *I* intend to anyway. I'm feeling *loads* better already. Where Martin's concerned, it's now time to fight back.'

'Does that mean you're going off to New York to get him back?' Adrian, coming in and catching her last sentence, sounded almost impolitely hopeful.

Abigail, still frothily excited by her new hair, skipped across the room and gave him a fond kiss on the cheek. He stepped sideways, alarmed, and crashed clumsily into the back of a sofa.

'No, not quite yet. Hair first, then it's time to deal with my body,' Abigail told him, looking down at her flat stomach and smoothing her hands across imaginary folds of flesh. 'I thought I might spend a few days at a health spa. Did you know they've turned our old college into one? I suppose it's because student teachers now get to go to proper universities. Anyway, it's called Chameleon, would you believe and supposed to be wonderful. What do you think, Stella, would you come with me? *Please?* I'll pay. They've got *everything*, or so it says. We'll be transformed, it would be such fun.'

Stella was immediately automatically thinking in terms of not having the time, huge expense, couldn't just go off like that and leave the family, but Adrian got in first. 'Good idea,' he said cheerily, adding, 'you could do with it, Stell,' prodding her bottom and grabbing some surplus flesh. The smile Stella gave him was so icily dazzling that he backed out of the room hurriedly, having accurately decoded its 'that was *unforgivable*!' message.

'Aren't men just ghastly sometimes?' Abigail sympathized when he was out of earshot. Stella collected her pages together from the fax machine and tried to recover her sense of humour.

'Oh, he just doesn't think,' she said dismissively, horrified to find that she was furious almost to the point of tears.

'Well, that's just the trouble. He *should*,' Abigail protested. 'Perhaps you should do something to remind him about that.'

'Like come to Chameleon with you and be made into a Whole New Woman?' Stella laughed.

Abigail looked thoughtful, 'Well, that wasn't entirely what I had in mind, but it would do just for a start.'

Chapter Seven

'Do you think it might be a bit too cold out here later?'
Stella asked Adrian anxiously. She always did this,
she thought, forcing guests out into the garden for
meals the moment the days were getting just that
tempting bit longer and warmer. Most of their friends
knew to bring extra sweaters when invited to eat with
them anytime between mid-April and late September,
just in case. Unless it was pouring with rain or they
could plead violent hay fever, they were whisked
through the warmth of the house and out to the big teak
table under the pergola. On the hottest summer
nights there was nothing Stella loved more than sitting
in the garden till the early hours, with midges dancing
above the lantern lights, nicotiana, honeysuckle and
stocks scenting the air, and wine, coffee and chat
flowing. The river at night made softer noises, small
gurgles and peaceful ripples, hardly enough to rock
the nests of roosting ducks.

'I'm sure I must have lived in the south of France in
my last life,' she sighed, surveying the table in front of
her, laden with bowls of marinading chicken and
prawns ready for barbecuing, slices of peppers,
aubergines and courgettes soaking in spiced oils,
tomato salad, potatoes with garlic and rosemary. A
spicy mixture of rice and vegetables was heaped into

the bowl she had bought from Willow.

'Or perhaps that's what you'll get in your next one if you're good. Especially if you keep on attempting to feed the five thousand. How did just having Abigail to stay for a few days turn into supper for thirty-two people?' he asked, mystified.

'Just trying to make her feel a bit happier, that's all. And she did more than her bit helping with the food. After all, she did come here to be cheered up. It seemed like a good idea at the time, the way these things always do. It *is* a good idea,' she insisted, even though he hadn't really argued that it wasn't. 'Anyway *do* you think it's too cold? Shall I take everything back into the kitchen?'

Adrian sniffed at the air as if from that he could tell if heavy dew and the temperature were both likely to fall steadily the moment it got dark. His hand was flickering in the air as if at any moment he might hold up an authoritative finger and check the wind direction. 'No, leave it – I'm sure it'll be fine,' he decided. 'They can always wander in if they feel the cold. You know what they're like, I once found Enzo sitting halfway up the stairs wolfing down a plate of lasagne.'

Stella smiled at him warily, still smarting from his remark about her being in need of a health spa makeover. She now felt that she no longer resembled a beachball, more an airship and that it was all his unforgivable fault. Perhaps she could actually go away, just for a few days. The family were all grown up, they could easily manage without her. A sudden feeling of bleakness hit her. The days when she, in person, was *necessary* were long gone. Her presence at home was now an optional extra. You can't have it both ways, she scolded herself, thinking of how often she grumbled that they all took her too much for granted, domestically. Perhaps, though, a conspiracy of humouring was going on. Maybe they only asked her to post things and fetch things, what was for dinner and were their best jeans dry in order to make her feel wanted. Certainly, if she died, or disappeared, they'd be sad but they'd manage. Adrian would find someone else after a short but decent interval – women, divorced, bereaved or purely adventurous would pounce on him like cats on a sparrow. She thought about poor Abigail, ousted by Martin's young blond. Where were all the men looking for women of a Certain Age? Being pussy-food, that's where, she concluded crossly. She watched Adrian wrestling with his state of the art all-gas, no-mess barbecue and wondered if, since his duties as impregnator were long ago finished, and since she just about earned enough to cope with the bills, he ever felt like that too. If so, that left the staying together part as a matter of sheer goodwill and the careful avoidance of boredom. She didn't get to hear of those sort of middle-aged problems in her job – teenagers who wrote to her thought terminal boredom was just one Saturday night with nowhere to go. The boyfriend who cruelly abandoned them at sixteen wasn't even remotely likely to be the last one they ever had.

Ruth came out of the kitchen carrying a jug of pink and yellow striped tulips which she put on the centre of the table next to the old wooden salad bowl Stella had filled with a mixture of rocket and various decorative Waitrose lettuces. 'Are these the colour tulips they call "rhubarb and custard" or something puddingy like that?' Ruth asked.

'I think so. Unless it's plums,' Stella told her. 'Will you be here this evening or are you off out somewhere?'

Ruth gave her a sly sideways look that Stella, counting forks, only just caught and noted. 'I'll be here, I s'pose. Nothing much else to do,' she replied with exaggerated nonchalance, tweaking at the arrangement of tulips. Stella recalled rather fearfully the sight of

Ruth at the boathouse gazing devotedly at Bernard. Just a crush, a passing fancy, she thought, resorting for comfort to the vocabulary of her own schooldays, words from the howling depths of history to her sex-smart *Get This!* correspondents. Ruth walked back into the house and Stella watched, marvelling at how her daughter managed to combine a heavy and large-boned body with the spontaneous grace of a panther. She was poised and supple like a dancer and tonight wore a long sleeveless green dress that seemed to have two layers, the top one of which was roughly crocheted and fraying into larger holes than it should have. One of the straps had fallen down her shoulder and rested on her creamy upper arm. She still has skin and flesh as soft as a baby, Stella thought, remembering suddenly how it had felt to hold Ruth, newly born, to her breast, to stroke the downy cheek with her finger and watch the instinctive hungry questing of her baby mouth in the direction of the touch. But Ruth was grown up now, capable of searching out oral pleasures that were best not, by a parent at least, thought about.

'You're not going to *eat* that, are you?' Abigail looked askance at Ruth as she tilted her head back, closed her eyes and aimed a hot dog stuffed with sausage, onion and oozing ketchup towards her mouth. Ruth stared at her insolently through her long black eyelashes, the hot dog protruding rudely between her teeth.

'Why shouldn't she eat it? It's her supper.' Bernard, glass in hand was sitting on the terrace bench watching Ruth's flamboyant performance with fascination. Her large red lips framed the bun, suggestive as a Chocolate Flake advert, and her pretty teeth bit delicately but hard, neatly chopping through the sausage. 'She does do it tremendously well,' he added admiringly, acknowledging a performance that was clearly just for him.

Ruth chewed and swallowed, smudged ketchup from round her mouth with the back of her hand then turned on Abigail, 'Yeah, why shouldn't I eat it?'

Abigail shrugged and drawled, 'Oh no real reason I suppose; I guess I just assumed you'd be watching your weight.'

'She doesn't need to. She's perfect,' Bernard chuckled, putting out a hand and kneading hard at Ruth's hip as if exploring the tenderness of a haunch of meat. Ruth shifted her body, leaning towards his outstretched hand like a caressed cat and although she looked as if she registered nothing more than the bliss of the moment, her half-closed eyes steadily watched Abigail for satisfying signs of envy.

Opening more bottles of wine over by the table, Stella made meaningless party conversation with Ellen MacIver and a woman who made suede cushions while her ears strained to listen to Bernard, Abigail and Ruth. She'd overheard Abigail's comment, felt Ruth's habitual pride in her looks wavering against an underlying sensitivity about her weight but could see from Ruth's expression that in the battle for Bernard, round one had gone to her. Bernard's hand was still running a finger idly up and down Ruth's thigh. Abigail noticed Stella watching and joined her to collect another drink.

'What is Bernard *doing*?' Stella hissed. 'If Adrian sees Ruth being groped at like that . . . I mean she's only just *seventeen*, for heaven's sake.'

'And he's what, fifty or so? A bit more?' Abigail mused, crunching loudly on a piece of celery. 'My first wasn't far off sixty, rather a good thing actually. He was one of my mother's and I was handed over for lessons one night while she went to the pub. By then they should know what they're doing.' She looked doubtfully at Bernard, 'Not all of them, of course; some never quite get the hang of it.'

Stella glared at her. 'You just wait till it's your Venetia's turn. Let's see if you're so casual about it then.'

Abigail shuddered. 'OK, I'll admit I wouldn't make him first choice for Venetia . . . OK, just for you I'll try and help. After all, I do owe you.' She grinned broadly, 'I have only two talents, pulling men and arranging flowers.' She looked more speculatively at Bernard as if, Stella thought, she was pricing up his assets. Perhaps she was.

'And tomorrow I'll have a go at re-doing that vase of tulips. I wouldn't want you to think I'm just here to be useless.' Abigail grinned at Adrian who approached them with a plate full of spiced chicken wings. 'And don't forget, Adrian, I'm counting on you to make Stella come to Chameleon with me. They're awfully good at cellulite. I realized what the word meant when I saw you trying on that red dress, Stella. Or maybe she could go there on her own and I'll stay and take care of you all, shall I?' Stella watched incredulously as she ran her hand lightly across his cheek. Her ears stung from Abigail's careless words and she hardly dared look around to see who else had heard.

'I'm sure she doesn't mean to be so tactless,' Ellen MacIver said sympathetically, patting Stella's arm, 'no one could be so awful. I expect she just thinks honesty is a virtue.'

'Well thanks, Ellen, that really makes me feel a whole lot better,' Stella replied with sarcasm so heavy that even Ellen couldn't misinterpret. Abigail was right, she decided, if even Ellen thought there was truth in it – she was getting fat and frumpy. There they were, the two of them, she and Abigail exactly the same age and Abigail was, with effortless confidence, about to swipe a man from a beautiful teenager. She watched, depressed, as Abigail picked up the nearest bottle of red wine, ran her tongue over her lips and fluffed her fingers through her short hair.

'Do let me give you another drink Bernard,' Abigail said, pushing herself firmly across between him and Ruth and topping up his glass. She leaned forward as she poured the wine so that he couldn't avoid peering down the front of her velour sweater and seeing a cleavage impressively jacked up, though he didn't know it, by a gold coloured silk Ultra-bra. She looked back at Stella and winked and then sat down next to Bernard on the bench, close up where her slim thigh in black lycra could squeeze hard against his and give him good cause to wonder about possibilities. 'Now, tell me all about your wonderful paintings,' she purred smoothly at him with her very best smile. 'I do so love to buy work from people I actually know . . .'

Adrian sat on the swing with Charlotte's baby on his lap. 'If I was a ninety-year-old Transylvanian refugee my paintings would sell like hot buns in a blizzard,' Charlotte was telling him rather forlornly. She sat on the damp grass at his feet picking at daisies in the half dark and watched her baby patting at his face.

Adrian sympathized. 'Perhaps you should tell everyone that that's exactly what you are,' he said, feeling dangerously close to adding, 'that's what I do.' He thought of the latest pseudonym he'd created for himself, Camilla de Mornay. 'She' it was who'd 'written' *Maids of Dishonour*. He tended to imagine her as a frisky woman just teetering on menopausal age with a lion-gold froth of hair, red ankle-strap shoes and spiky little knees. Her natural habitat was a smart hotel's barstool. Every day before starting writing, like a pantomime dame before a matinée, he psyched himself into character and changed, figuratively speaking, into Camilla. Sometimes in the High Street he even recognized clothes she'd like displayed in shop windows. He thought of her when he saw stockings (not tights, definitely not tights) with diamanté ankle motifs, black jackets with sequined lapels, broad gold bangles. Occasionally, perhaps in Milan or New York he even saw her, recognizing immediately a pert challenging bosom, a lazily swaying bottom, a leopard-print accessory. In the worried dawn hours he hoped and prayed that his imagination would hold out for the rest of his working life and that he wouldn't have to resort to actually dressing up, getting fully into character before he could commit words to computer. He put Charlotte's wriggling baby down and watched the child lurching unsteadily on the grass, constantly looking as if she was about to topple backwards or forwards.

'Such a funny stage in their lives. Why would any child who could crawl so fast and efficiently imagine that walking was actually a desirable alternative? They must be able to see into the future,' he concluded, wondering if he was on the way to being drunk. 'They must have more to go on than simply wanting to be like clumsy adults.'

'Perhaps it's true about them having knowledge of the mystical, still being in touch with their past lives,' Charlotte said.

Willow, in a translucent river-green and suitably flowing dress, joined them and looked at the baby. 'It's true, they bring with them knowledge of before their birth,' she stated solemnly. 'That's why they can't talk, so they can keep the secrets of the spirit world. By the time they have learned language, they've also learned to forget.' She gazed into the mysterious distance, looking as if she was searching out her own prenatal history. What her eyes picked up, though, was the unmistakable this-wordly sight of Abigail's gaze homing in on Bernard and Bernard's own gaze on the luscious form of Ruth. 'I can have any man I want,' Abigail had hissed to Willow on the terrace, 'just watch.'

Adrian could also see Ruth standing on the terrace talking to Bernard who sat on the bench. He was looking up at her, an expression of either frank lust or artistic calculation on his face. Adrian wasn't sure he liked either interpretation. He just hoped that Ruth, like babies, was equipped with some kind of useful and protective seventh sense. He then saw Abigail squeeze onto the bench next to Bernard and switch on her most seductive smile. Her long slim hand was already resting comfortably on his leg, just casually as if giving him time to realize what its being there might mean. He felt an unexpected pang of very old dormant envy. All those years ago he'd so often, from the safety of Stella's company, watched Abigail on the scent of a conquest and felt a thrilling vicarious excitement. And that, he knew quite well, was what had led to the Afghan coat encounter down by the lake. And *that* wasn't likely to happen again. The thought was unaccountably depressing, and he wandered off to look for Stella, for comfort.

Charlotte got up and followed her wandering baby towards the river where Enzo lurked with Toby, rolling joints and flicking bits of Rizla packet across Peggy's barge into the water. Ducks squawked, grabbing at the cardboard, thinking they were being fed and the baby pointed and squawked back at them excitedly. 'The grass is a bit damp,' Toby warned Charlotte, 'sit here on this step if you like,' then got up and left her and Enzo alone together, because they looked as if they should be. He wondered suddenly what had happened to Abigail. Looking up along the garden, he saw her, sitting close to Bernard with that look on her face as if she was all ready to laugh at the joke he hadn't yet told. Toby wasn't sure about her newly blond hair. There was something self-conscious and desperate about it. She reminded him of girls from the college, hanging around the common room with pale pouty lipstick and cigarettes and trying to look hard. One cutting comment, something like 'Ugh, gross acne' or 'Tree-trunk thighs' and they'd all be tearful jellies; he'd seen it happen. Abigail was gazing intently at Bernard with her head tipped slightly to one side, a budgie-like pose which always made Toby think was less about listening to what was being said than about *looking* as if you were listening. She'd looked at him like that in the wine bar, all that so-eager 'and what aspect of medicine fascinates you *most*' stuff as if she'd never been so interested in anyone in her entire life. All those little touches on the arm too, so fast you thought they must be accidental, each one like a tiny dart of static – he could see her now doing it all to Bernard. Perhaps she had lust potion on the end of her fingers, he thought, chuckling at the thought of what Willow-the-Witch, who was looking as if someone had just stolen her cauldron, would give for such powers. What, he wondered, would be the killer comment that would reduce Abigail to weepy adolescent mush.

'She's a complete cow,' Ruth murmured next to Toby. Toby looked at her in surprise.

'Is she?' he asked.

'More or less told me to my face that I'm disgustingly, shouldn't-dare-appear-in-public-like-this *fat*,' she continued, glaring across at Bernard and Abigail. A tinkling social laugh came from their direction. 'God, he'll be so thrilled, she's managing to laugh at his so-called *jokes*,' Ruth snarled.

'I thought you liked him.'

'Oh, I do,' she giggled suddenly, 'that's nothing to do with finding him stunningly witty. Actually, he's hardly got a sense of humour at all and that's because he takes himself so seriously. As an *artist*, brink of tremendous fame and all that.'

'I suppose someone has to . . .' Toby muttered,

wondering how else a stodgy middle-aged man could so easily get an endless succession of teenage girls to strip off all their kit for him.

'I'm not fat. I'm big. I like being big, it feels powerful,' Ruth went on, still glaring at Abigail.

Her eyes, Toby saw, glinted with unshed hurt tears. 'You're beautiful, you know that. *Abigail* knows that. She's just jealous,' he told her, touching her hand gently, hoping to impregnate her skin with sympathy the way Abigail had his with desire. He looked round the garden to where Enzo, Charlotte and the baby sat together like a new thrilled family, the MacIvers chatting animatedly with Peggy, all three of their heads nodding and pecking, over-emphatically agreeing some point or other, probably about the council, he thought. His mother bustled about clearing plates, pouring drinks. Enzo's sister, Giuliana, sat with Adrian looking terribly earnest and speaking as fast in English as she did with Enzo in Italian. She was sitting astride the riverbank wall like a passenger waiting for a motorbike to start. He pictured her with the wind streaming her hair out, with himself as the driver and her legs and arms holding on to him, lightly but securely. When he imagined Abigail in the same position, he could feel his body being trapped and powerless.

'Let's leave all the old people and go to the pub before it shuts,' Toby suggested, suddenly almost desperate to get off the island to somewhere without boundaries. 'Don't you think sometimes it feels like the river's a moat and we're all walled up inside a castle?'

'Is the moat keeping others out or us in?' Ruth asked.

'Both. I can't stand it, let's go,' he said, tugging impatiently at her holey dress. In the stifling, smoky atmosphere of the Red Lion, Toby felt he could breathe again. He sniffed the beery air and felt thankful that his favourite pub hadn't yet become either themed or

109

prettified. It had an honest, grubby Englishness about it, from its stained beer-and-cider mix coloured carpet to its tobacco mottled ceiling. 'When I'm in some bierkeller in the wilds of Germany,' he told Ruth as they waited at the bar for their drinks, 'this is the kind of thing I'm going to miss.'

'Is that all? Just a grotty pub? Aren't the English supposed to get all nostalgic for things like cricket and Earl Grey and oak trees and church towers?' she laughed.

'That's only what people say when they're trying to impress about being cultured. I bet everyone who travels really misses ordinary things like cheese and onion crisps and "Blind Date" and, well, pubs with warm beer.'

'And driving on the left,' Ruth added, her eyes full of anxiety, 'You will be careful won't you? *Really* careful?'

Toby smiled at her, fighting an urge to tease her about how parental she sounded, 'Course I will. I don't want to die. And by the time I get back you'll have passed your driving test too. You'll be buzzing around in your own Beetle, I should think. Or maybe a Fiat Uno . . .' He had a miles away look, the one he always had when thinking about cars.

Ruth sipped at her beer and felt rather like crying into it. She suddenly realized that after Toby left to go travelling, he'd probably never live at home properly with the family again. For him, after the trip would be university, then work, and grown-up life. They'd finished being children together, now they'd have to work out a way of being separate adults.

In a corner of the pub, Philip Porter, council spy, sipped delicately at a low-alcohol lager and lime and observed Toby and Ruth with fastidious distaste. He couldn't believe any female worthy of the name could actually go out to a public place in a dress that was

110

running into holes. The boy had engine oil smeared on his jeans and a pair of trainers so filthy he was surprised he hadn't been asked to take them off and leave them at the door. He shifted uncomfortably on the bench in the corner, worried about creasing the jacket he'd felt forced, because of the ingrained grubbiness of the place, to take off and sit on. All in the course of civic duty, he reminded himself, preparing to leave the pub and wait in his car to see how late these two, and any other island inhabitants, were prepared to disturb the neighbourhood peace winding the rackety, clanking chain of the ferry.

'Guess what!' Charlotte exclaimed, carrying her grizzling and tired toddler and accompanied by Enzo and Giuliana. Tumbling into the pub, they all began talking at once.

'That friend of your parents . . .' Enzo started, looking far more animated than his usual dour self, began.

'She's only gone home with Bernard, back to the boathouse to see his *etchings*.'

'"I think I can promise you'll find them *fascinating*" we heard him telling her.' Giuliana giggled, her long hair, blue-black like a magpie's feathers, falling over her face. Toby watched her, suddenly wanting to stroke stray hair from the corner of her open, mobile mouth.

'Not quite his usual age group. I wonder what he's really going to show her?' Charlotte said, catching Giuliana's laughter.

'Nothing she hasn't seen an awful lot of before,' Ruth stated grimly. A little worry nibbled at her, suppose he showed her his unfinished painting of her? Suppose she told her parents? Worse, suppose she *laughed*? Toby said nothing. He was taking some time to wonder if it was really so funny, two people of a similar age going off to spend some private time together. They'd all got so used to Bernard making out with teenage girls that anything else was practically deviant. He wondered if it was to do with living on the island, everyone breathing down each other's necks. He thought suddenly about the *Autoroute du Soleil* and his trip took on the feeling that he imagined went with breaking out of gaol.

'And the best bit . . .' Giuliana spluttered into her vodka and tonic, 'Ellen MacIver was listening too and she asked if she could go with them, said she'd be *thrilled* and *privileged* to have a special viewing of Bernard's work!'

'She should be so lucky,' Enzo said.

'So should I,' Ruth muttered.

Philip Porter sat in his car listening to a depressing play about Eastern Europe on the radio and rather wishing he got paid overtime for these extra observation duties. Of course no one knew he was doing them; office hours, and his hours, finished at 5.30 and all this was purely voluntary. Ted Kramer would have something to say when he saw the reports the next morning, he was sure: probably something like, 'Get a life, Philip' which was the flippant and irresponsible way he had started talking recently, since he'd joined the queue for early retirement and stopped wearing proper suits for work. Only two people had used the ferry in the past hour and if it wasn't for the tremendous row it made he'd have dozed off and missed them. But there was the smoke and the smell of spiced food from someone's barbecue, that was worth reporting on. It was a good point towards the council's case, the lack of proper access for fire crew should the need arise. So many valuable minutes would be wasted by firemen grappling with the ferry that would take no more than eight at a time, hauling heavy equipment over the water while perhaps lives were being lost. The whole island could burn down from one careless barbecue, most of the houses were built of nothing more than silly matchwood. He wrote all this down and decided, at 10.45, to call it a night. The left side of his groin was starting to get sore from sitting cramped in the car waiting for something to happen and he eased his body backwards and forwards to relieve the pain. A hernia probably, he thought, perversely pleased to have something to show for all this extra work, and he rubbed gently at the sore area as he rocked.

'Did you see that?' Enzo, slightly drunk and leaning on his sister, asked as they approached the island's shore, unseen by Mr Porter, by means of a considerately silent borrowed punt. They all turned and looked back at the white Nissan that Enzo was pointing at.

'Was he doing what I thought he was doing?' Toby laughed incredulously.

'Next time someone calls him the tosser from the council, they'll be completely right,' Charlotte giggled, hugging her sleeping child to keep her warm in the chilled night air.

Chapter Eight

'She'll have to go, Stella,' Adrian said in bed the next morning. 'Abigail. She'll have to go,' he repeated when Stella didn't reply. 'She's upsetting everyone. She always has, always will. She was always like that, pushing things just too far. I'm surprised Martin stuck it as long as he did.' Stella could just make out the deep furrow of a frown beneath his floppy fringe. Toby would look exactly like that thirty years from now, she thought. Adrian continued, making sure she got the point, 'I know she's said something awful to Ruth, I could tell by her face. Ruth spent half of last night looking as if she was trying hard not to cry. And Willow went home in tears because Abigail sauntered off to spend the night with Bernard.'

'You do exaggerate, Adrian,' Stella said, 'I know she's never been the most tactful person, but I'm sure no one living here is so thin-skinned as to take her seriously.' She wished she felt the same, though, she thought as she got out of bed and hauled on her ancient pink towelling dressing gown. The dressing gown wasn't at all glamorous: she looked in disgust at its pulled loops and trailing hem. Anyone looking at it, hanging shapelessly from its hook behind the door, would be able to identify her immediately as a woman not inclined to adulterous liaisons, at least not in her

114

own bedroom. Abigail would be ashamed to own such an object – it should be placed immediately, held by arms-length finger and thumb, in the jumble box in the cellar. She should treat herself, get something new and sexy that didn't make her look like a belted pillow. It would have to be simple and stylish enough to look appealing, but not so sexy that it smacked of middle-aged despair. She went to the window to open the curtains and let the sun in. Its warmth might help her not to feel so cross with Adrian who sat propped up on his pillow, content to have issued his request that Abigail should leave and confident that this was now Stella's problem to solve and not his.

'I know Abigail's tricky, but she's actually very unhappy,' Stella reasoned with Adrian. 'You can't expect her to pass up on a bit of comforting when it's offered. After all, she did come here so I could help her get through the Martin thing. And you can't expect Abigail to be responsible for Willow's failure to attract Bernard. There's nothing new there – Willow's been banging on that particular door for years and getting no reply.'

Adrian still sat frowning, as if he didn't quite understand. She continued, 'You don't mind me solving other people's problems at a nice safe distance for money, do you, but when there's a real-life person here needing a bit of support you can't stand the pace.' She sat on the end of the bed, the dressing gown falling open and revealing her thigh. She remembered what Abigail had said, and what Ellen had confirmed, and pulled the fabric across her legs, reluctant at that hour to be confronted with the podgy corrugations of cellulite. If she was honest she'd admit that, in terms of Bernard, 'comforting' hadn't exactly been offered either. In her well-practised way, Abigail had simply helped herself to the man like a skilled shoplifter breezing through the first day of a department store sale. Ruth had gone to her room the night before with much stamping on the stairs and slamming of doors but Abigail hadn't heard her because after Abigail had gone to the boathouse with Bernard she had not come home at all.

Down in the kitchen, Stella padded around making coffee, feeding Abigail's yowling cat and trying to make herself think about work when Ruth came crashing downstairs, clearly in no better mood than the one she'd gone to bed in. 'Your friend, Mum, she's a complete slag,' she stated with heartfelt force as she opened and shut cupboards and put together a breakfast of muesli and a banana.

'Hey, come on now, that's no way . . .' Stella said, secretly agreeing.

'Yes it *is*,' Ruth interrupted, slamming her bowl onto the table and splashing milk out of it. 'You know she's still out? She's only just *met* him, doesn't even *know* him. That's like one of my friends, Melissa, or me even, going out clubbing and stonking off to screw the first bloke that buys them a drink. *That's* being a slag, I don't care if she is old. *And* she left you her cat to feed. I bet she never even asked.' She waved the spoon accusingly at her mother, then plumped herself down hard onto a chair and snatched angry bites at her banana. Stella leaned against the dresser and studied Ruth and her pious fury. That made two members of the family asking her to get the woman out of the place. Perhaps Toby would like to come back from work and join in, add his vote one way or the other.

'Suppose Bernard had asked *you* to go and spend last night with him,' she asked, 'would you have gone?'

Ruth sat very still, her spoonful of muesli halfway to her mouth. Her eyes looked huge and incredulous, quite shocked, really, Stella thought. 'Me? Why would he ask me?' Ruth floundered, stirring her breakfast and chasing a raisin round the bowl with great concentration.

'You know perfectly well why,' Stella persisted, sitting down opposite Ruth and forcing her to look her in the eyes. 'You like him, more than a bit, I can tell. And from what I saw last night he seems to like you. What *would* you do? I'm just curious. I just want to see if you expect a different sort of behaviour from older women like Abigail from what you'd expect from yourself.'

'Well, for a start I'm not married to someone else and supposed to be pining over lost love like Abigail. Running off to sleep with the first person who asks, if he *is* the first person – might be the *twenty*-first for all we know – isn't much like someone who's really missing their husband.'

'That's not what I'm asking. What would you do?'

'OK, OK I know you're just trying to weasel out some hypocrisy,' Ruth sighed, 'but at least I know him. I didn't just go out and pick him up like a can of lager or something. Anyway, he wouldn't ask me. I think he'd be too scared of Dad.' She smiled, her fury calming.

Stella laughed at the thought of Adrian, gentle and dreamy with his long soft hair and baggy cotton sweaters, squaring up to the brutish caveman Bernard and demanding to know what he thought he was up to, dishonouring his precious only daughter. Adrian wasn't likely to want to know what was going on, if anything did happen. For the sake of avoiding conflict, he'd choose to pretend not to notice even if Ruth was sneaking out to the boathouse in the dead of night, pretend he was too absorbed in work. Stella would be the one who would have to deal with any resulting heartbreak and/or pregnancy, where've-you-been-all-night rows and battles about age difference and sleazy old men.

117

'It's Willow I feel really sorry for,' Ruth said, avoiding Stella's face in case she recognized a lie. 'She got really miserable and pretended she was getting hay fever and that she was going home for one of her remedies. She's *besotted* with Bernard, anyone can see that. You'd think Abigail would have noticed and kept her hands off. Not very sisterly, is she?'

'No,' Stella agreed, 'it's never been her strong point. She'd say it wasn't her responsibility, that the man was free to choose or not choose, and there's not much you can argue with there. And of course there's the Martin problem, which isn't as simple as you think. He's gone off with someone without a thought for Abigail and is having, we all assume, the time of his life. I suppose she doesn't see why she shouldn't grab some of that.'

'Well, why can't she go and grab it somewhere else then? Why does she have to do it *here*?' Ruth suggested through a mouthful of cereal, 'You should take her away before she works her slaggy way round to having a go at Dad. I bet he's next on her list, I've seen her the way she's always touching him. She even kissed him for lighting her cigarette. You'd think he'd given her diamonds.' Ruth spooned up more cereal, looked at it and put it back in the bowl as if the thought of Adrian and Abigail together was enough to put her off her food.

Stella grinned at her. 'Your dad's too lazy. And besides, if he'd wanted to do anything like that with Abigail, he could have got it all over with years ago.' Probably did, actually, she suddenly thought, glad that at a twenty year distance there was no need to feel pained about it.

'You should go to that place that used to be your college – the place *she* mentioned,' Ruth suggested, bringing her dish to leave by the sink till it found its own way, magically, into the dishwasher.

'What, Chameleon, the health spa?' Stella said. She

looked at her hands, red and raw from washing saucepans that didn't like the dishwasher. 'A decent manicure . . .' she mused out loud. Hair done, body toned, sleek thighs, no 'Dear Alice'. Tempting. 'Would you all be all right if, and it's only *if* I did decide to go?' she asked Ruth.

'*Mum*. For Christ's sake, take a good look at us properly for once. We're all *grown-ups*.' She laughed briefly, 'Even Dad.'

Abigail woke up with a headache and felt the sun blasting against her eyelids and making them itch. She didn't want to open her eyes, nervous about what she'd see. There was no one in the bed next to her, that was something, so he hadn't sneaked in and joined her in the night. He was a bit old for that kind of hopeful ruse – students had done that sort of thing, she remembered. On nights when she'd simply crashed out through too much drink or too much talk they'd slyly sidle into the bed beside her in the hope that once they'd got that far it was only the tiniest next step to having full-scale sex. Sometimes it had worked, but not as often as people had thought. Bernard's bed was just like a big version of a student bed. It had uneven hollows in the mattress, as if they habitually followed the lumpy contours of a body that wasn't anything like hers and there was a suspect smell she didn't like too, as if the blankets had spent a month or six on a forgotten dusty shelf in the back room of a vicarage, waiting for the Scouts' jumble sale.

'Cup of tea?' Bernard came and sat down heavily on the bed close, too close, to Abigail and she opened one eye experimentally. He might have perked up and be readier for action than he had been the night before, and after sleeping on that sofa, be sitting there, perhaps decked out in an antique Paisley silk robe that gaped open obscenely and uninvitingly. Instead, to her relief

119

he looked much the same as he had when he'd dozed off into an unattractive open-mouthed snore on the crumpled velvet patchwork at two a.m., unflatteringly soon after that Ellen-woman (*on* and *on* about the wonders of acrylic paint) had got out her trusty Maglite torch and trotted off home. He'd probably slept in his clothes – the mustiness might not be confined to the bed. She reached out her hand for the mug of tea, trying to avoid too close a look at his thick sandy beard, in case of lurking leftovers.

'Pretty cup,' she commented, feeling that some sort of good-mannered social interaction was called for. She wasn't very good in the mornings and much preferred afternoon lovers, especially after-lunch lovers who knew that conversation was allowed to stop the moment the restaurant bill was paid.

'Willow made it. I've got a lot of her things,' he told her.

'You should marry her, or at least let her move in,' Abigail suggested, wondering if even Willow, lovestruck as she was, would put up with musty bedding.

'Good grief, whatever for?' Bernard got up abruptly and strode to the balcony door as if an accidental touch from Abigail was going to bewitch him into instant betrothal to Willow.

'Because she loves you, that's why,' Abigail told him wearily. 'Rarer than rubies, women who love truly,' she muttered into her tea. 'And men who love at all are rarer still. But then I don't suppose Willow would mind too much about that.'

'No, I don't suppose she would,' Bernard agreed readily, nodding slightly. Abigail sighed and closed her eyes against the unappealing sight of bland complacency. Where was Martin now, she wondered, glancing at the little gold watch he'd given her just after Venetia was born. He was probably asleep, she

120

calculated, his perfect profile shadowed against a hotel pillow, the all-night buzz of New York thrumming gently through his dreams. Next to him she imagined the long lemony hair of Fiona, clean-smelling and crumpled into after-sex dishevellment. Tangled hair only looked pretty on the young, throwing into appealing relief their smooth and unlined faces. On women of a Certain Age it just drew attention to an overall slept-in hedge-backwards kind of look. She put her hand up to her own strangely short spiky hair and pulled at it, squinting upwards to try to see if its new colour was still there, or if it had dissolved in the night and turned steel grey as a punishment for her own sins. She couldn't see it, couldn't any longer put her head down and hide her face and her feelings. It occurred to her that short hair meant never again being able to lie convincingly, unless she was doing it into a phone. Perhaps that would be a good thing – forcing her into better behaviour. Who knew? It might become a habit, perhaps if she was a better person, she'd deserve more luck – maybe it really *did* work that way. She looked at Bernard who had gone down to the kitchen end of the long light room and was playing with the toaster, clumsily cramming bread in and out of it as if he wasn't quite used to having to work it by himself. She imagined his teenage conquests up early and still eager to please, bustling about playing house, carefully making him coffee and mopping up spills and drips they'd have ignored at home. They'd find his bread crock (also made by Willow) and cut Bernard's toast into crustless triangles, like their mothers' best tea-party sandwiches.

'Breakfast?' he queried, unenthusiastically, not looking at her. 'No thanks. I'd better go now, I think.' She climbed out of the lumpy bed and reached for the few clothes she'd thought it safe to take off. He still didn't look at her, whether out of politeness or lack of interest she couldn't tell.

'Mm. OK then,' he muttered, his head more in the fridge than out of it. Oh, OK then, she thought.

From Ruth's skylight window Adrian could just see the boathouse. He'd been looking at it for hours, he was sure, waiting for Abigail to come out. He imagined her, hurriedly dressed in last night's clothes (knickers inside out and her bra done up on the wrong hook) and hoping no one on the island was an early riser, creeping like one of Bernard's guilt-wracked school-girls down the outside wooden staircase from the balcony to the scrubby garden area beneath. He thought of her picking her neat steps carefully past the old pieces of broken cabin cruiser that lurked rusty and treacherous under the overgrown grass and finding her way to the path. Even from Ruth's open window he could hear the wind chimes clanging in the trees in Enzo's sculpture garden and caught the early sun glinting on twists of steel that might represent God in Mourning or might be, as Adrian suspected, a defunct manifold from a Ford Escort. In his mind, Abigail was stealing past Enzo's tumbling shrubs, careful not to be seen by him or Giuliana who liked to breakfast on their deck and feed bits of croissant to her hens. Time to get to work, he thought, time to start thinking about sex for pretend instead of for real.

Stella sat at her desk on the first floor landing and started working her way carefully through the pile of letters that hadn't made it to the 'Go Ask Alice' column. She divided them into heaps, the ones that needed the standard contraception leaflet, the ones that required helpline numbers, the girls who thought they were pregnant and whose replies would need an urgent first-class stamp. Then there were those without obvious categories who would need carefully thought-out individual replies – a thirteen-year-old struggling to mourn the death of a loved teacher, another whose father had taken up with a neighbouring man, and one who knew her best friend was secretly seeing her boyfriend. And I'm supposed to have all the answers, she thought, her mind still on Ruth.

'Hi Stella, I'm back!' Abigail climbed the stairs towards Stella's desk slowly, in the manner, Stella immediately thought, of a woman who hadn't had much sleep. Last night's velour sweater was falling off one shoulder, in a way that didn't suit mornings.

'Don't look at me, I look ghastly,' Abigail said, laughing and putting her hands to her eyes and hair. 'After a night in that dreadful bed, I couldn't even *think* of facing his bathroom. I'll just dash up and have a quick shower.'

'I fed your cat,' Stella told her, refusing to give in to curiosity about what Abigail had got up to with Bernard. They weren't students any more, she wasn't about to stare wide-eyed and eager at Abigail and urge her on with '*Well? And?*'

Abigail, now about to go up the next flight of stairs, hesitated, 'Oh, er thanks. Sorry to have left her to you. It was just so terribly dark over there, you see. It seemed only sensible to stay . . . better than breaking my neck on that path anyway. I don't know about a bridge, what you need over here is a bit of decent lighting.' She looked up the stairs rather nervously and half-whispered, 'Is Ruth still here?'

'No, you've just missed her. She's gone into college, for once. Toby's gone to work and Adrian's down in the summerhouse,' Stella added, though Abigail hadn't asked.

'Right. I'll be right back. No one phoned, I suppose?'
'Sorry, no.' Abigail's mouth drooped for a giveaway

123

second before she rallied with, 'Bastard!' and an attempt at a sod-them-all-especially-Martin grin.

Nothing happened with Bernard then, Stella concluded accurately as Abigail disappeared round the bend in the staircase and started clattering about in the bathroom. She felt ludicrously pleased about that, as if she was Abigail's protector, or even taking some kind of care of her on behalf of Martin. Ellen MacIver had presumably managed to get home though, in spite of the dark and the hazards of the pathway, so Abigail must have hung on at the boathouse in expectation of at least the faintest of passes. Abigail would probably say it was all right for Ellen, she knew her way blindfold. But even so . . .

Stella turned back to the letters and tried to work out a polite way of telling a fifteen-year-old that she should ask her sex-crazed boyfriend which particular aspect of the word 'no' he was having trouble with understanding. Whoever, she thought, would actually choose to be a teenager – or, she thought, as the shower started running in the bathroom above her, a betrayed, jettisoned, middle-aged wife.

Peggy rubbed hard at her stiff, sore knees, trying to numb them before she climbed the steps with the bucket. She'd have a rest on the deck, feed the bread scraps to the swans and see what was going on out on the river before she attempted to go back down again. If she thought it through carefully, which she'd never yet managed to do, she could carry up with her all sorts of things that she'd need for the day and, when the weather was as fine as it was just now, perhaps not have to brave those crippling steps again till bedtime. She gripped the rail hard as she climbed, thinking about throttling the horrible Mr Porter and his suggestions about sheltered housing. 'You'd have people to watch out for you. Help at the push of a button,' he'd told her. She'd got all the help she needed, thank you, she'd told him. She didn't want any help at all, that was the thing they couldn't understand. She could manage, just, and on the day she discovered she couldn't she intended to say her goodbyes, lie down and die quietly. She detested the housing schemes for the elderly, as he'd described them. What words had he used exactly? She recalled 'low-built', 'easy-care', 'economy-maintenance' – all compromise words that smacked of convenient cheapness as if a wipe-clean surface was the only spiritually gratifying thing to aspire to at her age. She didn't want to live where teams of petty vandals on community service came round and painted a whole street's worth of sitting rooms in job-lot magnolia. She even detested the word 'elderly', it was just a silly, stilted way of saying *old*, a jollying-along word. 'Senior citizen' was even worse – the pompous little phrase suggested a dignity and respect that old people didn't have and certainly weren't given. What had he tried to tempt her with, she tried to remember. Big windows you can be seen through, close neighbours who could hear you call through the walls, he'd said. They'd be able to hear what she liked on the radio too, she thought, hear her splashing in the bath, filling her kettle, using the loo, talking to herself, swearing at the fools on TV. They'd make her wear a panic bleeper round her neck, like being back in infanthood with mittens on a string.

'Good morning!'

Peggy banged her hip on the deck rail as she turned quickly to find the owner of the voice. 'Oh it's you,' she said, with hostility, recognizing the council man she thought of as Mr Nice. Perhaps the other one was dead, she hoped viciously, choked by his council biro perhaps, or his skull pulverized to mashed strawberry, falling down all three flights of the town hall stairs. 'What do you want?' she asked with suspicion. She wanted to rub at her sore hip, but didn't want to give him any ammunition about her frailty or show any sign of pain. They might be trying a new ploy, sending them in one at a time, the nice one first to get round her, and then the follow-up, all in together for the eviction kill.

'Nothing,' he said, smiling. He looked relaxed enough, hands in his pockets, no tie, a grubby Aran pullover that had seen a huge number of better days. 'Nice tug. What is it, about sixty foot, Josher?'

Peggy's suspicion increased still further. 'Yes it is. Been doing your homework? Softening up technique, is it? It won't work, you know, I'm not going. Not going *anywhere*.'

He smiled patiently. 'My brother had one of these. He died on it actually, doing that tricky bit on the Kennet and Avon. I think it was six or seven locks too many for his heart. Good little boat though.'

Peggy gave a grudging half-smile. 'Sorry about your brother. Not a bad way to go though. I'll probably die on mine too, though not doing anything more active than battling with your colleague.' She screwed her face up with anger, tempted to spit over the side of the tug in disgust at the council.

'What are you using for heating? A Squirrel?'

'Might be, why? Can the council get me for that too?'

He laughed and she felt confused suddenly. He had, for a nine-to-five office-boff, very much an outdoor face, all deeply ingrained with old sunburn. He, at least, must have a life outside the office and the regulations. There were a lot more lines when he laughed than when he didn't, which showed he'd been used to a lot of happy times. Perhaps, she thought, he'd got an allotment where he could escape from the awfulness of office life at weekends. The other one, Mr Porter, she remembered, was a poor pasty specimen, unhealthy looking, like a struggling seedling that's had too much

126

careful protection from direct sunlight.

'Cup of tea?' she offered warily, wondering if this counted as consorting with the enemy. The other one wouldn't be allowed so much as the toe of his over-polished shoe across her rail.

'I'd love one,' Ted Kramer said, climbing nimbly and eagerly aboard the tug.

In the college art department, silently fuming among the casually chattering students, Ruth sat concentrating and still, her deft fingers threading fine silver wire through the baked fimo beads and twirling the ends off neatly, ready for attaching to the hooks for pierced ears. I'm going to make a fimo voodoo dolly, she thought, with spiky blond hair and a long thin beige body and thread wire through all the most painful places. She felt exhilarated with hurt and anger. She willed the feeling to be still there the next afternoon when she was due to sit for Bernard again. Even he, who, for an artist, didn't seem to be blessed with great powers of observation, couldn't fail to notice how intensely full of passionate feeling she was. If he didn't notice, she'd just have to tell him. How dare he, she thought, take that scraggy old tart back to the boathouse and show her what he was working on. She'll tell Mum, Ruth thought suddenly, her hands faltering over the beads. She'll say something accidentally on purpose grossly stupid like 'Marvellous sketches of Ruth, though of course you'll have seen them – the finished painting should be *superb*'. She's been looking at me, naked, those eyes that don't care at all looking over my charcoal body and thinking about nothing but how fat I am. She probably even laughed. She *definitely* laughed. Cow.

Chapter Nine

'I suppose stocking up at the supermarket before you leave is out of the question?' Adrian hovered in the bedroom doorway watching Stella pack for her trip with Abigail to Chameleon. It had seemed the most tactful solution in the end, though Adrian had pointed out to Stella, rather peevishly, that he hadn't meant he wanted to evict *her* from the house as well.

She looked up from folding her new red dress and grinned at him. He'd got a nerve she thought, Adrian, who'd once had every badge the Scouts could offer and made the best Caesar salad this side of Le Caprice, should have found evolving into a New Man barely a challenge. He had his hands crammed into the pockets of his jeans and his body was hunched like a small boy feeling sorry for himself. Any second now he'd be asking if his football kit was clean . . .

'If you're referring to *me* stocking up as opposed to *us* then you suppose right,' she told him, shoving hard to get a sweatshirt into the over-full bag. 'You know where the supermarket is and the prices of everything in there better than I do. And not to mention that I, according to you, have already over-indulged enough in food so *I* don't need any, do I?' Her smile was full of a hard sarcastic sweetness that Adrian hadn't seen before. It didn't go with the soft shades of blue and white in the bedroom. Fabrics, the muslin curtains drifting in the breeze, the waves of frilled lace on the square pillow cases, seemed suddenly brittle and hostile. The whole house was ganging up, bit by bloody bit, on him. Not for the first time he put the blame on Abigail.

'It's your own fault, you shouldn't have said I was fat,' she reminded him cheerfully as she opened and shut cupboards briskly, collected moisturizer and make-up from the bathroom and found her swimsuit in the back of her underwear drawer. '*Especially* in front of Abigail. That was unforgivable – women have killed, *and* got let off, for less. Also you've made it quite clear you'd rather she was off the premises, so don't forget I'm doing you a huge favour.'

'I know, I know. And you know quite well I didn't really mean you were *fat*,' he said, sighing heavily. 'I just meant, well you know, none of us are getting . . .'

'Don't say younger, *please*,' she interrupted, hauling her pink Paisley quilted bag off the bed. It felt awfully heavy, considering it contained very little by the usual going-away standards.

'We can buy things there, I happen to know,' Abigail had told her, with that beady-eyed gleeful look that accompanied the thought of spending a lot of money. Stella had packed a few rather tatty old tracksuit and sweatshirt items for lounging around and being pampered in, plus an ancient leotard with very little stretch left over from Ruth's ballet days for exercise classes and a few circuits in the gym. Perhaps, in spite of the rowing, she was really terribly unfit and these few days of toning and honing at the spa were long overdue.

Adrian kicked sulkily at the doorframe. 'I wasn't going to say younger. I was going to say, well, having the skeletal Abigail around must have made me forget that it's perfectly natural to be filling out and drooping a bit by our age. She looks more than a bit ill if you ask me. You'd look terrible that thin, people would think you were dying.'

Stella found she was trying not to laugh. She almost felt sorry for him, digging himself deeper into trouble with every well-meaning word. She pulled a jacket out of the wardrobe, kissed him as fondly as she reasonably could and breezed out of the room. He flinched slightly as if scared she'd actually intended to give him a spiteful bite. 'Well you just keep on drooping away, my darling,' she said, 'while I spend a few days gathering up all my own loose body folds and tacking them back together. All right? Bye, then!'

'I feel as if we're running away,' Stella told Abigail as they drove away from the riverbank in Stella's sky blue Golf. Outside the rowing club as they passed, eight young women with sleek cycling shorts and tight firm bottoms bent and effortlessly lifted their boat, ready to put it in the water. Oh, to look like that again, Stella thought, resolving to buy something ridiculously outrageous at Chameleon, perhaps a pink thong leotard to wear at the exercise classes instead of the baggy old Pansy Island Arts T-shirt she'd packed. Baggy T-shirt, baggy body went through her mind like a new mantra.

'I know. Isn't it fun? We haven't been anywhere together on our own since the night before your wedding all those years ago.' Abigail sounded like an excited child on her way to a birthday party. Stella felt nervous, as if, like a warning mother, she should be saying that things might end in tears. If that happened, the tears were unlikely to be Abigail's.

'Hmm. Some matron of honour you turned out to be, telling everyone in the bar that we were on our way to Paris to work in a strip club and that it was our last night in England.'

'Got free drinks, didn't we?'

'We nearly got a lot more than that. When that bloke from the chemicals company started the bidding to get us to demonstrate our "act" I really thought you were going to get your kit off up on the table.'

'I would've, if they'd gone over £500!'

Stella concentrated for a moment at a tricky roundabout, then asked, 'And what about now?'

'Now?' Abigail gave a cool sad laugh, 'No one would ask me now.' She fidgeted with her seatbelt and added, 'And I know it's ridiculous, but I do *mind* about all that.'

'What? Fading attractions?'

'I suppose so. Time you can't have again.'

'We all mind about the *time* that can't be had, but you seem to mind about the *men*,' Stella said. 'Isn't that what's gone wrong with you and Martin?'

Abigail stared out of the window, so Stella couldn't read what she was thinking and said, 'I seem to have to keep checking that it's not all over. Like I said, really I'm starting to think I'd rather be you, all contented and snug with Adrian.'

Stella pulled a face at her and laughed, 'Ugh, you make us sound like the Flopsy Bunnies. The worst smugness of the nuclear family.'

'I didn't say "smug", I said "snug".'

'I know what you said. And you wouldn't rather be me, chasing my tail in that circle of working woman and household slave, forever guilty that I'm not doing either properly. Besides, you'd miss all that money.'

'Yes, I probably would, though it seems less important right now. And at least you earn your own. When you bought this car, you didn't have to smirk and simper and say *thank you*, ever so nicely with the sure knowledge in the back of your mind that you owed Adrian a session of very special sex. With me it's mostly all Martin's, apart from the house, of course.

131

Everything is like *presents*. And I'm pretty sure I'm only allowed to share it while he's there. Presumably Fiona will be getting all the financial perks now. It's not as if she needs them either. How can a girl of her age possibly need the cosmetic support that I'm used to having him pay for?' Abigail was inspecting her badly bitten nails. 'I mean, just look what he's made me do.'

'If Adrian had had his way, he'd have made me fill up the freezer with Sainsbury's ready-mades before we left. Don't you think that's worse than making you bite your nails?' Stella laughed at her.

'I told you before, you do too much for them all. It'll do them all good to fend for themselves. You need to spoil yourself a bit, everyone does.'

Stella felt quite excited as she drove into the pretty Cotswold village. The road sign saying 'Belstone College', once attached to the main street's only lamppost had gone. She wondered what else about it had changed. The college had occupied the eighteenth-century Belstone Hall, a run down once-stately home that had never quite recovered from being requisitioned by the RAF during the war. Its Adam fireplaces, magnificent oak staircases and velvet curtains, so threadbare that the sun shone through and faded the pattern on the old-rose wall-paper, had all sunk further into sad disrepair under the thoughtless treatment of exuberant students. Stella remembered cigarettes casually stubbed out on the library windowsill, coffee stains on the neglected oak flooring, beer in the workings of the rotting Steinway, hair dye staining a chipped marble bath. She trusted that all this had been meticulously salvaged by Chameleon.

'Hey, look, Mrs Berry's post office is now an Eight-til-Late. Remember all those old envelopes she used to add up on? I bet she can't cope with a till,' she pointed out to Abigail, slowing down and peering out of the window to see what other changes there were. 'The pub's looking much the same though, apart from all those hanging baskets. I haven't been back here since we left, have you?'

'Once, because I was somewhere round here and got a bit lost. When I saw the sign for the village I drove here to get my bearings again. But that was at least five years ago. Those new houses weren't there.' Abigail pointed to a small square of pale grey starter-homes, all neat with white paint and their windows awash with froths of flounced net curtains. 'The people living in those were probably at the church hall playgroup when we were here.'

I shouldn't be here, Stella thought guiltily as they passed the little recreation ground where, on a see-saw and holding a bunch of poppies from the next field, Adrian had asked her to marry him. I should be at home making sure Ruth isn't spending all her time hanging round Bernard's studio and neglecting her A-levels. I should be making a start on my next book and giving Adrian a bit of support with his. Or maybe I should be in Sainsbury's, she thought, more cheerfully, playing at good wives and choosing all the different shapes of pasta to disguise how often we eat it. She pressed the accelerator harder as she turned in through the vast black double gates with *Chameleon* scrolled out opulently in gold on each of them. Next to her, Abigail sighed as if she'd at last come home. Perhaps she had, Stella thought, perhaps this was her idea of checking in, like a rock star with 'nervous exhaustion', into a form of private psycho-therapy wing, only in her case it was her body that would be soothed back into shape, rather than her brain.

'This is just what you need,' Abigail said to Stella as they climbed out of the car, 'time for yourself.'

Ruth walked past the shampoo display in Boots the Chemist and stopped abruptly next to the Footcare stand where she gazed at the corn plasters and verruca lotions with deep interest.

'What are you doing?' Melissa asked. 'Why've we stopped here?'

'I can't buy condoms in here,' Ruth whispered. 'That woman behind the till, she's known me from way back, ever since nit lotion and junior Calpol.'

'Oh, don't be silly, she won't care.'

'She won't, but I do. How do you think she'll look at me next time I come in for just Hedex? She'll say something stupid and loud and all full of double meaning like, "Ooh, telling him you've got a *headache* now, are you?" You buy them for me.'

'What? Me?' Melissa's voice rose. 'No way. If you're too cowardly to buy them, perhaps you're too immature for sex.'

'I have done it before, you know, I do know what it's like.' Ruth's voice rose, in indignation, above normal conversational level and a customer in a red and white striped knitted hat browsed longer than she needed to by the hair sprays. 'When it's sex with one of *our* age, they've all bought their own, no big deal, which just about sums up the sex with one of our age too, actually. *His* generation think women are all permanently on the pill, all chemically ready and waiting in case some man wants to do them the big favour. For heaven's sake, he's so old his favourite music is *jazz*.'

'He sounds horrendous. I don't know why the hell you fancy him.'

Ruth shrugged and turned away to play with the lipstick testers. 'I know. And politically he's a bloody dinosaur. It's part of being a muse. I mean, look at Gauguin in Tahiti, and Picasso. They had these women who *inspired* them – drove them to paint, to fall in love.' Melissa looked terribly doubtful, which Ruth thought was very unflattering of her. 'What's the matter, don't you think I'm capable of being someone's great inspiration?'

'It's not that,' Melissa tried soothing her, 'it's just, well, I'm surprised you'd want to. You make really great jewellery, you paint really well – you should have them lining up to be *your* muses, not the other way round. I'm sure your mum must have mentioned feminism . . .'

'Oh, you just don't understand. Look, are you going to buy these things for me or not?'

'Not. You can get them yourself in the Body Shop or at the petrol place or out of the machine at the back of the Coach and Horses.'

'I'll get them for you, what do you want? Rough riders, flags of three nations, cherry cola flavour or what?' Peggy, wrapped as ever in her crocheted blanket, emerged from the back of the make-up display carrying a hot water bottle in a fluffy panda cover.

'You've been listening!' Ruth accused her, horrified at the offer.

'Well, of course I have, dear. How else does a woman of my age get her entertainment? And if the alternative is a nice girl like you getting herself pregnant, well . . .'

'You don't "get yourself" pregnant,' Melissa stated stroppily. Peggy gave her a weary look and Melissa fell immediately silent.

'If he was a nice young man, you wouldn't have to do this kind of shopping. In my day . . .'

Ruth smiled kindly at her and tried to feel more grateful than embarrassed. 'No, look, it's OK, Peggy, it's not a problem. I think I've gone off the idea now anyway. Come on Mel, we're late for college. Bye then Peggy and thanks . . .'

Ruth and Melissa fled from Boots, giggling frantically. 'Oh God, our *neighbour*, can you believe it?

Suppose she tells Dad? I'll just die, I know I will.'

'No you won't. And no, she won't either, won't tell your dad, I mean. She couldn't, could she, how would it look?' Melissa collapsed into another wave of giggles. 'And can you imagine if she *had* bought them, what the assistant would think, I mean at her age they could hardly be for her, could they?'

'I wonder if she realized it was Bernard I was talking about?' Ruth said as they walked up the road. 'I wonder if she's even surprised.'

'Probably not. That's the kind of thing you take for granted on Pansy Island. Everyone knows that, local den of vice.'

Ruth laughed and pulled at Melissa's sleeve as they turned the corner by the traffic lights. 'Come on, this way.'

'Why, aren't we going to the college?'

'Yes, after we've been to the Coach and Horses.'

Adrian paced up and down in the summerhouse and picked up the phone. Stella had left the number, 'in case of emergencies' she'd specified, which made him feel that ringing her just to say he missed her might seem more than slightly foolish. She'd only been gone a few hours, he thought, hanging up again, halfway through dialling. Of course what he really wanted to say was not so much that he missed her, but how much he *didn't* miss Abigail. Having her in the house was constant nerve-tweaking, like not quite remembering where you'd left a loaded gun.

He switched on the computer and re-read his last chapter. The book was nearly finished, it was just a question of sorting out how the favourite *Maid of Dishonour* should finally (and in a tumultuous scene of orgasmic triumph) dismiss her rivals from both the story and her lover's bed.

'Has she gone? That woman?' Willow's patchwork

136

hair, loose and wild, suddenly floated between Adrian and his computer screen. For a second he thought of the spilled out stuffing, the shredded horsehair of an old mattress.

'Willow, *please*. You almost gave me heart failure,' Adrian yelled, furious with the shock of being interrupted. 'Don't you know that crashing in here uninvited is like, well, like walking in on someone *wanking*?'

'What? Oh, I am sorry,' Willow said, unperturbed by his outburst. She put a hand on his shoulder and smiled serenely, which he assumed was meant to transmit calming vibrations, and smiled and looked out beyond him at the river. 'Pretty view from here. You must find it makes for wonderful creativity.'

Adrian groaned. 'I do,' he snarled, 'when I'm allowed to get on with it.'

'Sorry,' she said again. 'It's just, I saw them driving away. Was Stella taking that woman to the station? Has she gone? For good?'

'Not for good, no. I can't honestly say Abigail does anything for good, not in any sense.' Adrian flicked quickly at the computer's mouse so that the screen showed the previous year's Christmas card list for Willow, if she was feeling inquisitive, to catch sight of rather than the sordid sexual maelstrom he'd been working on.

'They've gone off to a health farm for a few days, a thank-you treat from Abigail for Stella, and then they're back for the open day. Why did you want to know?'

'I was hoping you'd say she'd gone for ever,' Willow said, her face disappointed like a child with the wrong birthday present. 'She's a witch.'

Adrian could feel his mouth twitching with a sudden desire to laugh and he had to fight the urge to say, 'that's rich, coming from you'. 'I hope she is coming back actually,' Adrian told her, 'but only to collect her cat. The bloody thing brought a dead robin into the house last night and took it all the way up to the top floor to eat under Ruth's bed.'

'Poor little creature, left all alone with strangers. It was probably trying to give Ruth a present.' Willow's many-ringed hands were flapping nervously around, patting down her wild hair. 'Would you like me to pop in and feed her for you?'

Adrian frowned. 'What, Ruth? Oh the cat . . . no thank you, Willow, I may be a mere helpless, useless man, but I do know where the tin opener is.'

'No, I don't mean you're *helpless*, I just mean you probably don't have the right kind of empathy with cats. I do, it's a gift, a bond, a harmonious sympathy . . .'

'OK, OK – you're probably right, but I've got Ruth. She's very good with animals, I'm sure the cat will be fine. And it can always make a start on the sparrows.'

He wanted her out of his room. He wanted to tell her to run off and play with someone else. Willow was probably almost as old as he was and yet she made him feel as if he was talking to a little girl. Her dress, faded lilac silk that had been made for a far bigger woman, smelled of damp old cupboards. On her feet were the usual painted boots, though he somehow expected that one day he'd look down and see her tottering around on a pair of glittering silver high heels, four sizes too big. She reminds me of Miss Havisham, he decided, wanting to evict from his light sunny room the feeling that she had brought in creeping seeds of decay.

'I'm just off to see Bernard,' she said, startling him into thoughts of mind-reading. 'He's asked me for an opinion on his current work. And I've got an idea for a little joint project. Body casting.' She wafted her hands down in front of her and swayed slightly, reminding him bizarrely of a belly dancer doing warm-ups. 'Perhaps I'll look in later and check on that cat.'

'Oh do, please,' Adrian said, hoping that would make up for his earlier hostility. Inside, he was willing her to leave him in peace and he had the eerie feeling that she could read this and was deliberately hanging around waiting to put a writers' block spell on him. As she went through the door (he was surprised she even had to open it) he exhaled carefully, as if afraid to add more chaos to the air stirred up by her mothy fluttering movements. He reached for the phone again and started dialling.

Stella lay fully clothed on her bed and stared up at what must, she guessed, be a hundred yards of finely pleated chintz forming a canopy over the bed. The last time she'd looked up at that particular ceiling, at least she *thought* it was this one – the place was almost unrecognizably renovated – there had been a huge patch of dark beige damp roughly the shape of Italy. The plain terracotta fabric was the lining to a pattern of swooping, stylized kingfishers, of climbing, twirling flowers and leaves so curled and twisted that if they looked like that in her garden she'd be looking up various pests and diseases in her gardening bible. At the windows, swagged and tailed, more kingfishers dived, held back with fringed tie-backs and defying anyone to dare to twitch at the drapes for the mere shutting out of light. She thought of her own sitting-room curtains, in plain yellow padded silk, that she'd made herself, entirely hand-stitched, and had had to move back all the furniture to wrestle with the great bulk of fabric laid out on the floor. They had greying marks now on the inside edges, where carelessly grubby hands had hauled them into place on cool winter evenings and blinding summer afternoons. Apart from when she'd spent a night in hospital with

Toby when he had his tonsils out, and a weekend at an advice columnists' convention, she couldn't remember a time when she'd gone off and had a night away from Adrian. He occasionally went away for work purposes, but she didn't count that – she'd rather luxuriated in being alone at home. Being away without him, especially in this place where they'd met and spent all their time together, felt quite peculiar, as if she shouldn't really be there but had gone there to wait for something to happen.

She swung her legs down from the bed and went to investigate her bathroom. There was to be no more trekking down the cold corridor, praying for the light bulb not to give out. Thank goodness, she also thought, she didn't have to share a room with Abigail. She'd probably packed several shelves worth of cosmetics, let alone the ones she was likely to pick up during the next few days of intensive make-overs. She unpacked her own selection of moisturizers and lotions and had a good close look at herself in the mirror, trying to calculate the youngest age she could reasonably hope to pass for. 'About ninety-five in the wrong light,' she murmured to herself. 'But maybe mid-thirties in the right one.'

'Fancy some tea?' Abigail's blond head appeared round the door and made her jump.

'I can't get used to you with that colour hair,' Stella told her, 'I keep expecting it to have gone back to dark red, as if you were just trying it on for size or something.'

'So do I. It's only been a few days and the roots are coming through already,' Abigail complained, looking at her hair in Stella's bathroom mirror. 'You'd think God would understand that I'm having a bad time and let me keep it looking good for a bit longer than this.'

'I don't think God cares about things like that,' Stella told her as they left the room and headed for the stairs,

'I don't think he cares enough about the big things let alone the unimportant ones. But never mind, at least you're in the right place to get your grey roots sorted. God's at least allowed you to afford to be where the experts are.'

Toby carried Peggy's shopping across the ferry and walked with her to her barge. 'Those council men were sitting in their car spying on us again, did you see them?' she asked him.

'I did. They're doing a survey, something to do with how much we need a bridge.'

'I know. I shouldn't have let you carry the shopping for me. That younger one will have put that down on his list – one more point towards sticking me into care, just like a homeless child or a delinquent teenager.'

'That couldn't happen, could it?' Toby really didn't believe it could, being sure that for absolutely everyone over the age of eighteen, the option of making one's own decisions about life was exactly the same.

'Oh yes it could,' Peggy told him. 'And do you know, I'm beginning not to care very much one way or another. I can feel something adventurous coming on. There are other places to be than here, you know.'

Toby did know. He had envied, that morning, the way Abigail and his mother had hurled a couple of bags into the Golf and just driven away. Abigail hadn't even looked back at all, and his mother, driving, could hardly have been expected to. He wanted to do that, now the weather was good, to get on with his trip and just disappear for a few months. He wanted to be where no one knew him, where no one from home would know where he was. Except perhaps Giuliana. He thought about how she'd been laughing at the pub, the night of the barbecue. She was older than him, but not that much and definitely not in the predatory, youth-leeching way that Abigail was. He remembered how he'd thought it would feel good to get sorrow-stricken Abigail to smile.

Now he knew any man could, simply by looking at her and waiting for her to want his attention. Giuliana smiled at whatever amused her, and presumably not at what didn't. Honesty seemed to be the difference, honesty, and, he reflected, skin as soft as peach suede and hair that gleamed like the morning river.

Chapter Ten

'Now let me just have a feel of your hair, Stella.' The girl in the shiny pink overall leaned forward to take hold of a strand of hair and her perfume wafted into the back of Stella's throat and made her cough.

'Oh, you haven't got a cold have you, Stella?' The girl stepped back with wide-eyed alarm, her long, shell-pink nails wafting at the air just under her nose. Those nails couldn't be real, Stella thought, staring closely and trying to see any joins. The girl's name badge said 'Charlene' and her piled up hair was like blond bubble bath secured with a gold and diamanté clip.

'No, I haven't got a cold, it's OK,' Stella reassured her.

'Any allergies, Stella, touch of asthma, that sort of thing?' Charlene's voice sang carefully up and down in the way that Stella had noticed at her local building society, on hotel reception desks and with airline check-in-staff. It went with the kind of phone answering that included a friendly first name followed by 'and how may I help you?' They must all go to the same place to learn it, she thought, like those horsy girls way back at university who you could tell had spent a couple of months being 'finished' because they all walked with their hips jutting out, an imaginary copy of *War and Peace* on their heads and their feet out at ballet class angles.

'Right, now this little checklist,' Charlene said, picking up a pink tasselled Chameleon-issue pencil.

'Would you say now, Stella,' she began, looking with serious concern at Stella's hair, 'would you say your hair was . . .' – she hesitated before launching into her script – '. . . bleached, permed or tinted; greasy, dry, sensitive; frizzy, flaky, flyaway, unmanageable; abused, damaged or distressed? Or just tired?' She paused for breath, her head poised on one side, waiting for an informed and helpful answer. Stella suppressed a desire to laugh at her profound professional seriousness. She'd quite fancied having her hair washed, an inch or so cut off, that was all, just like at any normal hairdresser. Here at Chameleon, as she should have known, nothing was that simple. You got the extra attention that you paid for. Her hair had a separate personality, as did her skin, her cellulite, her diet, stress level and muscle tone and they were all allocated a right to their own range of problems and therapies. She'd always thought her hair was more or less all right, so goodness only knew what would happen when they started work on her body.

'Distressed?' she queried, 'how can I tell, do I ask it? And actually, I don't want to be over-pedantic but isn't hair already dead? Or perhaps that counts as terminally tired?'

'Sorry?'

'No, I'm sorry. Oh never mind. I think it's just normal. Just, you know, hair.' 'Normal' was obviously inadequate. Stella wished she could come up with something more challenging, tell her it was premenstrual, or having a bad-human day.

'*Normal*?' Charlene scanned her list, looking worried. 'I don't think we've got *normal*.' Her big blue eyes scanned the vast glass shelves of hair products

144

arranged beside her, looking for something suitable for an awkward customer.

Stella felt sorry for her and tried to be more helpful, 'Well, let's put it this way, when I buy shampoo I buy the one that says "for normal hair" in the hope that normal hair is what I'll have.'

'Oh. Oh, right.' Charlene looked relieved, as if now that Stella had shown total ignorance of her own hair condition, she could at least do her job properly by putting her well and truly right.

'Because,' Stella went on, squinting up at a chunk of her brown hair, 'if I accidentally buy something that's for greasy hair, that's what I tend to get. I always think if you buy shampoo "for dandruff" you'll get that as well, you know?'

'Not really, actually, Stella,' the girl said, looking apologetically puzzled, the bubble-bath hair quivering slightly as if the brain beneath was trembling with the effort of understanding an alien sense of humour.

Stella decided to keep quiet and make more effort to relax and enjoy, as the brochure in her room had told her to. Lying back in the hair analyst's chair in the busy hair studio, wearing only her underwear and a white towelling robe with a pink and blue chameleon embroidered on the pocket, she felt like a captive hospital in-patient being queried by an absurdly young male trainee nurse about complicated gynaecological symptoms. In this room, she remembered, she'd had a weekly Anglo Saxon tutorial, uncomfortably close to lunchtime and she'd struggled with essay topics such as 'Is The Battle of Maldon an Anachronism?' while sniffing the aroma of long-boiled cabbage steaming up from the basement. There was no hint of the smell of unappetizing food now, nothing unsavoury lingered, left over in the atmosphere, only top-of-the-range, temptingly expensive cosmetics. She felt quite home-sick – not for the family just then but for Wayne of Hair

Today who knew exactly how she liked her hair to look and could be guaranteed, after an hour of undemanding chat about holiday plans, excellent coffee and just the right kind of hair mousse, to send her home feeling ten years younger, a stone lighter and ready, like Abigail after her afternoon sleep, for anything. Instead there was a constant stream of analytical experts, prodding at her nails, scrutinizing her skin, with little worried sighs to convey that for such a *little* effort (and such a *lot* of money), all was not quite lost.

'It's a terrible motif, don't you think?' Stella said to Abigail when they met later for their sumptuous calorie counted three course lunch.

'What? The chameleon?' Abigail asked, squinting down at the embroidery on her own towelling pocket.

'Horrible scaly things with bulging eyes and lumpy bodies. Do you think that's what we'll come out looking like?' Stella hesitated with her tray at the temptingly loaded buffet, her hand hovering between white wine (100 calories) and a glass of freshly squeezed orange juice (50 calories, though if she left the decorative cherry-and-mint leaf-on-a-stick it might be only forty).

Abigail (200 shameless calories of white wine on her tray, next to a salmon salad and mushrooms plus rice in filo pastry) giggled and looked around the room. Identical white bathrobes sat around, topped by various shades of pink and brown faces, some with their hair wrapped in towels, two wearing sunglasses. Conversation was at a low level. In the peach ragrolled dining-room there was a long communal table for visitors who had come to Chameleon by themselves, but mostly those who had seemed to prefer to sit at tables alone either with a glossy magazine or the simple meditation on ideals of toned slenderness and silken skin. There were only two or three men

146

among the many women, all of them seeming to be in attendance as companion/minder, pouring wine, arranging napkins and generally cosseting their various beloveds. Abigail eyed one of them speculatively, 'Perhaps you get one of those if you pay extra. Must be a special tariff,' she suggested, adding cattily, 'I mean, he'd hardly choose to be with *her* for free now, would he?'

The room, as Stella commented, couldn't even begin to qualify for its old nickname of the 'piggery', especially given the discreet dolly's-tea-party portions of the food. A soft slap-slapping could be heard as Chameleon-issue towelling flip-flops crossed the floor, backwards and forwards from the buffet table. Some people, Stella noticed, were making several quiet visits, collecting many more gourmet delights than the prescribed three courses.

'I think the idea is that we change from being grey and unnoticeable to something bright and stunning and *gorgeous*,' Abigail said.

'You've been reading the brochure. All that stuff about the precious jewel of beauty.'

'Yes I have, especially the bit about being pampered. I always enjoy being treated like a prize pet poodle. It makes a change from feeling as miserable as something that's been dropped off on the Battersea Dogs' Home's doorstep.'

Stella bit into a perfectly round Jersey potato (20 calories?) and frowned. 'I'm not so sure about that bit. It seems sad to think that people have to come and pay this kind of a fortune for the chance to feel treasured. They should be able to get all that at home, just a general feeling of being valued. Well, we all should.' She stopped and thought for a moment and then continued. 'In a way this reminds me of the fringe areas of prostitution, the sort where men pay to dress up as babies and be mummied, that kind of thing. The

147

paying is for the pretence of being cared for, nothing else.'

'Oh, I don't know,' Abigail grinned, 'the men at *those* places are paying for a lot more than that. There's no point being prissy about it either. If you can pay for it, any of us can have more or less anything we want, don't you think?'

Stella thought for a moment. 'Well, surely most of the things worth having, love and contentment and all that aren't for sale.'

Abigail came out with the kind of amazed laugh that had the rest of the diners turning their heads in the hope of sharing the joke. 'Of course they are. *Especially* love and contentment. How do you think Martin got me? If you offer people enough, a new lifestyle, cash, whatever it is they want, I bet there's not many who'd not swop lives with someone else. What could be easier or more *adventurous*. Don't tell me the idea doesn't appeal – I just *won't* believe you.'

'Well, it would take an awful lot to make me give up what I've got,' Stella replied, wondering if Abigail had gone mad.

'Oh, come on, don't be so boring,' Abigail argued. 'Suppose someone offered you, say, your own peace and quiet Caribbean island, rather than the suburban Pansy one with all its dull old English weather, in exchange for, well, not so much really.'

Stella could see her glossing over the details and smiled, 'Well, no one's going to, are they. They'd be crazy to want to take over what I do.'

'Not so crazy, I've already told you I envy you, not that it's that believable. Now, what have you booked in for this afternoon? I've got a gym session, facial and a leg-and-pussy wax.'

'I'm down for seaweed wrap, Aqua-splash and a sunbed.' Stella sipped at her wine and wondered about the possibility of falling peacefully asleep, bandaged in bladderwrack or kelp, whatever the seaweed was. It might not be very comfortable; it might be slimy and gritty, like a Cornish beach after stormy days and a spring tide. She looked at the other women in the room and wondered if those who'd been there for several days actually looked any better than when they'd first arrived.

'They should take photos of us,' she suggested, 'when we get here, I mean. So we can have before and after shots and see the difference.'

'We might want our money back,' Abigail said, 'and then they'd say that the difference can't be measured in mere physical appearance.'

Stella giggled, 'Oh yes, like it says in the brochure – "a profound and lasting feeling of well-being". I'm looking forward to that.'

Toby shoved the last hubcap into place and stood up. It just needed another wash and a final polish and then the car was done, all the months of hard work and being flat broke finished. He took a clean J-cloth from the pack on the workbench and polished the VW badge on the bonnet, suddenly feeling worryingly at one with all those elderly men who lovingly polished the silver badges on their ancient Rover bumpers and yearned for the days when the AA men stood to attention in lay-bys and saluted their members. Badge-burnishing was the sort of thing Fergus MacIver would do.

'It's *very* pretty,' Giuliana, black hair gleaming like the Beetle's paintwork, was standing next to him holding a cat basket that contained a very cross-looking chicken. She was *very* pretty too, he thought, the complete, uncluttered Italian-ness of her, the plain yellow linen dress, simple gold bracelet and her sheer cappuccino skin almost taking his breath away.

'Why have you got a chicken in the basket?' he

asked, wiping his hands on the cloth and wishing he was clean enough even to think of touching her. 'In England that's something you get to eat in a pub.'

She laughed, her small teeth showing one gold filling in a pre-molar, like a carefully placed extra jewel. He could imagine her biting quite ferociously into something on a bone, a drumstick or a chop, tearing at meat. He wouldn't mind her biting into him.

'Willow's cat hurt her wing, see?' she pointed through the wire door and the chicken squawked nervously. 'I took her to the vet. I think he thought she should be cooked in a basket in a pub too. But she's a good layer. I told him and so he gave her an expensive injection.' She smiled guiltily, and put her hand on his arm in a friendly, confiding way. 'I could have bought a lot of eggs for that – don't tell Enzo, please.'

Toby laughed. 'I won't tell, I promise.' His arm had the electric feeling it had had when Abigail had touched him but didn't leave him with a terror of being savaged alive. Though she must be inundated by offers – perhaps she'd even laugh at him. 'Sweet boy!' he could imagine her laughing if he asked her out. She'd be kind but direct with her 'no', and she wouldn't get tangled up in a transparent selection of excuses like an English girl who didn't fancy him would. But it would, he was sure, still be no.

'Your car is finished, will you take me for a drive in it?' She suddenly asked him. 'Not now,' she added, indicating the chicken, 'tonight perhaps?'

Toby looked round quickly and rather stupidly, as if thinking she must be actually asking someone else, some god-like stud, a passing Brad Pitt or Patrick Swayze.

'Sure,' he said, smiling more broadly than he could possibly help. 'We could get away from here for a bit, out towards some fields and a country pub.' She wouldn't, he guessed, much like being taken out clubbing like the college girls, but he hoped he hadn't suggested something too cornily, romantically middle-aged. He couldn't think why he'd even said it – unless it went with the polishing of car-badges. At this rate he'd end up hankering after string-backed driving gloves. To his amazement she was actually looking as delighted as if he'd suggested dinner at the Ivy.

'OK. A nice night,' she said, pointing at the clear blue sky. 'Till later – but, please, we don't eat the chickens in baskets.'

Abigail paced up and down her room after lunch and thought about phoning Martin's office. It wasn't good enough, she'd decided, that he should keep himself so utterly and irresponsibly out of touch. Suppose something happened to the children at school? Suppose James had one of those awful cricket ball accidents and was lying in hospital in a neck brace, being asked if he could wiggle his toes. She'd be all alone dealing with it, comforting and organizing and sleepless and trying to convince him that Daddy was coming, honestly, it was just that it was a terribly long way from America. She felt such anger with him for opting out so completely just for the sake of sex with a new person. *She* wouldn't do that. She'd always been far more considerate and had even made sure that any lovers understood that it was term time only, so that she wouldn't have to make complicated arrangements about the children. If he couldn't be more responsible than this, she was definitely better off without him. It almost helped, feeling like this. It meant she would be right to move on. She picked up the phone and dialled Adrian's number, hoping he'd forgive her for interrupting his work. A man's point of view was important; women friends were fine, but they did tend to try to find the *good* in everyone, including the errant

151

man. Men had a different outlook on things, more lateral, brutally analytical even, which was very satisfying. It was time to remind him how wonderful it was when it was just the two of them together. They had, after all, once been such good friends.

Stella was disappointed that it didn't actually look like seaweed. She'd quite fancied being swathed, Ophelia-like, in fronds of sodden, clammy leaf. Instead she was coated all over, except for the bit modestly covered by paper knickers that reminded her of being in hospital having the children, with a brownish-green mudlike substance that smelled faintly of a polluted beach.

She sniffed suspiciously. 'If I was sunbathing near this stuff,' she remarked tentatively to the girl applying the gunge (the name-badge this time was "Tanya" and the hair a pale, thin, ginger ponytail) 'I might actually wonder if there'd been a dog . . .'

There was a horrified gasp from Tanya, who'd had, like Charlene, a sense of humour by-pass. 'Oh no! You see it's an *algaeic* formula, *totally* sterile and absolutely beneficial for your skin,' Stella was told firmly.

Stella thought it would be hurtfully patronizing of her to point out that seaweed *was* algae and so she settled back, just as she had in the hair salon, to enjoy her own thoughts and to wonder if the speed at which the seaweed wrap dried would be any use in indicating the sort of weather that was to be expected for the following few days. If her whole body caked quickly to the texture of a parched riverbed, they might be in for a heatwave. Perhaps, though for that kind of thing, she'd need to be hung out of the window in a stiff breeze. Given the torturous nature of some of the treatments offered in the brochure, that didn't seem too far out of the question.

'How do we get this stuff off?' she asked Tanya, who smiled happily at client ignorance.

'You go in that shower over there, Madam, with a loofah,' she said, indicating a doorway in the corner of the room. Stella felt quite relieved, having imagined a nineteenth-century Baden-Baden scene involving a sadistic hosing down with storm-force jets of freezing water.

Once she'd completely painted her with mud, Tanya left Stella alone in the room, turning down the lights and turning up the music that was meant to be restful and soothing. Stella lay still and hoped she wouldn't get an itchy nose and concentrated on trying to find some sort of tuneful pattern to the music. It was probably something to do with whale-song, she decided, failing to identify a rhythm. Beneath the paper blanket, the edges of the paper knickers were beginning to disintegrate and reminded her rather disgustingly of an infants school lavatory accident. Ruth would love this, she thought sleepily, as would any teenager who'd still got a hankering after playing mud-pies.

Adrian drove fast for the first five miles and then slowed down considerably and started hoping he'd get lost enough in the rustic lanes to make himself thoroughly late. He couldn't imagine what he'd been thinking of, well he could if he was scrupulously honest, agreeing to meet Abigail. She'd been horribly clever, using just the right words to get him to come out to play – appealing to him for help (as a friend), all that stuff about a man's view of things, how much she wanted Martin back, true love and all that garbage. How awfully late in the day to have suddenly *discovered* love, he thought cynically.

She certainly hadn't had much of an opinion of it when *he'd* been briefly besotted about her. Not even so much as the equivalent of an agnostic about it, just bluntly, cruelly as dismissive as a dyed-in-the-wool atheist. Now he had a long evening ahead of him, miles from home, with a woman who terrified and attracted him and without even being able to drink himself into blame-free carelessness.

'What about Stella?' he'd said, 'What will she be doing?'

'Oh, she's already helped me *so* much,' Abigail had pointed out, 'I think she should have an evening off from me and my problems, don't you? She's going to the talk on Colour in Your Life in the Noel Coward Room, and she's been really looking forward to it, so she wouldn't have wanted to come out anyway.'

So considerate, Adrian thought now as he drove at 50 mph in the slow lane of the motorway, trying to make the journey last two hours instead of only one.

The restaurant Abigail had chosen had once been a large and impressive roadhouse, back in the days when travelling by car had been more of an adventure than a chore. It was, as he drove up reluctantly and slowly trundled the Audi round the car park, the sort of place that had only just escaped being turned into a theme pub complete with ye olde Englande serving wenches. He imagined it would be full of men of his age, but in grey flannel trousers and blazers with Rotary Club badges rather than the Levis and Gap cotton sweater that he had chosen. I might even be offered a tie, he thought with dread as he pushed open the stained glass swing door and confronted the mahogany reception desk with tiny pink table lamps at each end that gave an impression of an inadequately warmed winter evening.

'Adrian! I'm so glad you could come.' Abigail rushed out of the inner door and kissed him ferociously on each cheek, far more fondly than she had done at home when she'd been doing the wan, frail abandoned wife act.

'I said I would,' he told her sulkily, trying to avoid breathing too deeply and inhaling a choking quantity of her perfume. The amount he *could* smell made him feel a twinge of sadness, for she was wearing the same one that Stella currently favoured and he wished, quite fervently, that it was familiar, chestnutty Stella who was clutching his hand and leading him to a secluded alcove seat and not the terrifying, angular Abigail.

'Drink?' she asked, putting a hand out towards an approaching waiter.

'Just tonic, I think.'

'Oh but surely . . .' she smiled persuasively. He grinned at the waiter.

'Oh, make it a *double* tonic, plenty of ice and lemon please.'

'Well, *I'm* drinking, anyway,' Abigail said, 'I'd like a very large gin with a very small tonic inside it please.'

'How did you get here? Did you borrow Stella's car?' Adrian asked her. Abigail shifted and crossed her legs, her tight navy skirt riding up her narrow thighs. Lethally bony knees, he thought, crossing his own legs instinctively.

'No. I got a taxi. It isn't that far, fifteen miles or so. I do so *hate* being car-less. You will give me a lift back later, won't you, darling? The *hassles* of taxis . . .'

'Mm. Yes, of course I will.' Adrian mentally added thirty extra miles to his long homeward journey and wished he hadn't been brought up to be so good mannered. None of the over-assertive heroes in his books would be conned into such a thing, not unless they had dastardly ulterior motives at any rate. And he hadn't got any of those.

'It'll be just like taking a naughty runaway child back to school,' she giggled and Adrian felt nervous. *She* sounded like one of his wanton heroines out for ruthless seduction. A few slowly moving loose cogs seemed to click into place in his brain.

'Stella doesn't know you're out with me, does she?

Where does she think you are?' he asked. He'd been trapped, he realized gloomily, into a pointless conspiracy and he wondered how it would look if he made a bolt for his car and a cowardly homeward dash back down the motorway. Abigail made a bad-girl face and pouted across the table at him, confessing, 'Actually I told her I'd got rather a headache and fancied an early night.'

The waiter brought a fussy little tray of drinks with napkins, paper coasters, a mixed bowl of nuts and crisps. 'You can have too much aromatherapy, you know,' she added defensively, stirring her drink with the pink plastic spear provided. 'I expect it disturbed some extra stress,' she continued, rubbing delicately at her temple with her newly manicured nails.

'But you haven't *got* a headache.' Adrian leaned forward, gently moving her hand back down to the table, and reminded her, 'It's me you're talking to, you don't have to pretend. Anyway, what did you want to talk to me about that you'd rather say when Stella's not here?'

She looked at him intently and frowned. 'You men, you think it doesn't matter who says what to whom, don't you? Emotional stuff goes right over your heads. In an ideal world, I'd be out of your life and having neat, weekly appointments with some anonymous counsellor.'

'Oh, I don't know . . .' Adrian muttered, sipping at his unexciting drink and wishing he, too, had arrived by taxi.

'When I talk to Stella it's actually a bit off-putting. She said to me once, not meaning to do a put-down, I'm sure, "If you saw some of the letters I get from kids, you wouldn't even begin to think you'd got problems." She's two things: one is *professional*. You know, in her job, carefully trying to be objective? But then there's the second thing.' Abigail picked up the paper napkin

156

and started shakily folding it into an aeroplane. 'There's that thing women do, even if they don't mean to and I'm sure Stella doesn't really, which is deep down telling me that if I can't hang on to my man, it's probably all my fault.'

Adrian laughed suddenly, 'Well it is, isn't it? I mean what *have* you been up to?' He sympathized though, about Stella. Hearing him grumbling about work she was quite likely to dismiss him briskly with something along the lines of 'Well, just thank God you're not thir-teen and pregnant for the third time by your own father'. He often thought writing a letter that started 'Dear Alice . . .' would be the only way to get her full attention. He could just imagine her opening it and reading, 'Dear Alice, do you think you could make your mind up about whether we're going to Sardinia or the Seychelles this year . . .'

'I've done nothing,' Abigail was saying, 'that's it. Not for ages.'

'Ages, how long is that, a month, a week?'

'*Ages.*' She looked at the floor and scuffed her feet on the carpet. 'Martin is doing a much worse thing, he's claiming it's *love*. That way he gets to have it off with the sweet young thing and collect all the moral brownie points. *I've* never done that. Do you know, I'm beginning to think that I've only actually *loved* one man.'

Adrian sighed. 'Perhaps you should have told *him* that,' he pointed out.

'I think I'm about to,' she said.

Toby drove down the A423 with Giuliana next to him. They'd gone a long way from home, but he felt he could drive for weeks with her beside him. She looked delicious, as perfect as the Beetle's mirrored chrome-work. He glanced sideways and saw her cream skirt lying high across the tops of her smooth tanned legs.

She had *foreign* skin. She was lush European olive, not like stodgy British wallpaper-paste skin.

'You built the car really good,' she told him, shouting above the awful racket that was the classic Beetle sound.

Toby smiled at her. 'It took a long time. Lots of work.'

'I know. I watched. Every time I went on the island and off the island, there you were, in your car, under your car,' she laughed.

'We'll stop soon,' he said. 'Are you hungry?'

'*Starving*,' she laughed. 'What about that place?'

Toby slowed the little car and turned into the car park of the pub. It looked peculiarly old-fashioned, as if it was just a piece of scenery put there ready for a film to be made about the 1930s. At the side of the building, he thought, there'd probably once been a couple of early petrol pumps, the sort that had a shell-shaped glass top. There'd have been a respectful, cap-touching attendant too. He drove through the car park looking for a space and found one next to a dark blue Audi convertible. 'My father's got one like that,' he commented as they got out. He glanced at the number plate. It *is* my father's, he thought, somehow, with a sense of foreboding, not wanting to tell Giuliana that. Stella might have done a runner from the health spa and sneaked out to meet Adrian for an illicit extra-cholesterol supper. Or Adrian might be out with his agent or an old friend. Either way, tonight the last person he wanted to run into was a *parent*.

'Actually, why don't you just wait here and I'll see what it's like inside,' he suggested, jingling his keys from hand to hand nervously. 'I mean, I'm not sure it's our sort of place . . . and it might be really full . . .'

He dashed off, feeling crossly that he'd left behind with Giuliana an awkwardness that would need explaining later. Inside the building he moved slowly and furtively, as shifty as a spy. He didn't want to be seen. If his parents *were* both there they'd expect him and Giuliana to join them. They were that sort of family, he thought ruefully, cheerfully ignoring cross-generation restraints.

When he caught sight of Abigail's duster-yellow hair, he didn't for a moment recognize her. He just wondered, in a blustering sort of way, what the blonde was doing with her hand on his father's arm. Their heads were close together, and the talking seemed intense and conspiratorial. It was also clearly a table for two, with neither his mother nor Adrian's bald, elderly agent, anywhere in sight.

'Well? Is it nice?' Giuliana was waiting for him by the car, lipstick freshly applied.

He smiled feebly, out of breath from having fled the restaurant so fast. 'No. No, it's dreadful. Full of old men with women who aren't their wives.'

She giggled. 'Maybe fun . . .'

Toby opened the car door and she slithered back in. 'No, it's not fun. We'll go somewhere by the river. Somewhere we can breathe.'

Stella enjoyed the talk on 'Colour in Your Life', though felt it should have been called 'Colour in Your Wardrobe' as only clothes were mentioned. She'd thought of Willow's lovely pottery and wondered how important the speaker would have thought it, to have the right shade of red against the various greens of a mixed leaf salad. Would the same red be all right with lollo rosso, or Chinese leaves, or rocket? Did it matter, was it relevant to one's star sign or skin tone whether coffee was drunk from a pink mug or a blue one? She finished her spritzer, said good night to the speaker and wandered quite happily upstairs to her room. How was poor Abigail, she wondered, as she padded carefully along the corridor. Outside Abigail's door she waited for a moment

159

and knocked gently. She might be in need of extra aspirins or something, she thought. There was no reply. She must be asleep, Stella concluded, wishing her, through the door, a peaceful, head-soothing night.

Chapter Eleven

If Stella had been in the bed next to him, she'd have been seriously concerned at the level of dream-twitching Adrian was doing in the early hours of the morning. In his half-sleep he groaned loudly, thrashed his arms around and knocked the clock so hard off the table beside him that its battery and innards fell out and lost themselves under the bed. He muttered and grunted and twisted the pillow, trying to escape from what was going on in his head. He dreamed about being back under the willow tree with Abigail, observed by too many stars in a sky that was far too big, moonshadows criss-crossing the grass by the lake and casting great beams of wild light on the dead black water. There were carp down there as big as alligators, weed long enough to choke an elephant. Under Abigail, this time, was not his souk-scented Afghan coat but the classy tartan picnic blanket he took annually to Lords and unfolded for a champagne lunch on the Coronation Lawn behind the Warner Stand. Her unexpectedly schoolgirlish underwear in pink gingham was strewn beside her and she lay spread naked beneath him making gratifying gasping noises. There were daisies in her hair and the scent of summer-dry grass all over her skin. He could feel the skin, tight across her bones, through his sleep. Adrian writhed and turned in his chaotic bed, trying to get the dream to end. 'You see, there's still something there,' she was now purring to him.

His wits blunted by lust, he assumed she meant his penis. 'Of course there is,' he protested, 'it doesn't just shrivel away with time.'

He turned over again, and attempted mumbling different words to cancel out the others but his voice had forgotten how to make sounds. His head wagged from side to side, like a spaniel with a sheep-tick in its ear as he tried to cast out the awful mental pictures, and his hand flew up and hit the light switch on the wall, grazing his knuckles. Thankfully, at last his eyes opened on his familiar soft-edged blue and white bedroom and he stared, wide-eyed and frightened, at the ceiling, waiting patiently to unravel the comforting fact that it was, after all, only a dream. His conscious mind sorted itself out slowly and as it did he rubbed harder and harder at his sore hand, wishing he could numb his entire dreadful self. The whole sordid thing, every pink-and-white, earth-scented, moon-beamed, groin-nuking image, was only too horribly, detestably, obscenely, treacherously true.

'Are you feeling better?' Stella asked Abigail over the Chameleon breakfast. She eyed Abigail's plate as she asked, noting that the headache the night before couldn't have been one that involved much nausea, considering Abigail now felt able to eat scrambled egg, toast, tomato and mushrooms – cooked the no-fat way, according to the menu, though still surely several thousand calories and fearsomely unwelcome in a queasy stomach.

'I'm fine now, thanks. I expect I was just feeling a bit premenstrual or something.'

'I quite like feeling premenstrual these days,' Stella said, sipping her grapefruit juice, 'because in not so many more years from now I suppose all that will be over and I'll feel quite nostalgic for the awful mood swings.'

'I won't,' Abigail said with a shiver. 'Anyway I expect you still get them if you take tons of HRT.'

Stella considered for a moment. 'I don't actually know. And I don't know if I've got five fertile years left or fifteen. It's ridiculous really, I have to keep up with all the latest stuff about adolescents – I could go on "Mastermind" with what I know about puberty, but I've hardly got a clue about what happens at the far end f fertility. Probably because I don't want to make plans for the ageing process before it actually happens so that I can go on pretending it won't. When I'm really old, I'll always think they don't actually mean *me* when they talk about crusty old pensioners. Peggy on the barge is like that. That's why she won't give up and move somewhere easier.'

'Oh, she's just a stubborn old bat,' Abigail replied, reaching for another slice of toast and the no-sugar marmalade. 'She can hardly even walk. She just needs to live somewhere where the damp can't get at her joints all the time. Staying where she is will only make it worse. People really should recognize when it's time to move on. Everyone should.'

'I'm sure you're right. But then, you see, she'd probably just die.' Stella looked out of the window at the view over parkland and down towards the willow-edged lake. 'You know, I could get used to living like this. You'd never have thought they could make the old place as wickedly comfortable as this,' she said contentedly. 'All the waitress service and pandering to your every trivial want. It's funny to see how much the place has changed. When we were here it was always so cold, you just had to get through the work because the library was the warmest place.'

Abigail smiled broadly, 'I'm so glad you're happy. I

163

really did hope you'd like it. You could do a lot more of this sort of thing if you really wanted to, you know.'

'Good grief, I didn't mean it literally,' Stella laughed. 'I do have bills to pay, people to take care of, work to do.'

'And they all take you disgustingly for granted. But suppose you didn't have it all to do? Suppose you could just swap lives with someone? Wouldn't that be fun? I often think it would – and don't tell me you couldn't really be tempted by permanent luxury.'

Stella thought of home, the inter-artist bickering on the island, Adrian's sleazy career and the ever-present tide of sad letters from frantic teenagers that she had to deal with. 'You've got a point,' she conceded, 'perhaps it would be lovely to start again and try and get it right this time. But of course we can't. We all just have to muddle through with what we've got.'

Ruth missed her mother. She missed her shouting up the stairs that it was time to get up for college. She missed her writing down phone messages and leaving them on the Post-it pad on the dresser. She even missed Stella telling her off for leaving unwashed cereal bowls by the television last thing at night and for keeping five mould-gathering coffee cups on the window ledge next to her bed. She lay curled up snugly under the duvet, wondering what day it was and whether her first class was at ten or eleven that morning. Adrian was useless. He just opted out and went down to the summerhouse (and that was another thing that needed to be discussed with her mother there to back her up) to get on with his work, completely oblivious to the fact that there was anyone else in the house at all. Toby was probably asleep too, seeing as he hadn't come home till the birds were doing their early morning singing. He'd come slamming in, whistling and clumping up the stairs and not caring who he woke, which he wouldn't have done if their mother was at home. He needed reminding about consideration. Ruth felt grumpy and blamed everyone else. They were all out there having perfectly happy and fulfilled lives. She felt as if she'd got stuck somewhere along the line, with things all planned out that weren't coming together, for reasons that were not her fault. It was hard to forgive Bernard for being really pleased, the day before, that his painting of her was almost finished. 'All over soon, my love,' he'd told her, 'I expect you'll be delighted not to have to keep coming down here and stripping off.'

The automatic retort – 'I'm not your love' – had been on the tip of her tongue but left safely unsaid. After all, he was old enough to think she should take it as a compliment. Other than that, she hadn't been able to think of a suitable reply, short of the truth, which was that she felt positively insulted that he hadn't yet even suggested having sex with her. If only she had the nerve to ask him if he intended to – but she just couldn't bear the risk (and the humiliation) that he might say 'no'.

Ruth clambered out of bed and looked out of the window to see what the weather would tell her to wear. She still had the childlike instinct to assume that a sunny day meant a hot one which sometimes meant that in February she would go out into the blazing frost in something skimpy and thin and on humid, thundery summer days pile on layers of sweaters. Down in the garden she could see her father sitting on the wall by the river, throwing pebbles in and looking as if he'd decided to take the day off. He was wearing just a black T-shirt with his jeans so Ruth decided it was warm enough for something silky and sleeveless. She had a very old red dress with huge purple roses on it and dark green swirling leaves that her mother had once said were more suited to delphiniums than roses. Ruth wouldn't know, the garden was another of her mother's departments. She'd perhaps go and visit Bernard in the dress, she decided, let him see her looking like a bouquet. Perhaps he'd want to arrange her, she thought as she selected a bottle of coconut lotion to take into the shower, though hopefully horizontally on his velvety sofa rather than vertically in a vase.

Adrian threw stones into the water and then felt cross with the daft ducks who came paddling and quacking, thinking he was throwing them food. 'Stupid buggers,' he muttered at them, 'can't you see it's not food?' Of course they couldn't. If it was thrown into the water, their limited reasoning told them it must be bread. He sympathized — he'd had a couple of hours now in which to work his conscience round to deciding he'd been thoroughly conned. It wasn't his fault. When Abigail had rung and told him she needed to talk, he'd believed exactly that and he shouldn't have done. He should have said he was too busy, reminded her that she'd got Stella for confiding in, bollocks to all that man's eye view rubbish. Wasn't all that girls together stuff what they'd gone away for? He picked up another handful of stones, bigger ones this time to make a bigger, crosser splash, and started trying to make them skim across the river's surface, which was difficult from up high on the wall. The tide was quite low and he could see the muddy riverbed littered with bits of bent supermarket trolley, discarded bricks, an old car battery, and various battered tin cans. Peggy's barge rested on the mud and leaned at what must be a very inconvenient angle for her. Imagine being in bed and being tipped sideways in your sleep, he thought. He sighed again, wishing he hadn't thought about bed. Not even the word — it just made him think some more about Abigail. It was like chewing at a hang-nail, prodding at a bruise. He should have backed off and fled for home the moment she slid her tongue in his mouth outside Chameleon's gates. But then he'd tasted the feeling of being young and irresponsible again. Off they'd sneaked, just like teenagers avoiding homes full of watchful parents, back to under the willow tree where it had all happened before – gigglingly thrilled that it hadn't been pollarded or chopped down or incorporated into a golf course. 'There it is,' she'd stated triumphantly, as they stumbled to the lake edge and found the great tree, 'It's still there, this must be *meant.*' The silly, thrilling headiness of it. And she'd meant him to feel like that, that was what really infuriated him – under that tree was where she'd been aiming for all evening. She'd probably found it during an after-lunch stroll with Stella, wandering about exploring the old grounds with half an hour to spare between a gym session and a manicure. All that poor-me talk in the pub about how she'd got her whole life wrong, wished she could have another go and get it right this time now she knew about the things that really mattered. Why, she'd asked, had other people been born with some kind of instinct for a fulfilling, selfless life, or had they learned it from mothers who hadn't been selfishly negligent like hers? She was playing with him. She'd kept touching him in a just-being-friendly and confiding way so that he'd felt guilty excitement from not being sure whether she intended him to feel like that or not. If he didn't know better he'd have dismissed her as a time-wasting prick-teaser. But she never teased. All the buttons available for pressing were the right ones, the jackpot one being the persuasive reasoning that old lovers don't count, they don't add to the total. But of course he didn't want her, not really. He was, after all, one of those lucky people who knew that what they'd already got was what they'd always wanted. One of the people Abigail said she envied. He was pretty sure he was anyway.

He chucked the biggest stone in his hand at a cruising swan, not caring whether he hit it or not. They can break your arm, he remembered his mother, and everyone else's, saying. I wonder if it's ever actually happened, if there's really a sad little collection of people out there with swan-scarred arms and a permanent terror of big birds, he thought as he swung back over the wall to the garden and went to unlock the summerhouse.

Toby was also laying blame on Abigail. Down at the showroom where he and Nick polished a just-sold Renault Espace ready for its proud new owner, Toby rubbed viciously at the passenger door and gave the paintwork a sparkle it would never see again. He breathed in the luscious, expensive smell of new-car upholstery, of pristine vinyl and for the first time in his life failed to find it thrilling.

'What's wrong?' Nick asked, polishing the roof at the more peaceful pace they were both used to. 'You're going to rub it back to bare metal at that rate.'

'Nothing,' Toby lied, 'well, not much anyway.'

'Woman?'

'Yeah. Woman,' he admitted, gloomily enough to hope that his expression said it all and that he wouldn't have to. Nick was one of his oldest friends, right back from snivelling small-boy primary school days, but it would be impossible, terminally embarrassing to them both, to admit that the cause of his miserable moodiness was seeing Abigail and his father snuggled up together, all touchy-feely in a half-lit pub. Nick wouldn't want to know about that – that was just too personal. And that bloody dreadful pub-type place, Toby indulged himself with another bite of angry recollection, was so remote from home that to interpret Adrian and Abigail being together as any-

168

thing other than a treacherous, adulterous conspiracy, was just completely impossible.

Nick wouldn't want to know about that either. Nick was grinning and sniggering quietly to himself.

'What's so funny?' Toby glowered at him, starting to feel an urge to throw the cloth full of polish at him. He could almost *see* Nick's imagination running through the possibilities of what his 'woman problem' had been, probably stupidly picturing him failing to get it up with Giuliana. Well perhaps it was better, though only just, he supposed, to let him think that than have to tell him the truth.

'You should write to your mother about it,' Nick told him. 'You know, the "Go Ask Alice" column. She'll sort you out.' He carried on chuckling cheerily at his witty idea.

'Oh, ha-fucking-ha,' Toby snorted, hurling the cloth with pleasing accuracy at Nick's left ear.

'That friend of your mother's – Abigail, was it? – she said I should marry Willow, or at least let her move in. What do you think?'

Ruth rolled over onto her back and stared at the sloping ceiling. There were long, ancient cobwebs wafting up there, too high for anything to reach except maybe a duster on a very long stick. It crossed her mind, for the first time, that they looked shabby and grubby, swathed speckly grey and floating in the breeze like Enzo's wind chimes. Usually she thought the cobwebs were a symbol of the trivial domestic things that simply didn't, and shouldn't, matter to artists like Bernard. When she'd got her own place, they wouldn't matter to *her* either. Scummy, she now caught herself thinking. Probably even Willow, desperate to please, wouldn't want to bother doing anything about those.

'Ruth? What do you think?' Bernard stood at the

easel gazing at her face as if he could read her opinion long before she spoke. He put his brush (size 10, sable) in his mouth while he fiddled with the board and Ruth started grinning uncontrollably. He looked exactly, just for a fleeting second, like the jokey little self-portrait of Beryl Cook inside the back cover of all her books. He only needed a beret.

'You should get a proper artist's smock and a big floppy bow,' she told him, folding her hands behind her head to get more comfortable. She turned her head and looked at him. 'If you did live with Willow, would it be a marriage of true minds or just a convenient sharing of art space? I mean, her pots and sculptures would look pretty good down in the gallery with your paintings. Or you could turn this whole area up here into a gallery too and go and live with her in the cabin. You could make cute little arty babies. Or perhaps not, I suppose Willow's well past her sell-by.'

Bernard rubbed nervously at his beard. 'Oh, I don't think I could do that . . .'

'And why are you asking me anyway?' she continued leaning up on her elbow. 'My mother would just say if you have to ask yourself or anyone else whether you should get married, then you shouldn't do it. Not that it's any good asking her anything at the moment though, she's gone away and left us all for a while.'

'Oh, has she? So you're all alone at home then.'

'Well, there's Dad and Toby – but it's not the same,' Ruth confessed, wondering if it was too pathetically childlike to admit to missing your mum at seventeen. It certainly wasn't *sexy*, that she did know.

'No. No, it isn't,' Bernard muttered, putting down his paintbrush and wiping his hands on an oily cloth.

Ruth looked down the length of her body, studying it interestedly. Lying on the soft, velvet covered sofa, her pale naked tummy went pleasingly flat. She was glad she hadn't cluttered it up with a navel ring like Melissa's. Her breasts fell away slightly to each side of her, but were still firm and big enough to form good mounds. They reminded her of cakes on a wonky shelf seen plumply rising through the oven's glass door. She raised her left knee and inspected the flesh of her thigh. It was creamy and firm and so far unpodged with cellulite. The 'Go Ask Alice' page sometimes got letters from girls as young as twelve who already imagined they'd got the porridgy lumps that their mothers were probably always complaining about and rubbing useless expensive stuff into. Stella was constantly clucking away crossly about magazines conditioning girls into an obsession with the body perfect.

'So you think I probably shouldn't marry Willow then,' Bernard had moved away from the easel and was standing over Ruth, watching her watching herself.

She looked up at him and smiled lazily, pushing her arms behind her head and arching her back in one long languourous stretch. 'Jesus, Bernard, I really don't care. You can do whatever the hell you like.'

'I'm sure water aerobics isn't supposed to make you *hot*,' Stella panted as she swung her right leg up and down sideways through the water, along with Abigail and about fifteen other women. The steam was rising off the pool and the puddingy, early morning faces as yet undefined by make-up were going steadily pink. The water in the pool was warm enough to count as a bath. Stella assumed it was to soothe bodies tender from the various treatments. There was also the potential horror scenario of a guest being shocked to heart attack level by a temperature more usually found in the municipal baths that made the management feel anything less than 88 degrees might be a dreadfully expensive risk.

'I know. It's supposed to be kind of sweat-free – I

171

thought that was the idea. Might as well be pumping iron in the bloody gym,' Abigail gasped. '*He's* very cute though,' she nodded towards the tightly muscled young man who yelled at the class from up on the side of the pool.

'And nineteen, twenty . . . give me just ten more, *please* ladies,' the voice of the instructor seduced into his microphone. He wore a lilac lycra outfit, shorts and a vest top with black stripes down the side. On his wrists he had pink weighted bands held on with velcro, and his feet bounced comfortably on black trainers so huge-soled, vast-tongued and padded Stella assumed they could only be sports-code symbols of sexual showing off, the footwear equivalent of driving a long red noisy sports car.

'Hmm, not bad I suppose. Hard to take any notice of him while I feel like a lobster being slowly boiled,' Stella complained. She felt it somehow wasn't fair that being several inches shorter than Abigail, the clammy water came almost up to her chin, whereas on Abigail it was at a more comfortable chest height. On the other hand, Abigail's legs were longer and she therefore, Stella calculated, had to work harder to displace more water when she kicked out. All the tubbiest visitors to Chameleon had joined this class, she noticed, probably on the basis that an aerobics class where their bodies were comfortably hidden under the swirling water made them feel less self-conscious. She felt a surge of sympathy for them, wishing that no one on the whole planet felt awkward about their God-given body shape. On the other hand, she conceded, Chameleon wouldn't exist if they *didn't* feel like that and she would be back at home sorting through the multi-coloured envelopes containing this week's broken teen spirits. She and Abigail were easily the smallest there. If *they* all got out, she thought with a flash of unaccustomed cattiness, the water level might just drop to below her shoulders.

'And three . . . and two . . . and ONE and *turn!*' the young man with mahogany tanned legs roared at them. Obediently all the women turned to face him and he looked over the group with a professionally seductive smile which only just, Stella thought, disguised a certain amount of scorn. 'Stupid fat punters,' she imagined him thinking, though she noticed his expression brighten more genuinely as his gaze flickered across Abigail's blond head. Good grief, it really is true, Stella thought with reluctant envy. That's all it takes, just that one little treatment at the hands of a competent hairdresser. If you pointed out, she thought as she obediently swished her left leg up and down through the water, that what made most women's hair blond was basically the same bleachy stuff that scoured the nastiest stains off the bottom of the toilet, would they all suddenly prefer, oh shall we say, a rich deep chestnut colour? Sadly, she thought not.

'And TURN! Right, now all face me and it's *jog* time . . . UP and DOWN and . . .'

The instructor bounced up and down in an exaggerated on-the-spot trot which they were all to copy as well as to keep their balance in the water. His lycra shorts and their bulging and obviously unrestricted contents bounced with an impressive and independent enthusiasm all of their own. Stella, Abigail, and the rest of the class had no choice but to watch and admire the mesmerizing flop and swing of his genitals. Abigail, in an attempt to stop laughing, sploshed herself down into the water. 'Sorry, lost footing,' she apologized. Stella watched the bulge in the man's shorts with fascination.

'God, I'd pay folding money just to watch this, let alone all the body toning thrown in,' she whispered to Abigail.

'You've had such a sheltered life,' Abigail whispered back. 'There's any amount of this sort of thing out there in the big world.'

'Hey, I thought you were supposed to be repenting and giving all this up.'

Abigail smiled knowingly at Stella. 'It's not me I'm thinking of. All this stuff is out there just waiting for the new you.'

It's happening at last, Ruth thought. She lay spread out on the velvet, still with her arms lazily supporting her head, having *sex with Bernard* done to her. He seemed quite happy with her idle passivity, perhaps misinterpreting it as a shy lack of experience and giving him the chance to impress her with his reassuringly gentle (but it never fails . . .) technique. Unprotesting, but not quite yet deigning to join in, she allowed him to fondle and explore her body, run his hands and mouth (and that delicately rasping beard) wherever they wanted. Ruth's mind was still up on the ceiling, but instead of concentrating on the cobwebs, she was pretending she was detached from herself, that she was up there staring down at this scene, capturing it like a movie to be replayed and watched later. She saw their copulation as an art installation and wished she'd actually got Melissa perched up a ladder taking reel after reel of photos so she could make a montage for her final A-level assessment. Self-portrait was on the list of possible projects, to be tackled, according to her tutor, with originality and flamboyance. Well try giving *this* marks out of ten for an interpretation, she thought to herself happily as her mind was dragged from the ceiling to concentrate on the more delicious feelings going on down inside her body.

On the glass-topped table by the window, Willow's lava lamp went 'gloop' and the blob of oil inside it swung itself slowly to the top of the coloured liquid like a lazy goldfish casually seeking food. Willow sat hunched on her purple bean-bag and stared at it and wondered what would happen if she picked it up and threw it, very, very hard, at the wall. Her nervousness that it might explode with far more force than its gentle bubbles implied it ever could, meant that the perfect moment for the actual throwing had passed. Too old and sensible to throw things now, she thought miserably. Too old to be moping about over some man who simply isn't, and never will be, interested. She got up and went into her bathroom and opened the little cupboard that she'd painted with pearl-draped, slender mermaids. 'Nothing really useful,' she muttered, scrabbling though the tiny phials and jars of homeopathic pills, Bach flower remedies, aromatherapy oils, aspirins and Prozac. She closed the cupboard door and stared at the golden-haired mermaids, thinking about the awful Abigail and the confident, deadly ease with which she'd simply plucked Bernard from Stella's party and marched him back to the boathouse. 'What's she got?' she asked the mottled cat that sat primly in the bath watching her. 'Blond hair and a don't-give-a-toss attitude.' The cat started purring and kneading at the cold green enamel, assuming, with the kind of vanity that Willow also ascribed to Abigail, that if it was being talked to, it was being praised and petted. Willow caught sight of herself in the full-length mirror on the back of the door and grimaced. 'Matted as a cat, grizzled as a rat, matted as a rat, grizzled as a cat,' she chanted over and over, reaching back into the cupboard. She pulled out a pair of nail scissors and, almost trance-like with depression, began snipping at her hair.

Chapter Twelve

'So, tell me honestly, right between the eyes, that you didn't feel in the slightest bit attracted to that man by the pool this morning.' Abigail was nagging at Stella over dinner. Stella concentrated on her salad of grilled Mediterranean vegetables and stubbornly refused to play confessions. To her it seemed a tremendously long time since the water aerobics class. Such thinking as she'd done in this place where the normal use of brain power was entirely optional, had been about whether to have camomile tea or caffeine-free coffee, and whether to go for deep-cleansing exfoliation or an organic fruit-oxide gel mask. Since the morning she'd acquired pearly pink painted toe-nails, a complexion that felt as smooth as new petals, a navy blue thong leotard that was far more comfortable than it looked and a terrifically expensive pair of Capezio split-sole dance trainers. She wondered what Abigail had been doing all day that had kept her mind running on a pair of joggling testicles. Perhaps she'd wandered round the place, tailing the instructor and trying to drop her room number casually into conversation. Perhaps she'd even dropped her room key, much in the way that prowling ladies of the past might have 'accidentally' dropped a lace hanky at the feet of their desired one. Abigail pushed on at her, 'I could *tell* you fancied him. You looked as if you hadn't seen anything like it in years.'

Stella laughed, '*No one's* seen anything like that in years! Probably ever! Wobbling from side to side like that, and where else could we all look? I mean, when Linford Christie runs at least you're not practically on eye level with his . . . well, his tackle.'

'Everyone looks at it though,' Abigail said. 'It would be unnatural not to – it's part of the mating process, like dogs sniffing. Don't you *ever* look at men when you're out? I can't believe you don't even window-shop them in restaurants. Have you really only had eyes for Adrian?' Stella thought for a while. Man-watching wasn't really one of her hobbies. She would vote herself the person least likely to throw her knickers at a Chippendale – wouldn't even want a free ticket for the show. Catching sight of some gorgeous young hunk out of the car window was as likely to turn her head as anyone else's but she tended to think of them in terms of what Ruth might bring home, not for what she herself might be interested in. She was just as likely to look at women too, admiring (and envying) long legs in a short skirt or swearing never to be seen in *that* shade of green.

'Well, I suppose I have in a way. I mean, I rather liked the look of David Attenborough for a while, but then who didn't? All that sexy running commentary with wild animals *doing it*. Oh, and I've still got a soft spot for Mick Jagger, but that's just left over from way back then, in the same way that I still quite like to eat licorice allsorts in the car sometimes. I don't exactly get the hots for anyone these days, not even the *warms*, as it were. No, you're right, I've been boringly mentally faithful to Adrian ever since I was nineteen.'

Abigail looked astounded. 'If I announced that dreadful fact to this whole room I bet there isn't a woman here who wouldn't be simply appalled! I feel like getting up on this table right now and telling everyone how boring you are about men. It's disgusting, it's . . . well, it's smug!'

Stella felt as if she was getting a thorough telling-off and became defensive. 'No, it's not, it's just lucky, that's all. I've always loved him, he's always loved me, end of story. I'm not claiming it's all big deal romantic stuff. It just makes life awfully simple. You can get on with the other things when you know that bit's sorted.'

Abigail glared, 'Are you trying to tell me something?'

Stella looked puzzled. 'No – I'm not criticizing or even commenting in terms of other people, I'm just telling you that's how it's been for me. And for Adrian. You just haven't been that lucky, that's all. I get letters from kids who are like you – always thinking there's just one person out there with their name on, like a Christmas present. I get this feeling that some of them will *never* find happiness in the usual love-and-staying-together sense, because they think it should just *happen*, without any effort. Maybe you're looking for something story-bookish that isn't there at all, not for anyone.'

Abigail frowned, 'Martin went looking for something too. He seems to have found that it *was* there. I wonder what he's doing right now? Probably got his hand up Fiona's skirt under a lunch table. I bet he's even taken her to one of the places *we* used to go to – typical insensitive lack of imagination.' She pushed her grilled chicken round the plate with her fork, looking mournful and hard-done-to. 'You know, I really am missing the children,' she confessed to Stella. 'It wasn't *my* idea to send them off to a boarding school and more or less wash my hands of them for half a term at a time. Last autumn they took Venetia out to have her hair cut and I hardly knew who she was the next time I saw her. When I'd dropped her off at their door she'd had a pony tail and when I picked her up on exeat day she'd got this sort of page boy thing with a fringe. That's the kind of decision mothers and daughters should go out and have fun making together, isn't it?'

Stella nodded, though at the same time wondering when the last time was that she and Ruth had found it 'fun' to discuss any potential hairstyle or item of clothing. 'You don't get them for long,' she reflected, feeling genuinely sorry for Abigail, 'one minute you're wondering if they'll ever sleep through the night, and the next you wonder if they'll ever get up before midday. Why don't you go and fetch them out from school?' she suggested, pretty sure it should be that simple. 'It's not a young offenders' institute after all, is it? They're not locked in. And even if they don't want to leave permanently, surely you're allowed to take them out for a day or two now and then, aren't you? And if the school don't want to let them out, just mutter something about marital problems – that's the kind of thing that gets Matron rushing off and packing their bags for them.' She gave a rueful giggle, 'After all, what impending divorce usually means is that there's suddenly no money for school fees, so they'll be falling over themselves to help you sort things out.'

Abigail's face brightened immediately. 'You know, I never thought of that. I've always just waited for half term or the occasional specially allowed days, the way we parents are expected to. But then things are a bit different now . . . Will you come and get them with me? Please?

Stella sighed gently and thought of home and of work and the week's Jiffy bag of problems that must have arrived in the post for her by now. The Island Art Fair was less than a couple of weeks away too, and she wasn't there to stop Willow squabbling with Enzo about signposts and posters and music. Bernard would be stamping around being phenomenally insulting about the MacIvers' amateur efforts and loudly telling everyone that there ought to be some sort of quality control procedure and Ruth would need help persuading Adrian that giving up the summerhouse for just one weekend wouldn't instantly exorcize all his creative spirit from the room.

'I do have things to do, you know,' she protested to Abigail.

'No you don't,' Abigail argued, 'you've got things to do for *other people*. Even your job is about other people. When we came here you said it would do them good to get on with life by themselves for a change. If you go dashing back now, they'll hardly have had time to miss you. I bet Adrian hasn't got through all his clean socks yet. You're too willing to be put upon, that's your trouble.'

'No I'm not. And anyway, now you're doing the putting upon. All this pressure. And Adrian's extremely good with the washing machine.'

Abigail laughed, looked across the calm and peachy room and out of the window at two women in Chameleon tracksuits sauntering down towards the croquet lawn for some gentle after-dinner exercise. Down across the park, in the valley beyond, the sun was dropping over the lake and glinting orange streaks through the willows. 'Oh yeah? And what pressure would you rather have, home or all this?'

'So you don't mind if I stay away for a bit longer?' Stella lazed on the chaise longue beside the zealously-draped window in her room and chatted to Adrian on the phone. She pictured him in the cream leather chair in the summerhouse, his own telephone hauled out from under loose pages of a discarded chapter, unpaid bills and junk mail, magazines and newsletters from the Guild of Erotic Writers, all of which clutter convinced him that his office looked like an authentic businessman's. To him, it only lacked a set of Newton's Balls to play with. Probably a real top-of-the-tree executive would have a desktop supporting nothing but a minute laptop computer, a Mont Blanc pen and a left-over show-off boarding pass from a very expensive flight, Stella always thought, but as long as Adrian was happy . . .

'It's fine by me, honestly. Stay as long as you like if you're enjoying yourself.' Before Stella could reply he added, 'As long as you really *are* enjoying it. Are you?'

She felt quite touched by his concern, especially given the rather tense manner of her departure from home. She stretched out on the chaise longue's ocean-blue velvet and looked admiringly at her pearly toe-nails, 'Well yes, I am having fun, actually. More than I expected – this place is bliss. I'm not exactly a Whole New Me, I suspect I'd need about a year for that, but I certainly *feel* great. I'll only be an extra night or two away. The school isn't too far from where Abi and Martin live, but she doesn't want to stay there on the way so we're treating ourselves to one of those huge old Grand Hotels on the coast. Should be fun.'

She heard Adrian sigh long and loud, like a child who can't cover up tiredness. 'So if she doesn't want to be at home, where exactly does Abigail intend going after she's seen Venetia and James?' he asked. She could hear the undisguised dread in his voice and laughed.

'Don't panic, I'll try and persuade her that her own home is the best place to be with them – *for* them. It's only about ten days away from half term, so if I sort of suggest that Martin might happen to come back, at least to see the children, then she can work out for herself that she should be there playing happy families with them and reminding him of what he's missing. And if she *can't* work that out, I'll just have to help her to. It is supposed to be what I'm good at.'

There was another sigh from Adrian, this time unmistakably of relief. 'Right. So when you come back here, it'll just be you. No more Abigail.' He seemed to need a lot of reassurance on this point, she thought, wondering why he was suddenly so terribly eager to have her to himself. She felt quite flattered, so lucky to have a husband who still wanted her exclusive company. Abigail would probably dismiss it as his selfish need for her domestic services, a suspect and jealous reluctance to share her with her oldest friends. But then poor Abigail was bitter and bereft, she reminded herself, and not really thinking straight.

'Body-casting. A million emotions can sing from the body,' Willow declared. 'Body casting is quite a simple process really, but of course what you do with the basic mould once you've got it, that's where *art* comes in. It could be cast in bronze or simple plain plaster, or' – Willow's clay-streaked arms started to weave the air as she worked her imagination – 'or spread with streaky bacon and painted gold, or wax and lit as a candle, or chipped like spite, or made in chocolate for breaking off and eating . . .'

'We understand, it's OK,' Giuliana told her, putting up her own delicate tanned arm to half the flow. She was finding it hard, as were Bernard, Enzo, Peggy, Ellen MacIver and Ruth, to take her amazed eyes off Willow's hacked hair that was like the first stage of a terrorist's punishment. It stuck up in spiky, uneven clumps like a badly pruned shrub, coloured a patchy orange-blond and ginger where the lavishly applied neat peroxide had taken on the different shades of her hair. It simply resembled the same mottled old cat, but as if the poor creature had tumbled into a freshly bleached lavatory. Willow seemed to be oblivious to any change in her appearance, as if the crazed chopping was a perfectly ordinary everyday thing, not mad at all, though her eyes had a hint of a new fierce challenge in them, daring a comment to stumble out. Her audience, gathered in Bernard's gallery to discuss allocation of wall space, became collectively convinced that she had gone over the edge into complete loopiness and felt wary of upsetting her.

'I want to do *everyone*. Everyone on the island, and I want that wall for them. Arses!' She yelled the last word as if she'd been working up courage for months to be thoroughly insulting.

'What?' Ruth asked. '*Arses*, did you say?' She sniggered childishly and glanced at Bernard.

Willow flashed her such an ice-cold, demonic look that Ruth immediately stared at the floor, hurriedly crossed her fingers and started muttering the Lord's Prayer under her breath. She thought of the little Fimo voodoo doll of Abigail that she'd been making at the college, fearful that just by thinking a few mildly hostile thoughts about Willow, she'd shoved her over the edge. What, if that were true, would be the state of Abigail now? Hairless, padded-celled and ranting with pain, she must be. It wasn't too unpleasing a thought. Bernard nudged her gently, which made her feel better, though just for once she hoped Willow hadn't seen.

'Bottoms, bums, posteriors, *derrières* then, for those of you who prefer things minced up and flavourless.' Willow reeled off the words with undisguised scorn. 'I want to cast all the bottoms on the island, starting with . . .' she looked around the assembled group, all of whom immediately gazed at the floor like teenagers in class who haven't revised for a test. 'Yours,' she announced, pointing at Ellen, who flinched and stepped backwards, terrified.

'Me? Oh, not me, I wouldn't know what to do . . . I'd rather not . . . really, no honestly.' Ellen fluttered and flapped and the rest of them, relieved not to have been chosen, cravenly ganged up and cajoled her. 'Oh, go on, Ellen, you'll be fine, it doesn't hurt a bit,' Bernard encouraged her.

'I expect it's just like doing a face pack, but down the other end of you,' Ruth added.

'Christ, you only have to take your knickers off and lie down, even you can manage that,' Peggy declared rudely.

'And then it will be someone else's turn,' Enzo said. 'But you will be done, over,' he added.

'Done over, more like,' Ruth murmured.

'Yes, yes. You're a good sport, Ellen,' Bernard told her with a huge, persuasive smile, hugging her to him briefly and chummily. Ellen, whose team spirit and adoration of Bernard were easily appealed to, now looked quite honoured to have been selected. Willow looked deranged but triumphant.

'She won't get round to the rest of us, you'll see,' Bernard reassured Giuliana after Willow had flitted off to organize plaster supplies.

'No, because she'll be taken away in a bloody mad-wagon first,' Peggy said. 'I'm off before she changes her mind and comes back for *me*. There's something I've left simmering on the boat . . .'

'I know what she has cooking,' Giuliana whispered to Ruth as they left the gallery and went outside into the calming sunshine. 'She has a *man*. Toby told me. He is the council man, she has him tied up in her boat and she won't let him go.' Giuliana giggled.

Ruth thought about the bizarre encounter with Peggy in Boots and smiled, 'I'm not surprised. Peggy probably wants him as a sex slave.'

Giuliana's large brown eyes opened very wide, 'No – I thought she had him for a hostage, so he can't make her leave. *Sex* – it could be. In Italy,' she declared with pride, 'we are never too old. Not till we die.' She grinned, 'Maybe not even then, who knows?'

Peggy stumped off back to her barge and clambered aboard as fast as she could. Ted Kramer helped her down the steps and handed her a mug of tea. 'Have we got something to put in it?' she demanded, looking past him to the corner cupboard where her drinks supply (five brands of Scotch) was arranged.

'Famous Grouse?' he asked with a grin, sensing a crotchety mood.

'That Willow woman. You should see what she's done to herself. She was never a beauty, but what she's done's practically self-mutilation. Barking mad, she's gone.' Peggy poured a generous dollop of whisky into her mug and sipped deeply. 'So've I,' she suddenly added, looking at Ted as if seeing a large, leather-clad burglar instead of a benign leather-skinned man in a crumpled selection of old corduroy, 'Just now, I said, "Have *we* got something to put in this tea", instead of "*I*". Haven't done that since Bill was alive, oh twenty or so years since.' She sat down heavily on the arm of the collapsing armchair by the stove and looked shocked at herself. Ted was a comfortable person to be with, that was the awful truth of it, she realized. He kept visiting and talking. Even in the confined space of the boat he managed never to be in the way. He had economic movements, that was it, neatness, agility (oh, remember agility? she thought), dexterity. Quietly, almost stealthily, he'd cleaned the kitchen, swept corners that hadn't seen a brush in years, washed the windows, was there on the boat with her because he *chose* to be. One day, she thought, he'll not be here, because his job is all about getting *me* out of here. Off he'll go to his cottage in St Ives, job done, and I'll be in Acacia Close, doorway to death, where you pick up the phone and it's a direct line to the undertakers. He'd not only given her his time and his company, he'd given her someone to *miss* when he'd inevitably be gone. That wasn't fair. She had to make an effort, right now, to make sure that the 'missing' would be mutual, perhaps not even have to happen at all.

'Tell me about your cottage,' she asked him, 'I've always been fond of Cornwall.'

Toby carried the fat padded envelope into the kitchen, hauled off the parcel tape and tipped the contents onto the table. He looked around furtively to check no one was lurking at either the doorway or window and rummaged among the heap of coloured envelopes, searching out the one he had sent to the magazine. Clever thinking, that. It would hardly have done to slip one in that had neither stamp nor postmark – he might as well have dropped it on her desk while she was actually sitting at it. His own was electric blue, taken from the drawer in the sitting-room where Stella kept a spare supply of emergency birthday cards. One day, though not too soon, he hoped, she'd notice that there wasn't an envelope for the watercolour of Richmond Bridge.

Stella opened the door and went out onto the balcony to sniff at the sea air. There was the usual stiff British breeze that always sneaks most of the warmth off the coast. It's as if, she thought, we're just not to be trusted with the sheer, wicked heat of the Bahamas or southern oceans, that we need just a little puritanical cool reminder to keep hot thoughts in check. The early evening sun forced itself down quite strongly enough, though, on the parched hanging basket beside her, seaside-livid with salmon-pink geraniums, scarlet begonias and trailing pink and mauve surfinias. She fetched water from her authentically restored, gloomy Edwardian bathroom, trickled it slowly on to the dry compost and thought fondly of her cool garden at

186

home, where oozing tree-ferns and glossy-leaved acanthus flourished by the water and the purple-black clematis threaded itself through the weigela. Adrian would be strolling down the garden with a large vodka and tonic about now, perhaps taking one for Peggy and joining her on the barge's deck to watch the moorhens and the rowers and the passing cyclists, joggers and ponies on the opposite bank. She picked up the phone and dialled her home number, but gave up after fifteen rings. She wondered what they were all doing, all out being social without her. A small twinge of envy got at her – if Adrian was only on Peggy's barge he'd have easily been able to get to the phone in the summerhouse. That was the second time she'd phoned and he'd been off somewhere. They couldn't even leave the answering machine switched on for her to leave a message, couldn't be bothered to imagine or to care that she might want to. All of them, all were just too busy having fun with her out of the way. It's only for another night or so, she thought, as she dead-headed the awful plants, making up her mind to enjoy herself. When Abigail's got the children she'll be all right. She can take them home and get on with the rest of her life. There can't be anything more I can possibly do for her. And then I can go home.

'What are you doing? Are you ready to come down to the bar for a drink?' Abigail came out onto the balcony and watched Stella carefully watering the plants. 'You're always *tending* to something,' she commented, 'you're a complete born-again mother hen!'

Stella laughed, 'Oh, thanks a lot! And what would have happened if I'd refused to tend to *you* when you called up all desperate?'

'Oh, I don't need *nursing*, just comfort and company,' Abigail said breezily. 'And I'm getting much better. I can feel my spirits rallying. Chameleon must have done me more good than I ever thought possible.'

'Ready for anything now, are you?' Stella asked slyly.

'Suppose I am. *And* you've come out of it pretty well yourself, so don't pretend you were just there as my minder.' She consulted the little gold watch, 'Anyway, hurry up, it's past drinks time. Now we're actually *allowed* some, there's catching up to do. I'll wait for you in the bar.'

Stella took her red linen dress out of the wardrobe and held it up in front of her. Her hair, due to Charlene and her team who had, thankfully but unbelievably, known exactly what they were doing, looked glossy, shiny and somehow years younger. Her skin, thanks to several sessions on the super-fast Sunliner, had a long-weekend-in-Nice kind of tan, which suited Stella better than the heavier month-in-Marbella type. She put the dress on and applied her make-up (all new, the old stuff – blunt lipsticks, dated eyeshadows, clogged mascara – simply thrown out) with her newly acquired skill, then she stepped back and inspected the very pleasing results.

Chapter Thirteen

'And what are you two ladies doing? Here for the conference, are you?'

Stella, precarious on a bar stool, sure that her bottom drooped over its edges, looked up from her pre-dinner gin and tonic and straight into the slate grey eyes of the kind of excruciatingly correct man she imagined Abigail's Martin to have become since she last saw him. She recognized a type: early forties, smoothly good looking and smartly businesslike, an advert for a classy watch. Too neat to look convincingly comfortable in old jeans, he might collect coordinated designer leisure-wear and be a life-member of an expensive gym. This one had blond and brown discreetly streaked hair, too much of it, as if letting it grow thick and long for one last time before the baldness that ran in the family set in and youthful good looks were over. He wore a grey suit that was neither shined nor crushed, a soft white shirt and a knitted dark grey silk tie that even Adrian, who detested such superfluous and conventional things, would probably grudgingly agree to wear if an occasion demanded one.

Abigail, more accustomed and more bodily suited to perching prettily on bar stools, swung round and inspected him like a lion wondering about possible lunch. She smiled slowly and lazily at him, and then her gaze shifted to his darker haired, darker suited tall slim companion who hovered and glowered rather uncertainly just behind him.

'*Hello*,' she beamed, just like, Stella thought, an eager air stewardess welcoming first-class passengers aboard and sizing them up for date potential.

'The stationery fair? Is that what you're here for?' the grey suit asked.

'Er, no. Actually we're not, we're just . . .' Stella began.

'Oh no, we're here checking out property,' Abigail interrupted, smiling broadly, waiting for them to acknowledge her *double entendre*. Obediently (or just politely) the two men laughed. 'I'm Simon,' the grey-suited one introduced himself, 'and this is Geoff. And we *are* here for the conference. I'm software and he's techno sundries.' Geoff grunted uncertainly but held out a hand to Abigail to be shaken.

'I'm Anna and this is Samantha,' Abigail smoothly introduced herself and Stella without so much as an acknowledging blink at the lie. Stella choked over her drink and looked hard and long at Abigail. She had a devilish, sexy grin slapped across her face and her slim legs were crossed high and provocatively. She looked as if she was about to wink, though at whom, Stella couldn't have said. Her left shoe swung casually off the end of her foot, which suddenly looked as rudely inviting as if she was dangling her best knickers. She was enjoying herself in a highly practised kind of way, Stella thought, as if at last she was completely and utterly in her natural element. Stella felt thoroughly out of hers, a long way from home comforts.

'Your table is ready,' a waiter approached and murmured to Stella and she thanked him, thoroughly grateful to be rescued. 'Come on, er . . . *Anna*, food's ready.' She slid rather inelegantly down to the floor and as she staggered slightly her arm was firmly taken by Simon.

'You OK?' he asked quietly.

'Fine, absolutely fine, thanks, just tripped,' she said, smoothing down her scarlet dress and recovering her dignity. He did have awfully nice eyes.

Abigail unfolded herself like a cat stretching and smiled at the two men. 'See you later,' she said, her voice full of Mae West promise. Stella was quite surprised she hadn't addressed the pair of them as 'boys'.

'Abi, how *could* you?' Stella giggled when they reached the out-of-earshot safety of their table. 'I've never, not even in my wildest moments, seen myself as a *Samantha*.'

'Why not? It's a dead sexy name. Suits you, now you've had a make-over,' Abigail said, brutally ripping a bread roll in half.

'It's only sexy because it rhymes with "panther". Not a name I can even begin to do justice to. You could at least have let me be "Anna", you're much more of a "Samantha" than I could ever be. God, that man must think I'm well and truly pissed, sliding off the bar stool so clumsily. It's only because I'm too small to do it with grace.'

'No, it's because you haven't had enough practice,' Abigail said, laughing. 'There's a lot of things you haven't had enough practice at.' She waved the bread accusingly at Stella. 'What have you ordered to eat? The sea bass? Let's have champagne, that will go nicely. I'm having the *mélange de fruits de mer* as they so pompously call it – fish stew that isn't quite up to being called *bouillabaisse* probably.'

'OK. But *please* promise me we don't have to spend the rest of the evening with Messrs Software and Sundries,' Stella bargained as the wine waiter approached.

191

Abigail grinned slyly. 'I can promise not to *try* to spend the rest of the evening with them. But I can't promise they won't try to spend it with us. And of course, they might not be using their real names either, so it's like fancy dress all round, everyone pretending to be someone else. That way you get to *behave* like someone else too.'

'Are you nuts?' Stella said. 'Who in their right mind would *pretend* to be called *Geoff*?'

'Someone called Archibald?' Abigail suggested, laughing.

Stella glanced back towards the bar, which was now filling with conference delegates, some still wearing their plastic identity tags, as if so proud to have their status spelled out beneath their names that they couldn't bring themselves to remove them from their lapels. Perhaps they didn't have much status outside the boundaries of work – perhaps they spent so much time doing these trips away from home that they were treated like slightly inconvenient visitors when they got back home with their freebie offerings of multi-coloured notebooks, supply of fine-line pens and superfluous rolls of state-of-the-art parcel tape. There might be small children who'd grown out of the books Daddy attempted to read to them at bedtime, wives who spent treacherous giggle-and-tell time with girl-friends he'd never even met. She had an odd sneaky feeling inside, surprising herself, a stirring attraction to the man called Simon, although, or maybe because, he was everything that Adrian wasn't. Adrian would dismiss him as 'straight', assuming corporate dullness and a despicable in-car selection of easy-listening pop classics.

She'd liked his voice, his optimistic readiness to make an approach and enliven a tedious, away-from-home evening. Perhaps he got lonely, out there being successful at sales, she thought, trying to stay sensibly

192

aware that she was quite ridiculously inventing an entire life for him and his colleagues. He was, far more likely, just trying for an easy pick-up and some fast, anonymous sex.

'Not that it would matter if we *did* have a bit of fun with them . . .' Abigail was musing on, almost to herself. 'I mean, it's not as if anyone would ever know what we did. No one would probably care. Not in my case anyway. And where,' she suddenly demanded, 'was Adrian when you called him earlier? *He* could be out somewhere, up to any old thing, for all you know. He could be in a bar just like this one, making a new friend that he isn't going to tell you about.'

Stella took a mouthful of her tomato and avocado salad and thought about Adrian's idea of fun. It usually involved football, films, family. The other obvious 'f' wasn't, as far as she knew, an extra-mural hobby. 'I don't think so,' she laughed, 'Adrian couldn't be bothered. He's terribly lazy. Right now he's probably lying on the sofa with a Sainsbury's chicken tikka, Becks bottles all over the floor and a video of something with spies and Sharon Stone. That's usually his idea of a good night.'

'Don't you be so sure,' Abigail said, looking straight at her with unnerving seriousness. 'Wouldn't you advise your problem people never to be too complacent?'

The champagne arrived and Stella quickly gulped down half a glass. 'Yes I would, you're right,' she agreed. 'But they're not me . . .'

'And you're not Adrian either. Think about it.'

Stella didn't think about it. She didn't want to. She'd always assumed it was a comfortable, easy thing, living with someone you could trust. You needed to be able to picture what they were doing in your absence with some degree of accuracy, otherwise all was emotional anarchy. She didn't want to have to torture herself with mental pictures of Adrian and Willow rolling passionately in wet clay on Willow's studio table, or imagine him and Ellen MacIver thrashing in her rockery by the hygienically fumeless glow of her built-in all-gas barbecue. Abigail was telling her there was no such thing as trust and she didn't want the discomfort of even suspecting.

Around them, the dining room was filling with hotel guests. There was the usual out-of-season collection of elderly couples and threesomes of widows treating themselves to a break before the school holidays. Stella imagined them in minibus groups, touring gardens by day, snipping craftily at shrubs, taking illicit cuttings of species that caught their fancy and about which they would later brag coyly to their friends ('That choisya's from *Sissinghurst*, wasn't I naughty?'). Perhaps she and Adrian would end up like that, sitting opposite each other at tables heavy with damask layers and cumbersome cutlery, nothing to talk about but the day that had just passed, and hoping they'd still be alive for the next one. What use would secret fantasies be then?

'They might ask us to go to a club,' Abigail was suggesting as their fish arrived.

'And they might already have found someone a whole lot younger to ask,' Stella said glumly, pouring more champagne.

'Do you know, you sound as if you'd actually mind that,' Abigail commented with surprise. 'And there I was thinking you were just about to tell me you needed an early night and had a riveting novel to finish.'

Stella laughed. 'It's this place. It's so *staid* and *proper*.' She looked around at the eau-de-nil carpet, the muted rose wallpaper with cream and moss green flowers. 'The furnishings are so discreet, so utterly, offensively *inoffensive*. It's driving me mad. When we're older this is the sort of thing we're supposed to find tasteful. Where do people like us go?'

'Hell, eventually, if we're lucky. The Other Place will probably be just like this. Bland and boring and tinkling with shopping-mall music.' Abigail giggled, 'I think you're getting drunk. Here, have some more.' She leaned over and topped up Stella's glass. The waiter brought another bottle, shoving it quietly into the silver ice bucket and deftly whisking away the empty one, though Stella couldn't recall either of them ordering it. She ate her sea bass and ordered a chocolate truffle torte, recklessly obliterating the careful calorie counting at Chameleon. What difference could one little sin make?

Ruth was glad she hadn't, after all, rushed to phone Melissa and tell her about Bernard. Suddenly it was all deeply private, as secret as her first five-year diary, all locked up. She'd done her reporting duty by telling Melissa when she'd first had all-the-way sex, a rather rushed encounter in the far corner of the college car park, in the back of a Ford Mondeo with a blond dreadlocked boy from B.Tech Performing Arts. His frantic breath had sounded like Niagara Falls in her ear. She'd laughed when he'd told her she was beautiful, laughed because it had sounded as if that's what he, and his mates fresh from their terribly remote and famous boarding school, had decided was a sure way to get a girl to part with her underwear. His hurt, puzzled face had then told her that she'd been wrong, he really *did* think her beautiful and it was from that moment she'd stopped defining herself as fat, big, overweight, bulky, lumpy, all the words that could put her down. She was determined it would take more than Abigail's casually bad-mannered up-and-down appraisal and judgement to send her back to that kind of insecurity. She sat in the garden on the swing-seat, rocking gently and remembering Bernard's breath on her neck, calmer than the dread-lock boy's, perhaps, she thought, in fear of heart attacks. He must be that old, and her father was always saying he looked just like a battered apple, the perfect shape for a heart-failure man. His hands had left smudges of pinkish oil paint on her breasts, which, like a teenage pop fan who'd got close enough to touch her idol, she had been reluctant to wash. Eventually she'd scrubbed off the marks in the shower, determined that if she didn't, it would be like assuming that she'd never get the chance to lie naked on the velvet sofa with him and get smudge-marked all over again. She had to think onwards, not backwards. That was the kind of thing her mother was always advising.

'Hi. You OK?' Toby sat heavily down on the seat next to her and started swinging it to a different, more impatient rhythm.

'Yeah. I'm fine. Couldn't be better,' she told him, wondering if he'd correctly interpret her self-satisfied smile, 'What about you?' He looked down at the ground, picked up a couple of daisies and started shredding their petals. He didn't seem inclined to speak. 'You look like you're doing "she loves me, loves me not,"' Ruth said, wondering if he'd got something he'd quite like to say along those lines. She knew he'd been out with Giuliana. If he told her about that, she could tell him about Bernard, see what he thought, see if he'd betray her with distaste crossing his face, or if he'd catch how happy she was and be willing to share it.

'Giuliana?' she persisted, 'How did it go? I know you went out with her. Probably the whole island knows. Peggy saw you driving off.'

'Hmm,' he murmured. 'We just went to a pub. Had a pizza, you know.'

Ruth laughed, 'You took an *Italian* out for one of our English grotty *pizzas*? Have you got no imagination?'

Toby shifted on the seat, almost tipping Ruth onto

the grass. 'I didn't mean to take her there, we went to a stupid fucking great awful pub first.' He hurled what was left of the daisies onto the grass.

'So what was so stupid fucking awful about it?' she asked.

'*Nothing*. Sorry Ruth, just forget I mentioned it. Actually it was great being out with her, I really like her. But . . .' he sighed deeply and stood up, stretching as if he needed at least another twelve hours sleep, 'What's the point? I'll be going away soon. Last thing I need is to get involved. When you really like someone, they're never the ones who'll wait around till you get back.'

Deep, Ruth thought, watching Toby stride back to the house, hands in his pockets, back unusually hunched. 'Perhaps you should ask her to go with you!' she called up the garden. 'Then you'd have it both ways!'

'So, Samantha, how was dinner?' Stella looked up as the shadow of Simon fell across the table. She felt even smaller than before, sitting below him on the burgundy-striped sofa in the hotel lounge. In front of her were the ruins of coffee and the litter of silver paper from the stingy pair of chocolate mints. Abigail had gone off to the loo and Stella was alone on her sofa, watching the diners trail back out to the bar. She smiled up at him, habitually polite, which he took as an invitation to join her on the sofa. Her smile disappeared abruptly but it was too late, he was now leaning back comfortably, his legs manoeuvring themselves close to hers under the low glass-topped table. Any minute, she thought, suppressing the urge to laugh, he'd have his hand snaking across the back of the sofa behind her, like a nervous but determined first teenage date at the cinema.

'Oh. Hello again,' Abigail returned and sat down on

the sofa opposite from where she inspected Stella and Simon with obvious amusement. Stella glared.

'I was just asking Samantha about the food here. We tend to avoid eating in – spend enough time in these places and all you want is a sandwich and a pint.' He looked across towards the bar and waved at his colleague, inviting him over. 'Would either of you fancy a sticky?' he asked.

'A sticky *what*?' Stella asked, her thoughts racing to various sexual rudenesses. She blamed Abigail's presence for that; at any other time currant buns and flapjacks would surely have sprung to mind.

'A brandy? *Crème de menthe frappé*? *Parfait Amour*?' He leaned closer and smiled at her. He smelt of spearmint toothpaste and his skin was just lightly tanned and lined, like someone who played golf a lot and was careful to wear a hat and sun-screen. His ears, though, were as pink as sugar mice, as if they'd been left out of the skin care programme and were doing their best to let him know. They looked very vulnerable, those ears, she thought, and she had a shocking urge to kiss them better and tell them it was all right.

'Or we could go on somewhere else,' Geoff approached and made the suggestion, standing behind Abigail and looking down at her. Stella watched her face swivel, and, Abigail's eyes being on a level with the man's charcoal-suited crotch, saw a look of interested calculation cross her face as she focused beadily on the fabric and assessed its possible contents.

'Anna?' Geoff said, claiming her, his hands on her shoulders, looking down at her, 'What do you think? There's a great little bar not too far down the road.'

'Oh, why not?' Abigail said, looking across intently at Stella, 'A bit of sea breeze on the way – what do you think, Samantha?'

'Oh, I don't mind. I could do with some air,' Stella said, breezily, thinking that at least they'd be out of

198

this stifling place and she could breathe again. She was quite drunk, she realized, and needed at least a couple of hours before she went to bed. If she lay down now, there would be the inevitable whirling pit feeling, and if she sat still just where she was much longer she might doze into an unattractive dribbling, slumped heap among the cushions. Carefully, she stood up and with the others following, made her way towards the main door.

'I hope no one comes in and sees this,' Ellen commented nervously.

'Would it matter that much if they did? It's only your body,' Willow replied grouchily. She sounded as if she'd prefer silence, which Ellen felt uncomfortable about. She'd rather have the kind of conversation she got at the hairdresser, meaningless questions about holiday plans and weather, anything to distract them both from what was going on down at Ellen's lower back end.

Willow felt she'd got it all wrong. She realized now that she could have had any of them, just as naked as this stupid slack-bummed woman, lying on her table being smothered with Vaseline and vitamin E cream (in case of skin reactions) prior to the spreading of the plaster. They'd all been as terrified as each other. So terrified she could even, at last, have had Bernard. Not that there was much point in having him like this, she thought as she slapped on the goo – the only way she wanted Bernard lying naked and face down on her big table was if she was naked and face up beneath him. This Ellen, and she slapped a little more viciously, gritting her teeth against the resulting apologetic squeak of 'ouch!', was obviously the prissy type who referred to her underwear areas as Mrs Fanny and Mr Bottom, all that going into a corner to take off her clothes and then scuttling on to the table with her hands flapping. She ran a cruelly jagged fingernail down Ellen's spine, apologizing without sincerity as she did it, and wished she'd even got Ruth there instead. Ellen was such a waste of good angry spite.

Philip Porter was getting to like sitting in his car in the dark. He could use the miniature light that attached to his clipboard. His sister had given it to him for Christmas and this had been his first chance to have a go with it. He'd been fretting about that, hating to have something that had no apparent purpose, hating to have an item that had generated a thank-you letter and good intentions but which had still managed to languish untried in his glove compartment, next to the gloves and the folded duster. Now it perched triumphantly just to the left of the bulldog clip, in the half-dark successfully illuminating the page where the day's list of island visitors was neatly catalogued. He no longer parked outside the pub, not since the girls-only night when the police had come along and suggested that his presence there could be mis-construed to an unfortunate degree. Now he was further along by the rowing club, where his view of the ferry was only bettered by his view of several of the scruffier cabins on the island. The ridiculous bright blue painted one was blindingly spot-lit inside, which was unusual and potentially interesting. Most of the time, this particular house was lit like a dead hippy's shrine with dark red, slowly swirling lights, wobbling, jelly-like globules of colour reflecting on the main room's purple walls. Now the whole place looked as bright as a TV studio and, if he was not hallucinating, he could swear he'd seen a completely bare person, a woman, scampering across the room. He reached into the glove compartment and took out his little, but so handy, binoculars. This was the home of a very odd woman, he knew (Wilma Doreen Ellis), so he didn't feel in the least bit guilty, more that he was doing his duty as a good citizen.

If only Ted Kramer could see *this*, he thought excitedly, his binoculars almost twitching out of his shaking hands. If only he hadn't gone native and taken to spending all his time guzzling tea in the smelly depths of that old biddy's barge. What on earth was going on *now*? What was this woman doing to the other, the naked, one? What was she smearing on to her body? The only thing he could come up with was that Wilma Doreen was *icing* her neighbour, icing her bottom like a birthday cake, white and smooth and sticky. A smutty giggle rose up as he speculated on where she might put the candles. He felt a surge of unaccustomed sexual commotion – the kind of uncontrolled rush that had usually happened only in his clammy adolescent waking moments. And when the awful, heart-stopping knock on the car window came, he was right back there in his fuggy teenage bedroom with his mother interrupting ('time for school, our Philip'), as absolutely bloody ever, the very best moment in the day.

'I think we've had cause to speak to you before, haven't we, sir?' the policeman said, putting himself and his cap firmly between Philip Porter's binoculars and their extraordinary view.

It was years since Stella had danced this close to a strange man. It felt quite unreal, swaying slowly and with no particular direction in the dark as if the two of them were in a bad romantic movie. Anything that either of them said could only be false and corny dialogue and she was grateful for silence. She leaned against Simon's body and was back at the school dances, youth club parties, and college balls of her teens – the pre-Adrian days when every male she danced with had been simply an erection to squash against and feel slyly triumphant about. Even the music was the same, late night bluesy stuff that she'd liked then and still did. Just now she felt she rather needed Simon simply to prop her up. Tiredness had crept up and got at her and the air was thick with cigarette smoke and the stench of left-over alcohol. Most people had left and the few pairs mooching around the dance floor looked as if they, like her, were too exhausted to make a move to anywhere else. The right side of her face was steaming where Simon had his pressed against her and she could feel gusts of his hot breath in her ear, and her back was feeling overheated where his hands were splayed against her body. She wondered if the linen dress would be showing damp patches, hand-shaped. Turning her face towards his, she could see a sugar-mouse ear glowing in the dark. She no longer, she decided, had any urge to fondle it.

I'm not comfortable, she thought suddenly, and she pulled away a little to look around, peering through the haze, for Abigail.

'Samantha? Are you all right?' Simon's eyes were looking into hers and she tried to focus properly. Maybe I'm beginning to need reading glasses, she thought, as her eyes slowly adjusted to having his right in front of her. He was smiling, just a bit, just enough to make him look pleased with himself, as if the evening was going *exactly* as he'd expected – and would continue to do so.

'Mmm, fine,' she told him, unable to locate Abigail either on the minute dance floor or in any of the mostly empty velvet-seated alcoves. She was probably at the bar, or gone off to the loo, or even, she thought with envy, getting some air outside. This suddenly seemed a highly desirable option. 'I think I'll just go and . . .' she began, but, as if he'd sensed her reaching for the escape hatch, Simon's mouth swooped and landed with skilful accuracy on hers.

Well, this is interesting, Stella thought with detachment, joining in for the sake of politeness and to avoid an unseemly scuffle. It now felt even more like the youth club days, snogging a stranger simply because that was what happened next. Of course, unlike a teenager, it suddenly dawned on her that Simon was going to expect her to do a lot more about *his* erection than simply go to the bar for another Coca-Cola. She simply didn't fancy him *that* much. What would I advise the problem-pagers, she thought, as she felt his hands meandering down her back and pressing her more firmly against him.

'You can always say "no",' she remembered writing countless times, frustrated that they should still be asking, after the times she'd spelled it all out for them. 'The choice is yours. It's as easy to say as yes,' Extrication wasn't quite so easy though, she thought, peering over Simon's shoulder, still in search of Abigail. Perhaps she'd already escaped and gone back to the hotel to bed. Perhaps she'd gone to the hotel to bed with Geoff.

'I'll be back in a minute, promise,' Stella announced, unwinding herself clammily from Simon and making for the door marked Ladies before he could comment.

'Oh, there you are – I saw you all wrapped up with Mr Software.' Abigail was sitting on a rickety little chair smoking a cigarette underneath a machine that sold condoms. She looked like a doorkeeper in a brothel. 'Time to go?' she asked, before Stella had said a word.

'Time to go,' she laughed, 'Mr Software has become seriously Hard. How do we get out of here on our own? I really don't want . . .'

Abigail cackled and took a last deep drag on her cigarette before shoving it down the grubby sink's plughole. 'There's a window in that end cubicle,' she said, standing up and pointing to a graffitied door ('If you're into timewasting – shag Darren').

'A *window*? What, climb *out*?' Stella looked back at the door she'd come in through. Just beyond it lurked Simon, perhaps waiting with a result-clinching final drink. 'Of course he might have done a runner too, we could meet him legging it down the road . . .'

'No we won't.' Abigail sounded like the voice of experienced authority. 'You've let him think you're a certainty. It's your own fault, I was watching you dozing off out there propped up on his chest. If you use a man as something to sleep *on*, don't be surprised if he expects you to sleep *with*. Now, tuck your skirt in your knickers, chuck your bag out first and I'll be right behind you.'

Chapter Fourteen

'Now I really *am* tired,' Stella said, drying her sand-encrusted toes on the hem of her crumpled and sea-splattered dress. The salt water stung her ankle where she'd grazed it on the window catch as she'd climbed out in the escape from Simon. It had been less difficult than she'd expected: obviously time spent leaping about in the Chameleon gym, her hands clutching silly little blue weights, hadn't been entirely wasted. Not only had her body actually fitted through the small window without so much as a squeeze, but she'd leaped up onto the loo seat and the ledge with all the casual ease of a school PE captain. Lucky, she thought, that they'd been on the ground floor, though in her eagerness to escape she wouldn't swear she'd have found it impossible to dash across rooftops in moonless darkness and shin down a drainpipe.

'Don't you just feel so much better after a good paddle? It's like being a kid again. There's nothing like it.' Abigail sat comfortably with her legs splayed out, scooping at the sand either side of her like a child digging herself down into a hidey-hole. The sea swooshed up the beach, stopping only a few yards in front of them. There was a thin silver line of light beginning to appear on the black horizon, but it was still dark enough to imagine seeing dead bodies carried to the sand on the waves.

'Is it going out or coming in, do you think?' Abigail asked.

'If we sit here long enough I guess we'll know the answer,' Stella told her, squinting into the sunrise distance to see if there were any ships to wonder about. When she'd gone to the seaside with the children, when they were little she'd always pointed out distant boats and made up stories about where they'd been and where they were going. She'd told them about Russian trawlers, on freezing year-long trips away from home, the crew missing their babies being born, the seasons changing without them there to notice. The sea had no seasons, just weather – good or bad, stormy or calm. She'd made up stories about cruise liners, full of jolly widows looking for last romances at fancy dress parties where they dressed up as 1920s flappers and Charleston'd the night away. Ruth had liked best the quarter-mile oil tankers manned by only ten men who sped round the huge flat deck on bicycles. She'd imagined them playing bike polo, or having races and going too fast, too close to the edge. Toby had liked to hear about lone yachtsmen, sea-maddened and lost and down to their last Kit-Kat.

But just now, out beyond the pier which was neglected and skeletal like disused mine workings, Stella could see nothing but the illusion of whales and seals and sharks chasing among the waves. No traffic, no frigates chasing drug smugglers, not even a left-over lilo.

'They'll have locked us out,' she said to Abigail, turning to look back at the hotel. A few token lights showed, but nothing bright and inviting. From where she sprawled on the beach, Stella thought the hotel, looming with *faux* grandeur, looked like a Victorian temple to propriety – full of well-behaved people, who'd gone to bed at a sensible hour, having drunk no more than was good for them.

'No they won't,' Abigail assured her, turning to look at the building, 'There's a night porter. Think of all those civic functions people in places like this have to go to.'

Stella started laughing, a silly, young-girl snorting laugh. 'I always think *civic functions* would make a good name for a town square lavatory complex,' she spluttered.

Abigail hauled her to her feet, 'You're still pissed. You might as well have slept with that Simon bloke, you could have blamed it on the booze and felt no guilt at all.'

'It would have been my fault for being drunk though,' Stella pointed out. 'And what happened about the other one? Geoff was it? He looked all right. You don't usually go home alone, that I *do* know. Are you saving yourself for when Martin comes back?'

Abigail started walking up the beach, her shoes in her hand, 'Saving myself for the right man, yes. Perhaps I should have done it years ago, when I had the chance. Quite pointlessly, I'm making up for lost time.' She laughed, 'I'm enjoying watching you do the same!'

The cool air in the dead-fish dawn was restoring Stella back to a degree of sobriety. She felt Abigail's sadness and felt sorry she'd mentioned Martin. 'Oh he'll come back, you'll see,' she said, trying to instil optimism. 'He'll have to come back and see the children, and he'll remember what he's missing. As long as you make sure he knows he *is* missed.'

'Maybe. Though do I want him? Like I said, I should have settled for what you've got,' Abigail said rather grumpily, 'Come on, let's go in and get some sleep. If we sleep long enough, our admirers will be off for the day learning how to put envelopes in their windows or vice versa.'

'*Please* Dad,' Ruth pleaded over breakfast – the only time to catch her father before his brain was overtaken by the weirdnesses of his current plot and characters, 'it's only for one weekend, and I will clear everything up, and I'll make sure no one goes near your computer – I'll unplug it all and take it out and bring it up here if you like, and the printer as well.' Adrian continued looking distant and munching toast as if he didn't really have a clue, or a care, what he was putting in his mouth. Ruth sighed and persisted, in spite of warning faces from Toby who was making coffee behind Adrian. 'And I'll make sure all your work is completely locked away and give the whole room a special spring clean after, and put everything back exactly as you like it.' Still no response. She leaned forward and forced him to notice her, 'And I won't let anyone sit in your special chair or steal your sherbert lemons.' She sat back and waited, feeling there was no better offer she could make.

'You want the summerhouse?' he said vaguely, as if he'd only just caught a few of her words. 'To put your jewellery in for the Art Fair?'

'*Yes*,' she said, resisting the urge to bang both fists on the table with frustration, or possibly even on Adrian's befuddled head.

'OK,' he said simply.

'OK? You mean it?'

'Sure.' Adrian got up and went to collect a mug of coffee from Toby and then opened the door on a day glorious with sunshine. 'I'm off to do some work. Be a love and bring *The Times* down to me when it gets here, if ever. That kid gets later and later.'

'I didn't expect it to be that easy,' Ruth confided to

Toby as she watched Adrian loping down the garden path. 'You know how precious he is about his work space.'

'That's only because he doesn't want anyone to know about all the porn he's working on. It must be dreadful to feel embarrassed about what your job is. It must be how prostitutes with families to run feel when they go to things like the school fête. I wonder what Dad says at a dinner party full of strangers when someone says "And what do *you* do?" I don't suppose he tells them "Oh, I make a fortune writing wank-fodder."'

'That's only because he still thinks *we* don't know, as if we're still three or something. Otherwise I don't suppose he'd care who else knew. He's only scared they might tell us. I keep expecting Willow to, just out of spite. I get this creepy feeling she knows everything about everyone.'

Toby laughed. 'She knows why the newspapers aren't being delivered. The council man got arrested for spying on her while she plaster-casted Ellen and the paper boy's Mum won't let him come over here anymore. "Dodgy goings-on", Mr Karesh at the newsagents said that she'd said.'

'Not the *nice* council man? The one who's Peggy's friend?'

'No, course not. The spooky one who's always in his car, wiping his windows and wearing little gloves. It's no surprise, really.'

'No, I suppose it isn't. Toby?' Ruth looked around quickly to make sure they were alone, 'Do you think Dad's, you know, *all right*?'

'How do you mean, "all right"? Going mad, do you mean, or looking ill?'

Ruth considered for a moment, 'Mad, I suppose. He hasn't been the same since he went out the other night. He's going round looking like he's had a bad shock. I think something's happened. It can't be just that he's missing Mum.'

Toby got up quickly and took his mug to the sink. Noisily he started unloading clean crockery from the dishwasher, crashing around the kitchen putting things away.

'Here, you sort out the cutlery,' he ordered, hauling out the plastic basket and handing it to Ruth. 'I'm sure he's fine, just thinking about work or something, that's all. Don't worry about it.'

'I'm worried about *you* now,' she said, grinning at him, 'I can't remember a time when you voluntarily had anything to do with the dishes . . .'

Stella drove out of the hotel car park and wished she was going straight home. There was no reason why she shouldn't, she thought, cursing herself for being hampered by habitual kindness. She could easily just drive Abigail back to her house and tell her it was time she started practising coping by herself. It couldn't be that difficult, it wasn't as if Martin had *died*. But then she thought, how would it feel if Adrian went off with someone else, went off and left her? Wouldn't she even think she'd prefer it if he'd died, then at least there wouldn't be the dreadful grief of the death of love. She sighed gently as she pulled away from a pedestrian crossing light. She was being ridiculous. Of course it wouldn't be preferable to have him, or Martin dead. Abigail sat beside her, contentedly looking out of the window as they drove along the seafront, passing all the small hotels and boarding houses, all painted in a selection of sweet-pea pastels. She didn't, Stella thought, look as if she was actually doing that much anguishing about anything more hypothetical than the possibilities of what to wear.

There weren't yet many people about, even close to midday, not in the sense of families having their main summer holidays – those, Stella assumed, had flown off loaded with Factor 15 to the Spanish sun, but there were lots of little gatherings of older people, in optimistic floral cotton frocks topped with sensible cardigans or the inevitable beige Dannimac jacket.

'Don't ever let me buy a beige waterproof jacket,' Stella murmured to Abigail, as she stopped to let a collection of these cross the road. 'Just kill me if I ever do. Promise?'

'Good grief, darling, of course I promise,' Abigail agreed solemnly, understanding exactly. *That's* why I like her, Stella thought, driving away and feeling more cheerful.

Venetia and James were waiting to be collected in a small ante-room close to the main front entrance of their school. The pink and cosy study, haphazardly furnished with what were not quite antiques and cluttered with photos of and paintings by former pupils, was friendlier and less formal than a staffroom or Head Teacher's office. It was obviously the place where children were taken to have bad news broken to them, or to wait with their dire infections to be whisked off home to where they couldn't harm others. It was probably also, Stella speculated, the room where parents were informed that their failure to meet the fees could no longer be indulged, or that their child might flourish more productively in an alternative environment. Abigail and Stella walked in and were greeted by the house mother who looked anxiously at Abigail as if trying to work out the right words to deal with the situation. They probably weren't in her training manual, Stella concluded, watching the stocky woman's eyes darting here and there and avoiding quite meeting Abigail's when she talked. 'They're all packed and ready,' she said quietly, almost whispering, leaning towards Abigail in a confiding sort of way. Abigail pulled back slightly, as if terrified that it was *she* who was expected to do the confiding.

'Mum!' James, a gangly and heavy-footed ten-year-old, got up as soon as he saw her and rushed across the room, hurling himself against his mother, almost knocking Stella over on his way. 'Why are we going home *now*?'

Venetia, demure and strangely controlled for eight, sat coolly on a fringed velvet chair, her feet hardly touching the floor. She made no move towards Abigail, but smiled politely at Stella. Stella felt the child's tension and wished she'd waited in the car. She blamed Abigail for dragging her in, tempting her by telling her there was one of Bernard's early paintings over the fireplace. She looked at it with neighbourly curiosity, relieved that, more suitably in a school for such young children, it was an unchallenging, rather dull still life and obviously painted long before he'd discovered that teenage girls would cheerfully strip off all their clothes for him. Venetia, when she looked back at her, was still looking as uninterested as if she was waiting for a bus. I bet Bernard would never dare ask *her* to get her kit off, Stella thought.

'Darlings!' Abigail gushed, 'We're all going home, and then we're going to stay at Stella's house and visit her lovely island and all the artists on it. They're having a fair! You'll like that.'

Venetia's pretty lip curled and Stella wondered if the temperature really had dropped enough to make her shiver.

'With swings and rifles?' James asked. 'Can I win a fish?'

Abigail laughed. 'Not that sort of fair, darling,' she told him, hugging him fondly, thrilled at his enthusiasm. 'An *art* fair, lots of gorgeous things for sale, and paintings and jewellery.'

'Will Daddy be there?' Venetia slid down from her chair and stood in front of Abigail, looking, Stella thought, like a sulky little girl reluctantly about to present a bouquet to a visiting Duchess. There was a sharp intake of breath from the house mother, who was waiting behind them all, hovering in the doorway, anticipating drama, hoping to have to do mopping up of emotions.

'Er . . . no, I don't think so. He's working, in America. It's too far.'

'I expect he'll bring me a present then,' Venetia declared confidently, the hint of a smile drifting across her face. Goodness, Daddy's girl, Stella thought, she's going to be no end of trouble, and troubled if Martin doesn't come back.

'I'll go and turn the car round,' she told them, escaping out into the daylight.

They were very *good* children, Stella could only think as she drove them the thirty-five miles back to their home. James and Venetia said little, didn't whine for crisps or chocolate or turn a nerve-wracking shade of green in the back of the car. Through the mirror she could see Venetia sitting with her arms folded as if she'd got a grudge about something and was biding her time before coming out with it, silently watching the countryside pass by. James, who had developed manners acute enough to want to avoid silences, politely answered questions his mother hadn't actually bothered to ask about sports teams and friends and the horrors of early French. During the quiet moments, she could feel him *not mentioning* something, and wondered how many chilling hints his house mother had been unable to resist dropping in the hope that he could, even at his age, fill in the interesting newsy gaps.

'Where's Cleo?' was Venetia's only comment when they arrived at Abigail and Martin's palatial but spookily deserted house. She dashed off to run from room to room searching for her cat, speeding and

213

looking and slamming doors and sending hollow echoes down the long, broad passageways. Stella heard and felt her small pounding footsteps overhead, and then on up to the attic level where the suites of children's rooms and the former nanny's quarters were. Venetia hurtled down the stairs and then darted back to the hallway.

'Sorry, darling, what did you say?' Abigail was busy pressing buttons on the Ansaphone and not listening to her child.

'*Cleo!*' Venetia shouted, bunching up her fist and thumping viciously at Abigail's thigh, 'Where's my *cat*?'

'She's at my house, on Pansy Island,' Stella explained quietly. 'When your mummy came to stay she didn't want to leave Cleo here all by herself so she brought her along to us in a basket. She's very happy there, really. You'll see her very soon.' She smiled at Venetia, trusting she was being reassuring.

'Have you got Daddy there too?' the child demanded, frowning.

'No, just Cleo,' Stella told her.

'*Fuck*,' Abigail muttered. Venetia smirked and flounced off up the stairs again. 'Not so much as a "hello, how are you,"' Abigail complained, switching off the machine. 'In fact, "Hello, how are you, the house deeds are in the safe," would be nice.'

'Almost as nice as "Hello, I'm coming back"?' Stella asked, grinning.

Abigail laughed, 'Oh *much* better than that! Come on, let's find you the very best of the spare rooms and then we'll go into the garden and see what the pool temperature is. If the thermostat's working as it should be, it'll be warm enough for a lovely, lovely swim.'

Adrian typed the words 'The End' at the bottom of the page, leaned back on his ergonomically perfect leather chair and closed his eyes. Behind the lids, where he'd trusted he would see nothing but reddish-black blankness, he pictured Abigail's small breasts gleaming in the moonlight like smooth pale stones on a sandy beach. They were only breasts, he told himself, just quite small, ordinary breasts, no more magical or different or more thrilling than anyone else's. What on earth had he hoped to discover inside that pink and white gingham bra? What soul-transforming, life-enhancing, holy treasures had he expected to find in there? It was as if he'd gone right back to being a horny nineteen-year-old again, constantly checking that women would really *do it*, as if nothing useful, not one sense-endowing truth had been learned in between. He rubbed his eyes, trying to erase the pictures, and stared out of the window at the river, rising fast on its afternoon tide. The roof of Peggy's boat was bobbing on the rising tide just visible over the low wall and he wished that the rhythmic movement didn't remind him of youthful sex in the backs of cars parked alongside others, rocking in the misty dark in quiet lanes. It's only because I've finished the book, he thought, looking at the rather childlike 'The End' declaration on the screen in front of him, like a neat, keen schoolboy triumphantly underlining a piece of difficult Latin prep. Any other time he'd be grateful to have his surroundings make him think about sex, terrifically helpful for his job.

'You look as if you have the problem,' Giuliana's soft voice interrupted Adrian's thoughts and made him jump. When, he wondered as he swivelled the cream leather chair, had it become customary for people to start wandering in to see him, not just carefully, apologetically, but without even knocking? So pretty, though, he thought, admiring Giuliana's carelessly piled up hair, skewered loosely into place with a piece of metal that could easily have been purloined from one of Enzo's mighty works. She had such a long neck, he thought, such a perfectly free-moving, uncomplicated body.

He smiled at her and waved her into the ancient cane peacock chair. 'What problem do I look as if I have?'

She shrugged and sat down, her long slim feet neatly side by side as if she was waiting for a job interview. 'I don't know, just a problem. You look like you can't mend it.' She laughed suddenly, 'I know, you must ask your wife, she does the mending the problems – you ask her.' She leaned forwards, her hands resting on the chair either side of her thighs and he tried not to look down the front of the simple cotton singlet she was wearing, just in case he glimpsed yet more disturbing pink gingham. '*I* have a problem,' she confided and he held his breath, 'I can't find Toby and he said he would be here.'

'Isn't he in the house?' Adrian asked, rather stupidly. After all, the summerhouse would hardly have been the first place she'd look. She smiled, looking kind and he felt immediately very silly. 'This morning,' Adrian managed to recall, 'he did say it was his turn to go to Willow. Perhaps he is still there.'

Giuliana laughed, her one gold filling catching the sunlight. 'I'll go and find him. I shall watch him being plastered.' She got up and went to the door, looking back and giving Adrian a wicked, all Italian glance, 'It's now the time that I see his body,' she said, grinning at him.

Adrian watched her stroll elegantly up the garden path, slowing to stroke the foxglove flowers and trail her hand along the tops of the geraniums. He wished Stella would come home. She should be at Abigail's by now, he calculated, looking at his watch and picking up the phone. He wanted to tell her he'd finished the book, wanted to tell her he missed her. He flipped open his diary and started tapping out the number, but hung up quickly halfway through, realizing that the person who answered would most likely be Abigail. He opened a new folder in his computer and started experimenting with a few thoughts towards a new piece of work. It might, he thought, involve a lot of pink gingham underwear . . .

'This is absolutely *definitely* the life,' Stella stated, shielding her eyes from the sun and watching Venetia dive like a pink seal into the swimming pool. She reached out to the table beside her and picked up her iced white wine. A few freezing drops spilled from the edge of the glass and went through her swimsuit, giving her tummy an icy chill on the outside to match the cold on the inside as she drank.

'Comfortable, are you?' Abigail teased, 'Anything else I can get for Madam?'

Stella stirred lazily on the cushioned steamer chair and stretched out a foot to admire her Chameleon pedicure. 'No, I don't think so, thank you, just for the moment. Though perhaps a little later a well-muscled slave could come over and waft a large, cooling fan across my sun-kissed body.'

They both giggled, looking across the lawn to where Abigail's young, blond gardener, naked to the waist and gleaming from effort and heat, clipped carefully at the yew hedge.

'He's awfully good,' Abigail said, still staring admiringly at him.

'What at?' Stella spluttered into her drink.

'Gardening, of course! Whatever did you think?'

'You know what I thought. In fact, was he one of the ones?' she asked out of simple curiosity. Did people, people like her really have sex with young and gorgeous men or was it just tabloid talk? Surely Abigail couldn't really still be that promiscuous, not at her age. Grown-ups just weren't.

'What a thing to ask!' Abigail put on a mock-shocked face, 'I told you, he's here for the gardening. You should see his red hot pokers . . .'

'Oh should I,' Stella laughed, feeling that one way or another she'd been done out of the truth. Would she, she wondered, have told Abigail if she'd gone off to bed with that Simon the night before? Probably not.

'I'm bored.' Venetia's face bobbed up by the pool steps and she stared at her mother, expecting instant relief from her problem.

'How can you be bored?' Stella asked her, appalled. 'It's such a lovely day and there's so many fun things to do.'

Venetia ignored her. 'I'm *bored*,' she insisted again, glaring at her mother.

Abigail sighed, 'Are you, darling? I'm sorry about that but you'll just have to amuse yourself for a while. Why don't you go and find James? Perhaps he'll think of a game you can both play.'

'He's in his room with his computer. He's boring.' Venetia started slapping her hand up and down on the surface of the water, slyly watching the small droplets, calculatedly just not quite enough for complaint, landing on both Stella and Abigail.

Stella felt a small nag of impatience with the child. Hers had never been allowed to say they were bored. Her own mother had said, and she could remember it clearly, 'Only boring people get bored – they're the ones who can't think for themselves what to do.' 'You could read a book,' she suggested, 'or make something.'

'*Make* something? Like what? How?' Venetia stopped splashing and her face expressed a wary interest. Stella thought quickly, rifling though her memories for the entertainments she'd helped Ruth with.

'I know,' she said, 'paper dolls – the ones with

218

tagged clothes. Have you ever played with those?'

An extra big splash followed along with a scowl and, 'They're *boring*.'

'Not if you make your own, they're not,' Stella said patiently. 'Not if you decide just what you want them to look like and design all their outfits yourself. They can be space people with green faces or they can look like your best friend or your cat, whatever you like. If you go and get paper, coloured pencils and some scissors and bring them out here, we can sit under the big umbrella and I'll show you what to do.' She closed her eyes, giving the child time to think over the idea and after a moment or two heard her climbing out of the pool and padding past her towards the house.

'You're so good with her,' Abigail said. 'With me she'd just have demanded a trip to the nearest shops to buy five minutes worth of rubbishy plastic toy. Martin, of course, would probably have driven her up to Hamley's. She should have had you for a mother, not me.'

'Garbage,' Stella told her, putting her face up for the last moments she was likely to get of the sun that afternoon. 'She just needs a bit of company, that's all.' She smiled, loving the heat on her face and feeling recklessly heedless of wrinkle danger.

'We really should swop places,' Stella heard Abigail say. 'You'd be so much better at my children and my house than I seem to be. I bet you could even keep Martin here too.'

'You make him sound like a straying pet. And what would you do, exactly, while I'm swanning about taking over all you possess?'

'Oh, I'd be all right,' Abigail assured her. 'I told you, I'd be really, truly happy with exactly what you've got. We really should swop. Tell me honestly, you wouldn't mind living here, would you?'

Stella sat up and looked around the vast garden.

Beyond the yew hedge where the young gardener was clipping at off-shoots, was the all-weather tennis court. The garage block, outside which gleamed Abigail's little silver Mercedes, (complete with new front wing) was just the other side of it. The L-shaped house, the colour of Cornish cream, immaculately maintained, beautifully tended by a team of cleaners, was the sort that featured in the most up-market decorating magazines. When it came up for sale, if ever, it would merit a whole page in *Country Life* and would be so expensive that a price would not be mentioned. Whoever had to ask how much wouldn't be able to afford it.

Stella thought about the island tides, the cobwebs in her kitchen, the petty squabbles about the proposed bridge, Peggy's scruffy barge, Bernard's pathetically inflated ego. 'Well, of course I wouldn't mind living here. Who would?' she declared. 'You didn't even need to ask.'

Chapter Fifteen

Ruth lay face down on Willow's big table, resting her chin on her hands and staring at the patterns in the wood grain. I'm at her mercy, completely, she thought. Too late to back out now, she could only trust that what Willow was smearing greasily all down her back, bottom and thighs really was protective vitamin E and Vaseline. It could be anything, Ruth thought dreamily, enjoying the procedure and the possiblity of danger. It could be a dollop of Toby's precious Beetle's axle grease laced with loo bleach, or some kind of evil acid that would etch down through her skin and burn huge layers off. Willow wouldn't need to do a cast then, she could simply hang up the peeled and ragged skin and call it an art piece. Perhaps she collected them from all her rivals in love, like scalping, for trophies – there might be a lifetime's collection of other women's bug-chewed, leathery skins heaped in a trunk under a bed, ready to be hung and displayed at Willow's old age retrospective exhibition. She imagined them smelling slightly rancid, like Adrian's old Afghan coat that still waited in a bin liner in the cellar, ready for many years to go to a jumble sale. They'd probably need ironing, like mildewed sheets, Ruth thought idly.

Willow's hands worked rhythmically and neatly, like a masseuse late for the next client, and Ruth felt quite sleepy. She wondered if Willow had any idea that only half an hour before she'd been having sex with Bernard on his velvet sofa. As their bodies had moved (unnecessarily slowly, she'd thought, Bernard chuffing like an old museum steam train), she'd watched little clouds of dust motes puffing upwards from the fabric and frisking above them in the sunlight. They had reminded her of Melissa telling her that flying dust was a complete pain if you wore contact lenses, and she'd wondered if it was normal to think about such stupidly ordinary things while you were supposed to be totally abandoned to passion.

'Has he finished doing you yet?' Willow's abrupt question cut through Ruth's dozing.

'What?' Ruth half-flipped round to look at her, to see if she was correctly interpreting the question as the depths of crudeness. Willow briskly slapped her thigh, 'Stay *still*!' she ordered. 'Bernard's painting – is it nearly finished? He's certainly taking his time with you.'

Ruth smirked to herself, recognizing envy and feeling triumphant, not just over Willow but over all the girls who'd presumably been sketched, seduced and discarded in mere days – some even in *hours* it was rumoured. The feeling was short-lived though as Willow followed up with, 'Though there's an awful lot more of you to paint than most people, isn't there? I'm using twice the plaster on you that I did on that scraggy Ellen MacIver.'

'Well, I wouldn't want *any* bits of me to look like any bits of *her*,' Ruth stated grumpily. Willow ran her hand across Ruth's left buttock, deliberately slowly as if to emphasize how far the distance was, '*Bits* isn't the word I'd use. *Lots* perhaps. Now keep completely still, I'm starting on the plaster.'

Ruth ignored her instruction and turned her head as far as she could so that Willow could see just how angry she was. 'Look, do you want me just to leave right now, because I will if you carry on slagging me off. *I* know my body's OK, right? It's young and supple and soft and gorgeous. *And* I'm not the only one who thinks so.' The words 'so there' hung unsaid and childish in the air. Willow stayed silent, which might be ominous. Ruth bit her lip, wondering if, without doubt, she had now let herself in for the torture of the peel-and-scalp treatment. It wasn't her fault, Willow deserved it. She shouldn't be so fucking personal. She shouldn't be so fucking obsessive about Bernard, not without going and doing something about it, at least *telling* him, not just twittering about making him vases and bringing him flowers. Her hair looked just ridiculous too, Ruth thought, a hacked-up, spiked-up copy of Abigail's. It looked as if she'd torn it off in a rage rather than cut it with scissors. Perhaps she had, she wouldn't put it past her. Perhaps she'd used the ripped-off bits to stir into a love potion for Bernard. She could just imagine her mixing it up with his toenail clippings filched from the bin in his bathroom, and chanting and swaying over a boiling pot. Whatever happened to old hippies being gentle old souls permanently tranquillized by too much dope and forever into peace, love and hugging the trees?

Willow silently and swiftly skimmed plaster over Ruth's bottom. Ruth kept obediently quiet, in grudging but genuine respect for a fellow artist's concentration. It felt cold and creamy, and the chalky hardening process began almost immediately, like a good quality face pack. 'There, it's done,' Willow said, wiping her hands on a damp cloth. 'Now just lie really still for a while till it dries and I'll be back later to take it off. Just don't move at all, remember, OK? No tightening your butt-muscles or the final cast will look as if you've got a million billion wrinkles all over you and you won't want that . . . I'm just running out to see someone. Won't be long.'

Not so much as a cup of coffee, Ruth thought with disgust, dropping her head comfortably down on to her folded arms and closing her eyes.

Willow scampered down the path, as fast as her clumpy purple and silver boots would take her. Enzo's wind chimes clanged discordantly in the wind, like a storm warning, though to Willow, exhilarated and joyous, they sounded encouragingly like wedding bells. Sounds of drilling and metallic hammering were coming from his workshop and Giuliana's hens clucked close to the escallonia, as if trying to attract someone to rescue them from Enzo's artistic din. 'Oh, the glorious humming of the creative process,' Willow sang to herself delightedly as she trotted along, skipping girlishly over an old propeller shaft lurking dangerously beneath the fronds of cow parsley and the pink campion.

Bernard was on his balcony sipping an early Beck's and looking out across the river for inspiration. A young, slender woman strolling on the opposite bank with her baby in a pushchair was quite unaware that Bernard was using her to ponder the relative perfect distances between chin and nipple, nipple and navel. Ruth's finished portrait stood on the easel close to the table, which meant that it was still officially work in progress. Every now and then he glanced at it, trying to catch it with an objective eye, trying to decide if it really was as finished as he'd decided it was, or if just a little more tweaking was required. Thinking about this, and concentrating hard on the woman across the river, meant that he didn't hear Willow coming up the spiral stairs and into the room. Usually, by means of the sound of her boots, she gave him several thought-gathering seconds of notice in which he could choose quickly whether to indulge her with a bout of quasi-mystical heavy conversation (especially if she'd brought him a nice present), or fend her off and pretend he was just going out. This time he heard nothing till she stood behind him, filling the space with the sound of her breathing. He heard nothing because she had removed the boots and for luck had removed everything else as well. For a split, silly second it crossed his mind that she was naked so her clothes would make no warning sound – a pretty drastic measure if all she wanted was coffee and a chat or to borrow some linseed oil. It was with an uneasy sense of dread that he dared himself to turn and face her fully, and properly take in the bizarre sight.

'We are all a gift from nature,' she stated, her hands hanging simply by her sides and her feet close together. Her eyes looked straight ahead of her, just missing Bernard's and staring out past him to the horizon. She looked like a schoolchild at a medical about to have her height measured, Bernard thought. He slugged down the rest of his beer and put the glass on the balcony ledge.

'You'd better go further back inside,' he told her, looking nervously across to where the woman on the bank, thankfully oblivious, still pushed her sleeping baby.

'Why? Am I not something to be seen? What is to be hidden?' she asked, forcing him to look at her properly. Terrific tits, he caught himself thinking, to his own surprise. Her crazy hair was haloed with a circlet of ox-eye daisies. Smaller daisies, the child's daisy chain type, were looped round her wrists and ankles and threaded through her pubic hair. 'Peter Blake did one of his Alice paintings like that,' he commented feebly, wondering how he could decently get past her to the fridge for another, much needed, beer.

'Er, sit down, why don't you, I'll get you a drink.'

'I don't want a drink, I want to be painted,' she demanded.

'What, *now*? Just like that? Come on, Wills, you know better than that. Preparation, forethought, all that.' Just like sex, he thought, wondering if the same idea was going through her mind. Of course it was, why else was she there? He sidled past to the fridge and slyly checked out her back view. Great rear end too, worthy of casting in solid gold. Muscle tone most women would kill for – must be something to do with humping all that heavy clay around. He fumbled in the drawer for the bottle opener and thought of her working, sitting upright and braced at her wheel, legs apart, concentrating with those big teeth biting the bottom lip and hands moulding and tending the clay, teasing it up into shape. He thought of her doing all that as she was now, fresh-naked. Something stirred, at last, and he realized she'd won. Though the defeat, now it had come, wasn't so bad. A small, but vitally conceited part of his mind fast-forwarded to the grand and celebrated old age he'd planned for himself, to future Sunday supplement profiles, to Desert Island Discs, to speeches at his knighthood celebrations, at his Royal Academy presidency acceptance dinner – all the folklore-ish anecdotes and rumoured notoriety. Think Eric Gill, he mused, think Gilbert and George, Ruskin, Picasso, Dali, Warhol – man's fame, in art, depended on so much more than his work alone. Willow, capable of gestures such as this, could become quite an asset for him. She was certainly a more than worthy match.

Stella, arriving home in the middle of the afternoon, immediately missed the council man's car parked outside the rowing club. There was no longer any sign of the pristine Peugeot. He must have finished surveying us, she assumed as she parked opposite the ferry. She wondered what conclusion he'd come to, and if it was either accurate or useful. Toby's garage was closed and padlocked, all work on the Beetle finished too. She'd missed the little car's inaugural run, she realized with regret as she stacked her bags onto the ferry raft. She'd have liked to see it go, polished and immaculate, so different from the sorry wreck that had been towed in a year before, bought more in a spirit of hope than reality from an advert in *Wheelspin* that promised it was ideal for a 'ground-up body-off resto project.'

She turned the ferry handle, wondering if she was imagining that it was less of an effort than usual or if she was simply trying to justify the expense she and Abigail had gone to at Chameleon. The island seemed very quiet, with no sounds of human activity at all. She could just hear Enzo's chimes from the far end and the squabbling cackle of ducks close to the bank. It was almost as quiet as a dormitory suburb, as if everyone had at last given in and got themselves proper jobs and gone off to city desks. There was a scent of sleepy summer, warm dank leaves, overlong grass and musky wildflowers.

Fresh from the calm of Abigail's pale and empty house, a silent haven of peace where there was so much space that even the shouts and tantrums of the children seemed to be diluted and diminished, her own home seemed crumpled, noisy and crowded. It wasn't a matter of the number or sounds of people it contained – Stella felt crowded in from the moment she stepped into the front garden and had to battle through the overgrown weigela that had taken the opportunity, the moment her back was turned, of reaching out its pink-flowered branches to try to join forces with the cotoneaster on the opposite side. No one in the family, of course, had thought to cut it back. They must simply have shoved it out of the way every time they passed, in the sure unthinking confidence that Stella would deal with it when she got back. On the steps she fumbled in her bag for her door key, noticing that two bulging bags of old newspapers lay abandoned in the porch, too late for that week's collection by the recyling company which picked them up outside the rowing club if anyone remembered to drop them off. No one had, and what else, she wondered, as she let herself in, had they all forgotten to do? She felt a quiet resentment bubbling away, quite obliterating the lovely looking-forward-to-seeing-you feeling she'd carried with her all the way from Sussex. Now she simply envied Abigail her domestic organization. There was not the slightest sense in her immaculately run home that any member of the oh-so-efficient staff could forget to top up the Rinse-Aid in the dishwasher, or allow ten (as they had here) rinsed empty milk bottles to accumulate beside the sink. Mrs Morris had presumably been along to clean as usual, but the family knew she didn't do milk bottles – these had to be hauled along to the stack of empty crates by the ferry where the milkman eventually picked them up. The house could have done with a make-over, too, she thought, wondering how long the efforts of a team of professional Mrs Mops would last, and feeling immediately daunted by the amount of pre-cleaning that would have to be done before any such team could be invited to tackle the job.

She hauled her bags up the stairs and decided to unpack and calm down before going down to the summerhouse and finding Adrian. She didn't want to confront him immediately with trivial domestic grievances – that would be shrewish. She'd work those into general conversation later, when they were all assembled for a decent family telling-off. Much better to present him, as she'd intended, with her newly beautified self, give him a chance to be happy – no, positively invigoratingly *thrilled* to see her. She pottered reasonably happily around the room, stuffing underwear from her bag into the laundry basket and putting the crumpled red dress on the bed, ready to take along to be dry-cleaned later. She picked it up again and sniffed at it. There was still a salty, seawater scent lingering on it, still a trace of sand dropping flecks onto the white duvet cover. Simon, she thought, with a guilty smile, was one of the past week's activities that would be better never mentioned. She'd have to stick to telling them all about Aqua-splash aerobics, seaweed wraps and the hotel restaurant's outrageous mark-up on a couple of bottles of Pol Roger.

Stella was just thinking about trawling through the pile of problem letters that she knew would be waiting for her out on the landing, next to her computer, when the kitchen door slammed violently and a desperate wailing sound filled the house. It soared upwards towards her, the kind of awful it's-so-unfair keening that small children specialize in when their best friend has stolen their favourite toy, followed up by their mother believing the blatant lie that it was a *gift*.

'Ruth? Whatever's wrong?' Stella hurtled down the stairs and gathered her sobbing daughter into her arms. Only then did she notice that Ruth seemed to be wearing only a fringed Paisley bedspread wrapped round her trembling body. Behind her, leading to the back door was a trail of what looked like white chalk, interspersed with sugary lumps of plaster.

'Where are your clothes?' Stella demanded, wiping the tears from the girl's face, 'Is this anything to do with Bernard?' she then asked suspiciously, trying hard to keep a rising defensive anger out of her voice. It was important for Ruth to be able to tell her if something dreadful had happened, not to be put off by hostility.

'Willow,' Ruth eventually managed to splutter. 'She

went and left me. She went *hours* ago.' Stella felt mystified. 'She didn't come back *on purpose*,' Ruth went on, the sobs renewing their vigour.

'Come on, let's get you upstairs and find you something to wear.' More plaster cascaded from under the Paisley cloth and Stella began to feel seriously alarmed. 'What is this stuff? Why are you covered in it?' she asked.

Behind her, Adrian came in from the kitchen. 'What's going on? I heard someone crying and saw a blanket flapping past the summerhouse . . . Hello, Stella. God, Ruth whatever happened? Allergic to plaster?' Adrian, treacherously Stella thought, seemed to think the sight was amusing.

'If you think this is funny . . .' Stella hissed at him.

'Well it is, isn't it? Oh, you don't know, I suppose, Willow's taken it into her head to plaster-cast everyone's rear end. Looks like it was Ruth's turn.'

Ruth glared at him coldly, gathered up her fringed cloak and stamped off up the stairs.

'Now look what you've done,' Stella accused him. 'Don't you have *any* sensitivity?'

'Oh, and it's lovely to see you too, darling,' he said sarcastically, his amusement vanishing. 'I'll assume that the weight you lost at the health farm consisted entirely of your sense of humour?'

'What's so funny about our daughter crying? I don't care what Willow's arty-farty plans were, there's no need for her to send Ruth home in this state.'

She turned and left him standing uselessly at the bottom of the stairs and followed Ruth and the trail of plaster chippings to the top of the house. She could hear the shower running in the top bathroom and knocked on the door.

'Ruth? Do you want to talk about it?' She bit her lip and wished she didn't sound so absurdly *sharing*. The crying had stopped at least, though behind the gush of water from the shower there could still be some desperate sniffing going on.

'No,' Ruth yelled, following up with, 'later maybe.'

Adrian had disappeared, back to his summerhouse refuge, Stella assumed as she trailed back down the stairs. He'd walked out leaving her the two stair carpets and two hallways worth of plaster hoovering that needed to be done, in the same thoughtless way that he and the others had left the milk bottles, newspapers and the overgrown plants for her to deal with. The plaster would probably block up the drains after Ruth's shower too and then it would be *her* they'd all come and complain to. Perhaps she could get Willow round and force her to pick up every white crumb in her wolfish bloody teeth. She sighed and reached into the under-stairs cupboard for the vacuum cleaner, feeling resignedly that this at least she would make an initial effort to get sorted out quickly and neatly. No one else was likely to.

Adrian leaned over the river wall and wondered if Peggy was in her barge and willing to give him a cup of tea. He hadn't seen her much lately, she seemed to have taken to going off into the town with her new friend from the council. She'd also taken to wearing a selection of new clothes – a proper jacket instead of simply wrapping herself in the crocheted blanket, and a new pair of navy blue deck shoes instead of the Wellingtons padded with tweedy-knit socks. There was no sign of life inside the barge, but he climbed over its deckrail and sat on the far edge, looking out into the deeper water. The tide was at mid-point, so the still water reflected his face and body back at him, darkly and blurrily, but well enough for him to see an ageing, miserable expression of malcontent on his face. 'I'm getting old,' he said out loud, experimentally. 'I no longer know the right track for my life,' he went on. A swan sped across the water towards him, stirring up ripples that destroyed his reflection. Feeling sorry for himself, he thought the fracturing of his watery image to be entirely appropriate.

Stella took the Jiffy bag full of mail down to the kitchen and made herself a cup of tea. Someone, she noticed, had already opened the bag, but she didn't mind – she and Adrian often absent-mindedly opened each other's post. Sometimes it was just as well – he had once filed away her unopened bag full of problem mail among the many manuscripts he had received from aspiring but unsure erotic authors hoping for guidance and praise. She sat down at the table and tipped out the envelopes from the bag and mechanically, out of duty for once rather than real interest, started opening them. She read a few letters about faithless boyfriends, over-strict parents, and a teacher with a grudge, all the time keeping her ears and eyes tuned for the return of either Ruth or Adrian. Just as she was opening a large, dark blue envelope, Ruth appeared looking sad but clean, her hair just starting to twist into its mass of curls as it began to dry.

'Tea?' Stella offered, shoving the envelopes to one side. 'Shall I make you some?'

'Yes please,' Ruth sat down, obviously in a mood to tell her what had happened. Stella said nothing, just waited.

'Nothing really happened,' Ruth volunteered, staring at the table and picking at the wood. 'Willow put the plaster on, to make the mould, and said she'd be back soon and then she went out and never came back. It was *hours* ago. It was this *morning*.' The sense of humiliation was still in Ruth's voice.

'Perhaps she had an accident,' Stella reasoned, bringing Ruth's tea and sitting down again. 'I'm sure she wouldn't leave you on purpose.'

'Oh, she *would*,' Ruth insisted, her eyes blazing. 'It's because of Bernard.'

'*What's* because of Bernard? Is she jealous because he's painting you? I mean, I know she likes him,' she grinned at Ruth, trying to jolly her along, '*everyone* knows she likes him!'

'It's not just the painting,' Ruth admitted half under her breath, looking up briefly and meeting her mother's eyes for the shortest of all-telling seconds. Stella tried to breathe calmly and take in what Ruth had implied without exploding. She took her time, reasoning that it wasn't as if this was a total surprise, that Ruth was seventeen not seven and that she herself was supposed to be a liberal, liberated, understanding, parent.

'Oh,' was all she could come out with. For someone who dealt with a vast range of problems for a living, it didn't seem, even to her, to be a very constructive comment. She wondered what the questions were that she was supposed to ask now. Should she ask if he was Ruth's first lover (Did she really want to know if he wasn't? Suppose he was the twentieth?), if she was remembering to be careful, if this was a serious or casual relationship – or were any and all of these things absolutely none of her business?

'So you see, Willow's just jealous and now she probably thinks she's got some kind of revenge.' Ruth got up and took her cup to the sink, 'Stupid cow – I mean what a pathetic thing to do, really. She'd better not try asking me to come back and have another go with the plaster.' The hurt had now completely vanished from her voice, Stella noted, glad to hear a rallying tone of angry recovery. 'Anyway, I'm off. I'm supposed to be at a French class right now,' Ruth said, smiling a goodbye at Stella. 'See you later, thanks for the tea.'

So that's that then, Stella thought, admiring youth's powers of fast recovery and turning back to the post sorting. Your teenage daughter lets you know she is sleeping with a middle-aged, promiscuous artist and

233

there is nothing more to be said. Obviously she should, she thought, concentrate on those who really did have problems to discuss. She opened the blue envelope.

'Can we start again? With hello and it's lovely to have you back?' Adrian crept in with pretended nervousness through the kitchen door, holding a ragged bunch of geraniums, buttercups, cow parsley and forget-me-nots in front of him which he offered to Stella along with a mock-humble smile.

'Oh, they're lovely, thanks,' she said, beaming at him and getting up to give him a hug. He put his arms round her and squeezed her tight against him. 'Hey, can't you feel how much thinner I am?' she said, laughing, 'almost down to Abigail size.'

Adrian groaned. 'Don't ever go trying to be like her,' he pleaded, 'she's got too many sharp edges. In mind as well as body.'

Stella pushed him away, laughing, 'And how would *you* know?' she teased.

'I'll put these in water,' Adrian offered suddenly, picking up the flowers, 'You know what the wild ones are like, they wilt so quickly.' He bent to find a vase from the cupboard under the sink, 'Anything interesting among this week's problems?' he asked.

'Don't know yet, so far it seems like the mixture as usual.' She picked up the blue envelope, opened it and started to read as Adrian rather clumsily plonked the flowers into a blue Art Deco vase, found years ago at the church jumble sale. 'Though there's this one, from someone called "Alex", can't tell if it's male or female but that doesn't matter, listen to this: "My mum's best friend is having problems with her marriage and Mum's been helping her out. Now I think the friend's having an affair with my dad. I saw them out together, though they didn't see me. Should I say anything? And who to?" Some friend,' Stella commented. 'What do you think he or she should do?' she asked.

234

Adrian looked blank, 'What, you're asking me? *I* don't know. You're right though, not much of a friend. I mean, who'd . . .' He stopped and fiddled with a drooping buttercup, then suggested, with a flippant grin, 'Perhaps the kid should have a word with the dad. Might be worth a bit of extra pocket money . . .'

Stella laughed, 'Adrian, how could you be so cynical! This is a child, worried the family might break up.'

'No, no, that won't happen. Not in a million years. Tell it to keep quiet, let things pass,' he said, 'It'll be all right.'

'Huh, one thing I can never promise any of these kids,' she said, waving her hands over the heap and adding the one from Alex to the rest, 'is that anything can be guaranteed to be "all right".'

Adrian's face acknowledged the truth of that. He smiled, rather wanly and said, 'Then I guess you'll just have to tell him or her that then, won't you?'

Chapter Sixteen

Toby looked around furtively to see if there was anyone he knew in W. H. Smith before picking up a copy of *Get This!* If the security camera saw the guilty expression on his face, he thought, they'd have a store detective tailing him within seconds. The shop was busy, and he had to slide his hand carefully between the bodies of two stout and browsing women to reach the display rack. The magazine was unmissable, all pink and purple with pzazz! headlines in lime green. He couldn't remember his own sister ever buying anything so lurid – Ruth seemed to have graduated straight from *Beano* to *The Face* with no stopping off in between for these pre-woman lessons in make-up and man-trapping. Although the cover featured two giggling girls in citrus-fruit beachwear, there was clearly no way he could pretend he'd picked it up mistaking it for the comfortingly blokeish *Surf's Up*. Caught by a friend now, (or worse, Giuliana), all credibility would be shot to pieces. Around him women flicked through *Hello!* and *Tatler* and took no notice of him. He sauntered to the far end of the aisle to hang around next to men choosing car magazines and computer manuals so as to look less conspicuous before opening *Get This!* and nervously thumbing through to Stella's 'Go Ask Alice' column. He wasn't sure, not really, if his letter would be in this week, or even at all – perhaps it was too feeble to rate a mention, although he knew Stella worked to a pretty close deadline. 'Couple of odd problems in this week's batch,' she'd mentioned over supper the night she'd got back from Abigail's, as if she'd wanted a general discussion, which she sometimes did when something unexpected was sent in. Once there'd been a girl who was terrorized by her stepfather's dog, and then there'd been another whose mother had told about (and shown) her newly implanted breasts to just about everyone who called at the house, including the girl's boyfriend. This time though, just as Toby could feel his face turning pink and his appetite going, Adrian had butted in quite rudely and started talking to Ruth about rearranging the summerhouse for her jewellery.

The letter *was* in. He felt almost as thrilled as if he'd submitted a whole article. It didn't have top billing as the five-star problem (that went to a girl who'd fallen in love with her boyfriend's sister and didn't know how to tell him – tricky one that, Toby conceded), but given plenty of attention halfway down the page. Toby read slowly and carefully the advice his own mother was giving him.

You should remember that you might be mistaken about your father and this woman. She might be just as much his friend as your mother's, with nothing terrible going on . . .

'Shit!' Toby grunted, feeling thoroughly told off. 'Keep your trap shut, mind your own, time will tell,' was the essential message. She's so *innocent*, he thought, despairing of Stella. If he even came right out and *said* to her that he'd seen his dad snuggled up with Abigail in the pub, she'd probably just breezily say, 'Oh, I expect it was just some other couple who looked a bit like them,' and not give it any more thought. Well, I'd want to know, he thought, flinging *Get This!* down on top of a pile of *Literary Reviews* and walking very fast out of the shop.

Willow had taken to singing. Her voice, unexpectedly loud for someone so generally fey and whimsical in expression, could be heard over the entire island. She began her songs the moment she woke up in Bernard's sagging bed and went out onto the balcony to water the trough of tomato plants she'd wheelbarrowed along from her own garden. She specialized in old Simon and Garfunkel numbers, trilling 'Scarboro Fair' and 'Bright Eyes' across the river, the sound water-amplified to the far bank and then back across the rest of the island. Ellen MacIver, with unusual sarcasm, put in a request for 'The Sound of Silence'. She was driving Peggy crazy on her barge. Ted, who had now more or less stopped going home except with bags full of laundry, found it fascinating, a real live piece of the eccentricity the island was famous for. Enzo thought her showing off was despicably un-Italian – the worst kind of English trait. He sneered at her when-ever he met her on the path, intending to convey that Italians were so accustomed to permanent sexual fulfilment that they didn't need to go around singing and looking ecstatically smug about it. Willow's cats, too, were neglected and running wild, savaging two of Giuliana's poor hens and frightening a broody one away from her snug nest beneath a rusty Ford Capri bonnet. Willow spent more and more time at Bernard's studio, moving a lot more than the tomatoes onto the premises. Over a week, she'd staggered along the path with most of the contents of her own workspace, all the pots she wanted to exhibit for the Arts Fair, along with the finished plaster of six residents' bottoms and three more moulds (including Adrian's, which he had agreed to for its potential as research for his own work) ready for casting. It was almost as if she was weighing

Bernard's premises down with her possessions, anchoring him and his home as hard as she could so that he'd find it impossible to shift her out again. 'Is your friend, oh, I can't remember her name . . .' Willow twittered excitedly to Stella as they both crossed over on the ferry one morning, 'is she coming back for the Art Fair?'

'Abigail?' Stella reminded her coolly, knowing full well that Willow wasn't likely to have forgotten that particular name. 'Well, she said she was, and bringing her children too, just for a night or so.'

Willow looked gleeful, 'Oh, I am glad, I'm sure she'll enjoy it.'

'You're *glad*? Not so long ago you said she was dangerous and destructive and shouldn't be allowed on the island at all. Don't you mind about "devil spirits" any more?' Stella asked. They reached the main bank and Willow sprang off, agile as a schoolgirl.

'No. No, I don't. After all, they have their uses,' she declared mysteriously, skipping off towards Marks and Spencer, a selection of plastic shopping bags fluttering from her hands, the picture of domestic organization.

Stella felt furious with her. Ruth had pleaded with them all never, ever, to mention the humiliation of being abandoned on Willow's table covered with drying plaster, in the belief that the whole world, bar no one, would be creased up with laughter about it, and she'd die, absolutely die of humiliation. But it was terribly tempting to make her own feelings known. Willow, in her new-found bliss, was oblivious to innuendo and implication and supremely unaware that to Stella, Toby, Adrian and Ruth she was the object of angry hostility. What Stella wanted to face Willow with, mother-protective and still carrying the memory of Ruth's distraught sobbing, was something along the lines of 'How dare you go off and abandon my child, naked on your table covered in plaster and ordered not to move?' She'd practised the words in the car, going over them in differing orders to get them to sound right, but had come to the conclusion that actually stated out loud, in spite of Ruth's trauma at the time, the situation became just too funny to keep a straight face about. That, of course, made Stella even crosser – she hated to feel so powerless.

'Painting all finished then?' Melissa asked Ruth as she watched her in the college common room, twisting the final strands of silver wire round the last pair of earrings for her exhibition.

'What do you mean?' Ruth looked up and glared at her.

Melissa's hand flew up defensively, 'Hey, what's the aggression for? I only asked . . . It's just that you haven't missed any time here this week to go along and pose for that old bloke – and usually you do. That's all.' Melissa slumped down on the bench next to her and fumbled in her bag for cigarettes. 'Smoke?' she offered, hoping to buy an explanation and a better mood.

'No. Given up,' Ruth said sulkily. She put the earrings away in her bag and sat hunched over with her arms folded across her body, staring ahead in the general direction of the food counter. Melissa, who was studying psychology A-level, took this as hostile and uncommunicative body language and knew that Ruth would almost literally have to be unwound before she'd tell her anything.

She tried flattery: 'You've made some great stuff. I expect you'll sell it all, no problem, and then you'll be rich. Do you want me to come over and help you on the day?'

'If you want.'

'Did your dad let you have his summerhouse?'

'Yep.' Ruth unthreaded one of her arms, but only to push her hair out of her eyes.

Melissa persisted, 'And will we all get to see the great portrait?'

'Which one?' Melissa let out an exaggerated sigh and raised her eyes dramatically heavenwards. Ruth still glowered.

'Of you, *stoopid*,' Melissa said bravely, 'the one this great and famous artist has done.'

'Dunno.' Ruth at last unfolded her arms and uncrossed her legs and stood up. 'You know, Melissa, I think you're confusing me with someone who gives a flying fuck about what Bernard does with his stuff once he's finished it.' She picked up her bag and strode off towards the door, body language telling Melissa once again that she wasn't in the mood to be accompanied.

Ruth couldn't believe she'd been so abruptly discarded by Bernard. I suppose he makes every one of us think we're going to be the special one, she thought as she walked slowly along the road, reluctant to be heading back home. 'The painting is finished. I'm really pleased with it – an exciting departure in style,' he'd told her on the phone when she'd gathered the courage to call and ask when she should come again. She'd heard all about him and Willow. That was where the cow had gone off to, leaving her plastered and helpless on that bloody table. In bed late at night, with grumbling pigeons roosting on her skylight above her and sleep impossible, she'd wondered if Bernard had actually managed immediate sex with Willow that morning, only about an hour after he'd done it with *her*. Probably not, she'd concluded. Perhaps he and Willow had a relationship on entirely another plane, something mystic and spiritual – that would be why Willow was looking so superior. She couldn't believe that the clapped out old hippy had actually achieved

241

moving in. But then he hadn't suggested she, Ruth, should come back at all – in fact, as they'd been talking he'd sounded slightly distracted as if there was someone there with him, someone who he'd like to get back to, quickly – Willow – she now realized painfully, forced to accept the truth. Willow was now never *not* there.

'*What* style departure?' she'd asked him, having thought the painting of her looked exactly like all the other ones she'd seen of girls like her, but giving him the chance to invite her round to explain.

'Oh, bigger scale, bolder colour, that sort of thing,' he'd said vaguely, obviously not in the mood for deeper discussion. Now, miserable and bereft, she interpreted this as him implying that it was actually *her* that was a bigger scale, bolder colour, and felt doubly humiliated.

'I even feel a bit sorry for that awful Abigail now,' she confided to Toby out in the garden on the swing seat that evening.

'Christ, don't bother wasting sympathy on her. She doesn't even halfway deserve it.'

'Well, at least I know how she feels, someone she'd cared about just going off and leaving her for someone else.' She couldn't quite bring herself to say 'loved'. Even she, immersed in the drama of a severed relationship, wouldn't have claimed that she'd *loved* Bernard. The idea, all along, had been that he should love, adore, idolize, *her*. Surely at his age, he should have been grateful to have had the chance.

'Well, I suppose Martin was – is – Abigail's husband. It's got to be a *bit* different,' Toby said, unforgivably in Ruth's opinion. 'Anyway, she's a complete bitch, I think she was only pretending to be so miserable. She seemed to make a pretty good recovery while she was here.'

'Yeah, chasing after Bernard and eying you up. I saw

242

her, all those little pattings at you whenever she wanted you to listen to her. I even wondered if you and she might, well, you know . . .' Ruth sneaked a grin at him but he wasn't smiling.

'Chasing *everyone*,' he interrupted her. 'She's one of those women, the ones who can't bear to see anyone else happy. She has to go and wreck things.'

Ruth assumed he was talking about her and agreed, 'Well, I'm not happy now, so when she comes back perhaps she'll be a bit nicer to me. She'll probably even think I'm her very best friend,' she laughed.

'Don't count on it,' Toby warned.

In the secretive safety of the downstairs loo Adrian flicked through *Get This!* to the problem page and was surprised at how disappointed he was that the letter he'd written hadn't made it to the 'Go Ask Alice' column. It was a stupid, puerile thing to have done anyway, he decided, following up on a whim after Giuliana's flippant suggestion and writing to his own wife, pretending he was sixteen. Perhaps she hadn't read it yet. Probably this universal, ordinary, commonplace quandary, the brief and guilty knocking-off of the girlfriend's best mate, appeared in one guise or another in Stella's column every couple of weeks. After all, he thought, in teenagehood the best pal's always around, talking about the boyfriend, talking about the friend, there's bound to be more than a bit of sneaky juvenile curiosity on both sides. A boy of that sort of age couldn't really be expected to resist – he'd be so sure that every fold and freckle of his dick had been discussed and analyzed by the terrifying posse of two, it was hardly a major step to let the girl check out what her best friend was so enthralled by. Only he and Abigail, this time, were a long way from the excuse of being juvenile, he reminded himself. He had no excuses at all. If Stella, when she got round to dealing with it, only knew who'd sent the letter, and who it was about . . . He probably wouldn't have bothered if he hadn't just finished the book and was feeling loose-endish. Appalled to realize he'd started making notes for a new book that was based on that tumultuous forty minutes with Abigail, he'd consigned the words to the computer's waste-bin and instead written a 'Dear Alice . . .' signing it 'Pulp fan, Richmond'. It would probably turn up with the next bagload. Interested, he took a look at the problems and identified the one from 'Alex' that she'd shown him. 'Sensitive response,' he murmured to himself approvingly, glad that if anyone in the family *had* chanced to see him, Stella wouldn't thank them for rushing up and telling her. He flushed the loo, shoved the magazine up his sweatshirt and went to put it back in the kitchen.

'When did Abigail say she was coming back?' Adrian asked Stella as they started clearing out the summerhouse to accommodate Ruth's jewellery. He bent to clear up scattered papers from under the desk and added, in hope, fingers crossed, 'Or has she changed her mind now she's got the children with her, after all it would be a bit of a hassle, wouldn't it, dragging them over here.' I don't even mind if we keep her cat for bloody ever, he thought to himself, silently offering a comprehensive service of pampering, vet-bill-paying, flea-spraying, worm-treating cat-care to the gods in exchange for their indulgence.

'Friday,' Stella told him, making his heart plummet, '*Tomorrow* that is, I suppose. Which reminds me, I'll have to ask Toby to move out of his room for her children. Perhaps he can go off and stay with Nick for a night or two.' She flicked a duster over the newly cleared window ledge and asked him, 'Why isn't Ruth out here doing this? How is it we're fixing up the room for her?'

'She's suddenly, mysteriously, got an essay to write,'

244

Adrian told her. 'She also had this idea that it would be better if you and I did it all so that I'd know just where everything had been put away so I could find it again on Monday. Devious, huh?'

'Wonder where she gets that from,' Stella commented, causing Adrian's blood pressure to rise to a danger level. Abigail had been ringing up daily to report that Martin hadn't been phoning at all. Adrian thought he'd been clever, avoiding answering the phone round about six o'clock drinks time, but then perhaps that had been unwise, for whatever else had she been saying to Stella?

'Do you ever think you'd like a bit more space?' Stella suddenly asked, flinging the duster down on the desk and flopping into Adrian's big cream chair. She looked really small in it, he thought, really vulnerable like a child pretending to drive a car. He'd hate to hurt her, but, since Abigail, had been scared to touch her.

'What sort of space?' he asked warily. She might mean 'space' as in time away from each other, separate rooms, homes, miles put between them. She gave him a perplexed sort of look, as if wondering why he suddenly didn't understand plain English.

'You know, just *space*, more garden, more room in the house. A bigger house, I suppose. Somewhere with room for a proper study each, so you wouldn't have to trail down the garden in all weather.' She was smiling at him, quite tenderly really as if prepared to be patient with his lack of understanding of simple words.

'Oh, that sort of space,' he sighed, relieved. 'More room space, more land,' he muttered, repeating for reassurance.

'Well?' She was waiting, still patient. 'We could afford it, I've been doing some calculating.'

'I'm not sure. I quite like coming down the garden to here. It's like actually going out to work, closing the door on home life like the rest of the real grown-up world does. What about you, though, would *you* like to move away somewhere?' There was an element of wondering what was the right reply, he thought. Was he ticking the correct boxes? Stella wasn't looking at him, so it was hard to see what she was thinking. Her gaze was way across the river, miles away past the woods on the opposite bank.

'I'm not sure,' she said eventually, 'it's just when I stayed at Abigail's and there was so much room, and everything so fantastically well organized. I mean, if *her* daughter was doing this exhibition, there's no way Abigail would be scrubbing out *her* summerhouse. She's got staff for that sort of thing. It must be bliss. If we were that well organized I could be indoors at my computer right now starting on another book. So could you. This isn't the best allocation of time or talent.'

'That's nothing to do with how many bedrooms or acres we've got,' Adrian pointed out, perching himself on the edge of the desk where he could keep a close eye on Stella's expressions. 'It's more to do with not having the nerve to ask Mrs Morris to abandon washing the kitchen floor and come out and do this instead, in case she takes it as an insult and leaves. It's all about staff relations.'

Stella hauled herself out of the chair and picked up the duster again. 'I suppose so,' she agreed, wiping half an inch of dust from the top of Adrian's filing cabinet. 'But it's also to do with Abigail. People want to do things for her, she assumes they do, and they all collude. I do it too. I wish I'd said she couldn't come this weekend. I could easily have got Toby to drive down to Sussex with the cat.' She grinned at Adrian suddenly, 'He could have taken Giuliana. Did you know about those two, by the way?'

'I think so . . . Yes, of course I did, now I think about it. It's just one of those things that seemed to happen, without anyone telling anyone anything.'

'He seems to like his women a bit older,' Stella said with a grin as she opened the summerhouse door and stepped out with relief into the dust-free sunlight. She looked back at Adrian who wasn't smiling at all but just standing looking vague and startled as if he couldn't decide whether he'd just been told good news or bad. '*Toby*! Your son! Heavens, where is your brain today?' She reminded him softly, 'I mean, he seemed pretty much attracted to Abigail when she was here and now he's going out with Giuliana . . .'

'That's completely different,' Adrian suddenly cut in, rather crossly, defensively really, Stella thought. 'Giuliana isn't twice his age, hardly more than five years older, I'd say. I don't think Toby is the older woman type. No, he's not. No, I'm *sure* he's not.'

'OK, OK! Don't over-react!' Stella said laughing. 'Is this some male terror thing that I don't know about?'

Adrian stamped out of the summerhouse and slammed the door shut. He stalked past her and headed back towards the house, calling back over his shoulder. 'No, it's bloody *not*.' He stopped next to the agapanthus and turned round to face her properly, saying, 'Look, just because you're a sodding agony aunt, it doesn't mean that this household is full of mad fixations and hidden bits of devious behaviour. This is just ordinary *real life*. Nothing special.' He turned and strode off in through the kitchen door and Stella stood looking at it, wondering if that too would be slammed furiously. God, what have I said now, she thought.

Abigail muttered out loud as she packed. 'Not too much stuff,' she reminded herself, removing a lemon-coloured silk bra from the bag and flinging it in roughly the direction of the enormous chest of drawers that took up the whole end wall of her dressing-room. 'Mustn't frighten Stella.' She zipped up the bag, looked at it for a moment as if expecting it to open all by itself, unzipped it again and then walked back to her wardrobe, opened a door and took out another couple of slim, summery Ghost dresses. She folded each of them down to the size of a handkerchief and stuffed them into a corner of the bag, just next to her cream shoes. 'Can get loads of new clothes,' she murmured, smiling prettily at the mirrored wardrobe door for self-reassurance, 'when everything's settled.'

The bag wasn't too heavy when she lifted it from the peach-flowered sofa and carried it to the top of the stairs. She put it down and looked back towards the bedroom, automatically expecting Martin to come and offer to carry it down for her. 'Silly thing,' she admonished herself, 'no Martin, remember?'

Downstairs in the hallway, the children sat silently on the uncomfortable Regency sofa by the front door and waited patiently with their bags of haphazardly chosen and packed clothes and favourite toys. James swung his feet idly, kicking at one of the sofa legs in the unusual certainty that this time he wouldn't be told off for it. His mother no longer seemed to care about that sort of thing. His gerbil had escaped in the kitchen the day before and instead of going ape, as he'd assumed, terrified, that she would, she'd simply said that it was a good thing it had gone off to fend for itself, one less thing to worry about. Venetia picked at the skin on her forearm and timed how long it would take to make it bleed. 'I bet she won't even offer me a plaster,' she said to James as a satisfying jewel of blood welled up.

'No, I don't 'spect she will,' he agreed, and they both grinned happily at each other, pleased at the new and carelessly anarchic regime in the house.

'Ready?' Abigail said as she clattered down the stairs with her big squashy bag, stuffed with what she'd selected as life's essentials. 'Got everything you want? I hope there's not too much.' She looked hard and long at Venetia, biting her lip with uncertainty as if trying to remember if she was actually *hers*. Venetia ignored her, licking at her bleeding arm and savouring the taste of blood.

'It's all right, Mum,' James told her, doing some expression-interpreting, 'I helped Ven with her stuff. She's got enough knickers and things.'

'Oh. Oh, that's good.' Abigail replied vaguely as if she'd already forgotten what they were talking about. She turned to the table and pressed a number of Ansaphone buttons. 'Don't suppose anyone will call, but who knows, and really who cares . . .' she said, changing her mind and pulling the plug from the wall.

'She's mumbling away again, she keeps doing that. I can't hear anything she's saying anymore, not really,' Venetia whispered to James, 'Can you?'

'No, but don't worry, it's all right. People quite often do talk to themselves,' he reassured her. Mad people do anyway, he remembered his house mother telling him, and bravely he didn't share this information with his sister.

'Oh and passports . . .' Abigail muttered, opening a drawer in the table and searching through papers. 'They should be here . . . oh yes. Good, just in case. And lots of credit cards . . .' she stuffed them in her handbag, picked up her Mercedes keys and looked at the children. 'Right. Shall we go?' she said brightly, 'Say "good-bye, house".'

Venetia and James exchanged nervous glances, 'Good-bye, house,' they chanted obediently. Crossing his fingers for luck, James added in a whisper, 'See you soon, I hope.'

Chapter Seventeen

The island was almost ready for its influx of visitors. Ancient, faded and tattered bunting, long ago handed down from the town's carnival committee, did its brave best to look festive, swathed rather haphazardly from tree to tree along the path all the way from the ferry to the boathouse. Willow returned home briefly to tend to her yowling cats and to hang up a gaily painted sign re-directing old and new clients to her new premises in the boathouse gallery. The sign showed two silhouetted figures, based on the dancing ones on the front of her house, holding hands and decked with garlands of flowers as if they'd been met at a Hawaiian airport by an over-eager welcoming party. She had several moments of doubt and regret as she looked at her gloriously vivid garden, all the nasturtiums and calendulas rioting together with the unchecked dandelions and buttercups and the cornflowers and nigella wantonly self-seeded everywhere in between. She missed all this rampant fecundity, down at the other end of the island. Bernard didn't really go in for gardens; he seemed oblivious to the scruffy patch of parched bare scrubland surrounding the boathouse. It looked as if it was still expecting to have boats hauled out of the water and jacked up for repair. 'It's in keeping,' he'd simply insisted firmly, when she'd tentatively wondered if the area might be jollied up, 'refoliaged' as she'd laughingly suggested, mocking council-speak in an attempt to disguise nesting. Wisely, after his reply, she'd abandoned the subject, but only till later, however much later it had to be. Her own garden, at least, was still there to be visited and savoured. And she had, after all, got exactly what she'd always wanted.

'Love in the Mist,' she murmured, wandering through the grass, tenderly stroking the feathery nigella fronds and hoping ahead towards dank autumn evenings, snuggled into the boathouse flat with Bernard. Perhaps she could also do some subliminal persuading about colour, she thought, admiring her cobalt blue walls and candyfloss-pink framed windows, perhaps he'd understand, eventually, that there was more to life, where wall paint was concerned, than white.

Giuliana painted a long sky blue and cream silk scarf with her name and telephone number on it and, after she'd photographed it to make publicity postcards down at the local Print-Out, hung it across the gateway to show customers what she did and where she was. She, like Willow, also stood at the edge of her garden having doubts and regrets. The pretty, delicate banner fluttered nervously over an untidy brutal heap of abandoned car engines, twisted pieces of car wheel and fourteen dented aluminium dustbins that Enzo had begged from the council tip and then decided not to use. He reminded Giuliana of their Italian grandmother who had hoarded scraps of fabric, kept every cast-off piece of worn-out clothing, every dour black peasant-widow's dress she'd ever owned, just in case there was ever another war like the one where she and her family had gone ragged and cold through terrified mountain winters. But fabric was foldable, storable, just about possible to keep under some sort of domestic control. Enzo's precious unprecious metal simply piled its ugly self up and rusted and got in the way and made Giuliana depressed. She even hated the way he worked, the constant high-pitched squeal of power-tools, whining like an amplified dentist drill. She didn't want to live like this anymore, she decided as she picked her way across what could have been a bed of roses, or even cabbages and beans. It no longer suited her soul. She thought suddenly of fields of pungent lavender, of long, overripe plum tomatoes, zucchini, peppers, southern groves of olives and felt peculiarly homesick.

Stella rowed slowly round the island early on Friday morning and tried to look at it with a stranger's eye. Charlotte's prayer flags hung festively from the cherry tree in her tiny garden beside the cut and looked, from even quite close up, just like knickers drying in the sun. People will assume her washing line's broken, Stella thought, wishing she had a more appropriately artistic view of things. To her, the various flags and lines of bunting made the island look like a crumpled parcel wrapped by a team of mischievous five-year-olds. Ellen and Fergus MacIver had sneakily, she noticed, set up half a dozen white plastic tables and chairs in their back garden, suspiciously close to their freshly spruced-up barbecue. No one else would have seen that, the garden only being visible from the main-stream side of the river. They're not having a party, Stella thought to herself as she rowed past, or at least not one they've invited anyone on the island to, so they must be planning a secret batch of catering to capture and keep potential buyers. Their French doors stood wide open and Stella could just see, beyond the gently flapping floral curtains, the eau-de-nil walls hung all over with their year's work, scenes of the river from all possible angles, ducks and geese of every type, nesting, roosting, diving, mooching about – everything but flying. Fergus had once declared he didn't like painting a whole wingspan – it left too much space on the blockboard to be filled in with irrelevant reeds and trees. Draped along their front path, rose-arch to door, both sides, guard of honour style was a complete set of carefully ironed nautical flags. The place lacked only a double line of naval cadets, oars crossed. 'Dressed over-all!' Fergus had declared proudly the evening before as he stood outside his gate, waiting for his display to be admired.

Stella was depressed. Adrian was in a strange and remote mood, jumpy if the phone rang, vague in conversation and perversely touchy. She had tried asking him what was wrong and he'd told her, very brusquely, to save her concern for her job. He, apparently, didn't need it.

'Is she staying long?' he'd demanded for the third time that morning before Stella went out to row and to think.

'Abigail?' she'd asked, thinking surely he remembers I only answered this question an hour ago.

'Yes, of *course* bloody Abigail! Unless you've got more friends in sodding need, coming to leech your everlasting sympathy.'

'She can stay for as long as she likes,' Stella had hissed back at him, infuriated by his unpredictable temper – it seemed so childish. 'What exactly *is* all this sulking and stropping about?' she demanded. 'Surely it's not just because I went away and had a self-indulgent good time without you? You've been acting odd ever since I got back. I can't believe you've turned into that kind of man, not *you*.'

'No. No, it's not that,' he'd admitted but just as she'd thought he might be about to shed some explanatory light he'd changed his mind and gone stomping out to the summerhouse from where he'd forgotten that all his work had been removed for the weekend. Perhaps it was that, perhaps without his office he felt ousted and rootless, Stella concluded as she rowed round the northern tip of the island and headed back down towards the rowing club and the ferry again.

It was the thing Abigail had said, that was what was troubling him. Adrian sat on the wall by the river, wishing he knew quite how to interpret it. It was when he'd answered the phone, when Stella had gone off to the Post Office. He'd forgotten that he was supposed to be avoiding it. He'd felt stupid, nervously standing next to the kitchen phone and awkwardly pretending not to notice its ring while Ruth, an extra couple of yards away from it, got up from a chair with dramatic fuss and flounce, crossed the room to answer it and then asked him with deserved sarcasm what his last slave died of.

'Well, it's never usually for me anyway,' he'd tried as an excuse to Ruth in what he thought was a jokey sit-com father-of-teenagers way. But of course this time when it rang, with no one else around and the possibility, indeed likelihood, that it would be his agent, Adrian had no choice.

'Oh, I did so hope it would be you,' he'd heard Abigail's voice with a brittle but horribly intimate laugh. 'I think it's time, now, don't you?' she then said mysteriously while he wondered what it was time for. He caught himself looking at his watch, thinking that there might be a train he should meet, or another he should catch.

'And, of course, this time it's yes,' she said, the laugh sounding through every breath she took. The laughter made him feel there was an uneasy joke that only she was party to. If there was, it was obviously on him. She sounded odd, manic. She might have thought it funny to put a bomb under his wheel-arch, send a circular to the neighbours telling the shaming truth about his job, anything. Anything but, please God, don't tell Stella about that night . . .

'Yes to *what*?' he asked, terrified as to what the question had been that she was saying yes to. He couldn't think of one. He forced himself to go back over the best-forgotten facts. All he could remember was that he'd asked her if she was comfortable enough, that night under the willows (the recent night on the Lord's picnic rug, not the long-ago one on the Afghan coat – that had been back in the days before such middle-aged concern), and he'd asked her in the pub if she fancied a bag of dry roasted nuts. She hadn't, as far as he could recall, found either question particularly hilarious, and they hadn't been particularly memorable. If there were any nuts to say yes to now, they were obviously going to be *his*.

He was being horrible to Stella and he hated himself for it. She hadn't done anything to deserve his mood, she was just *there*, being normal and wonderful and all the things he loved her for. She drifted round the house, looking better than she had in ages and he didn't even dare touch her. It felt all wrong, after what he'd done. He felt like someone who'd gone and won a new car the day after they'd lost their licence. None of the characters in his books ever went through all this – as their creator, and mindful of sales, he'd obviously had to make them far better endowed with penis than with conscience. Right now, he wondered if he'd be able to write one of his tawdry, guilt-free books, ever again.

'Cup of tea?' Stella put a mug down next to him, climbed onto the wall and sat beside him, waiting for him to be companionable, out of his black mood, back to normal. He shifted up slightly, scared of being thigh to thigh and feeling her tempting warm skin. Perhaps it would be better if I just came out and told her, fast and honest and over in a second, he thought, like having teeth pulled. But who exactly *would* feel better after – probably not Stella, certainly not him, not for long, not after she'd told him to get lost, started divorce proceedings, changed the locks and thrown his computer into the river.

'Do *try* and be nice to her, won't you,' Stella began, 'it's not for long, and the children are quite sweet. They've no idea their daddy has gone off and left them.'

Adrian smiled, rather sadly she thought, but then said bitterly, 'There you go again, trying to get everyone to be nice to each other. You'd live in a real little Pollyanna world if you could, wouldn't you?'

'*Bastard*,' Stella suddenly shouted at him, viciously knocking his mug of tea out of his hand into the river. Adrian licked at his scalded hand and peered down in blank surprise, watching the blue and white mug drifting through the shallow water to join the riverbed debris. Stella climbed back off the wall, 'You're so knowing and *smug*, Adrian. What's so Pollyanna about having your marriage break up? If it happened to me I hope *I'd* have friends who'd take a bit of care of me, not give me three days max, followed by making it clear it was chucking-out time.'

She was halfway up the garden by the time Adrian thought of something to say. It was a feeble 'Sorry' that probably didn't carry that far. The kitchen door slammed and Stella disappeared, leaving Adrian alone on the wall, feeling a lot sorrier about the wasted tea and lost mug than he did about his attitude to Abigail.

Ruth and Melissa struggled from Toby's car with the first pair of dressmaker's dummies, borrowed after much persuading, from the college's textiles department. 'How many are there? How many trips will this take?' Melissa gasped as she hauled a stained and torn old beige torso onto the ferry. 'Pity they don't have hands, then they could hold onto the safety rail all by themselves,' she added, putting an arm round one to steady it. 'They don't seem too steady on their feet, I think they're pissed. Keep still, Mabel!' she ordered with a giggle, as the body tottered on its stand.

'Sorry. There's only the other two back at the college – and Toby said he could manage those on his own,' Ruth said, plonking another one down next to the first. 'As soon as I saw them I thought they were just so perfect for necklaces, or brooches or whatever. They're genuine old pre-some-war, not those tacky plasticky things with two hundred little screws that you get now.'

'Necklaces I grant you, brooches definitely,' Melissa commented, 'bit bloody useless for earrings though,' she said, patting the headless neck. 'They're gross, like rotting old bodies the river police wash up.' Melissa turned the ferry handle while Ruth pretended to dance with her dummy. 'Come fly with me, let's float down to Peru . . .' she crooned to its rigid body. 'Maybe I should have music in the summerhouse too. It's so awful looking at things in complete silence. When I'm in a quiet shop my tummy always rumbles, extra loud, does yours?'

'Mm,' Melissa agreed vaguely. 'Look, over there, getting out of that silver Merc by Toby's garage, isn't that the friend of your mother's that was staying here before?'

'Oh shit. Yes it is. I'd forgotten she was coming back. They've turfed Toby out of his room so her brats can have it. That Abigail cow is going to be just across the landing from me. I don't know if I can stand it.' Ruth jumped off the ferry, dragging the dummy with her. 'I wish we could cut the ferry chain, then she couldn't get over here – but then neither could all the people who are going to make me rich. Tell you what, I'm going to sleep in the summerhouse till she's gone again. I'll tell Mum I'm guarding my work.' She giggled, 'Just me and these headless women.'

'What do you think?' Willow asked Stella who had called at the gallery to see how the exhibition was looking. At least one sample of every artist's best work was included, both as a taster for the public and to show off the wide range of talents. The press preferred everything to be in one place too, then they didn't have to trek from house to house pretending they were really fascinated. Charlotte's scenes of the town made the place look bright and jolly and Enzo's 'First Supper,' a massive construction of agonized metal and rotting wood, extended almost to the ceiling. Stella wondered how on earth he'd got it in at all, and then noticed large strangely workmanlike bolts connecting the top half to the bottom. The stark long white side wall opposite the door (prime site, as ever) was hung, at intervals large enough to suggest he'd been seriously slacking, with Bernard's big canvases covered in splody nudes of his various teenage models. Some, she thought, were on the candid side, though she didn't want to appear prudish. It was just that these girls were so obviously very young. But she supposed if it was artistically essential for a girl to spread her legs *that* far (congratulations to her for even being able to, in the one where a leg was held above her head against a wall, like someone warming up for a vigorous cancan) it would seem philistine to complain. At the far end of the room, hanging like bas-relief on the white wall, was Willow's collection of plaster bottoms.

'They've turned out different from how I'd first imagined them. But of course that's *art*, it's all about *progression* in concept and application,' she explained earnestly. 'I meant to do all sorts of things with them, casting some in bronze maybe, or chocolate, whatever the owner of each of them suggested.' She looked round towards the door to see if anyone lurked and listened, 'Ellen MacIver, now *hers* was crying out to be painted exactly like a wet dishcloth, don't you think? A *trompe l'oeil* of a J-cloth perhaps? But in the end, I just thought, well white plaster – it's so honest. This way you can admire the differences in shape and structure without being distracted by fancy techniques. And I haven't had much time, of course.' She smiled a secret little smile. Stella watched her hands stroking lovingly over one of the plaster buttocks. It was the smoothest and tightest and its solid muscle tone could be seen clearly. 'It's your Toby's,' Willow suddenly said, startling Stella, 'I put it next to Giuliana's, hers is just like a peach, don't you think?' She patted it softly and added in a loud whisper, 'I hope putting them together will work. They do *go* so well, don't they.' Stella could only agree, though the 'going' that they did so well, just lately, had started to involve the studying of maps. The night before, there they'd been at the kitchen table, talking about whether Luxemburg was worth a visit, and whether it was politically all right to have a quick look at Turkey. It made her sad, especially with Adrian being so distant, to think that her son was now seriously organizing his long-awaited getaway. Like Ruth in the pub, she realized that this was a true leaving of home, that he would never really settle with them back on the island again. She wanted to talk it over with Adrian, see if he felt the same but he continued to be jittery and unapproachable. It was just possible, she thought, more in hope than in certainty, that he was feeling the same despondency about Toby's going, and perhaps not wanting to dump that feeling on her if she hadn't already felt it. Interpreting his mood that way felt like straw-clutching.

She wandered home from the boathouse, slowly and miserably. She knew she'd get over Toby going away, convince herself in time that it was a natural process, she wasn't really losing him. What crossed her mind though now, was that she might instead be losing Adrian and that, she was sure, she wouldn't get over.

'Stella! Lovely to see you again!' Abigail was at the gate when she got back, about two hours earlier than she'd said she'd arrive. She rushed up and hugged Stella. 'The children are *enchanted* by the whole place, adored the ferry and Venetia's thrilled to see her cat again.'

Stella smiled as brightly as she could, trying to be welcoming while her heart sank at the prospect of Adrian's venomous hostility to Abigail. God, she thought, how long can a weekend be?

'Have they found their room?' she asked, resorting to neutral hospitality. 'Will they be all right with Toby's shambolic mess? I did try to get him to tidy it up. He's promised to stay somewhere else for the weekend.' Leading Abigail into the kitchen, she said, 'Let's have a drink,' glancing at the clock and not caring that it was only four o'clock. She pulled a bottle of white wine from the fridge.

'This is my fault, isn't it,' Abigail said, reaching into the cupboard over the sink for glasses, 'giving you afternoon drinks at my place, decadence by the pool.'

Stella's bad temper snapped, 'No it's *not*. I can make decisions myself, you know. I'm not some easily-led child. I just fancy a drink *now*, that's all.'

Abigail looked contrite and pulled up a chair close to Stella. She put an arm round her shoulder and looked at her closely, 'I'm sorry. Look what's wrong? Is it us being here, because if it is . . .'

'No. Sorry, it's nothing. Just a bit pissed off, you know.'

'Yeah, I know,' Abigail grinned, removing her arm and playing with her little gold watch. 'It's Adrian, isn't it? You don't have to tell me, I recognize that "bloody husbands" look. Tell Auntie Abigail all about it. It'll make a change for it to be this way round.'

Stella didn't, on consideration, think she could tell Abigail anything at all. On the one hand, she didn't want to hurt her by confessing that Adrian just didn't want her around and that that was what it was all about, but on the other, it was Abigail she blamed for having to battle with Adrian in the first place. Abigail was looking at her expectantly, eagerly, waiting to hear that she wasn't the only person in the world who couldn't keep a husband. She's waiting to gloat, Stella thought crossly, looking at the excited eyes, the flickering hands. Deep down she's just waiting to be able to say, 'See, not so smug now, are you?' And no, no she wasn't smug but she sure as hell wasn't going to have Abigail point it out to her.

'No it's OK,' Stella said brightly and decisively, getting up and deciding that making a start on supper for later would be useful occupational therapy, 'I'm fine, really. Nothing's wrong.'

'Adrian hasn't said anything then?'

Stella turned and looked at her intently, wondering what on earth she could mean but Abigail still looked just the same, slightly manic and glittering, but otherwise more or less as usual, 'Like what?' she demanded.

Abigail did a silly sudden giggle with her hand over her mouth like a schoolgirl. Stella wondered briefly if she was actually losing her mind. Abigail was looking out of the window, down to where her children were creeping up on the summerhouse by way of the shrubs to where Ruth was arranging her jewellery.

'Well, nothing, I suppose,' she said, flapping her hands dismissively, 'I mean, I thought you must be upset about something he's said, that's all. It usually starts with something they say, doesn't it – I find that's what happens anyway.'

'*What* usually starts with "something they say"?' Stella persisted.

Abigail frowned, looking suddenly impatient. 'Oh, *everything*,' she shrugged. 'Just rows, general domestic battles, nothing important. Don't make such a thing of it, I didn't mean anything special,' she laughed. 'God, what perfect utter bliss you two must live in, to get so upset about some little falling-out like this.'

Stella sighed and gave up. She couldn't cover for Adrian's hostility, didn't even, on reflection, think she should try. He and Abigail would just have to muddle along as well as they could.

Ruth, arranging her jewellery and feeling just like she had as a little girl playing shops, could hear the children scraping at the bottom of the wooden wall outside the summerhouse. She wondered if she was supposed to be keeping an eye on them, make sure they didn't try and climb over the wall, jump down onto Peggy's barge and fall in the river. The tide, at the moment, wasn't very high – they were more likely to smash their skulls on the old bricks littering the river bed than to drown. She tried to decide to have nothing to do with them, they had a parent, however lousy, useless, slaggy and painful a one Ruth considered Abigail to be. The children were her responsibility, not Ruth's. The scratching and scraping grew louder, accompanied by some weird whispery noises. Ruth smiled to herself – they were playing the games she and Toby had played when they were little and lived at their other house, where Adrian had worked in a chilly room in the cellar. They'd crept around pretending to be ghosts, trying to get him scared enough to think it just might not be *them*. Sometimes when he'd left his desk – gone off to the loo or to get a cup of tea – they'd sneaked down the stairs and hidden in the dusty alcove behind the old fireplace, scratching and rustling when he came back and trying so hard not to giggle. He must have heard every breath they took, she thought now, smiling and turning her back on the noises and pretending not to hear, just like her dad had done.

'Ooooh, oooooh!' came the soft owl-like notes that small children think represent the undead. Ruth obligingly dropped a necklace (a carefully pre-selected unbreakable one) to the floor and put on a look of exaggerated terror, hand to chest and her eyes wide.

'Who's that?' she called, looking round wildly. An uncontrollable giggle came from the door, a boy's giggle, halfway to an adolescent guffaw.

'Oh, you *stupid bugger*, James. Now she's *heard* you!' A small cross face appeared at the window, a pretty but sulky little girl's face, with Abigail's big dark eyes framed by far more naturally blond fluffy hair.

'Did you hear that?' Ruth opened the door and carried on the pretence. 'What do you think it was?'

'It doesn't matter,' the girl sighed, 'we know that you know it was us. Men, huh?' she said, folding her arms and looking to the heavens, 'Mum's always saying they're no use.'

'I'm Ruth,' Ruth told her, 'and I suppose you must be James and Venetia.'

'Yes, I'm James,' the boy said, holding out his hand with odd formality.

Ruth took it and shook it while Venetia looked scornful. 'Of *course* she knows you're James,' she sneered at him, 'you could hardly be *Venetia*, could you?'

James looked very pink suddenly, as if he might cry. Poor boy, Ruth thought. 'Come in and have a look at what I've made,' she said, hoping to lighten the mood. It was bad enough having Abigail around again, without having her witch of a daughter stirring things as well. 'Do you like jewellery?' Ruth asked Venetia.

263

The child stood in the doorway, taking a quick and doubtful glance round the room.

'Mummy says it has to be real gold,' she warned.

Ruth smiled, 'Yes, "Mummy" would.'

'I like these. What are they for?' James asked. He stood by Adrian's velvet-covered desk holding a small, brightly-coloured fimo doll. It had long black legs, a honey-coloured body and arms and bright spiky blond hair. In one hand it clutched six pins with black pearl heads, and in the other six pins with white heads. Ruth had enjoyed making them, enjoyed the feeling of power it gave her to arrange their faces, give them expressions. They all had large brown eyes and sly smiles. She'd especially liked making the smiles. Just now Ruth frowned. She could hardly tell the trusting and rather sweet boy that each and every one of the ten of them was his mother, his mother in all her witchy awfulness. She could hardly explain the idea of a voodoo doll, which was that its owner, wanting to do evil to someone, should stick it with the black-headed pins, but that to do good and to help they should use the white-headed ones.

'They're just dolls,' Venetia said dismissively, her attention on earrings shaped like humbugs. 'I'd like earrings shaped like gummy bears,' she declared. 'Will you make me some?'

'What's the magic word?' Ruth asked, wondering why she should care whether the child had manners.

'Abracadabra,' Venetia said cheekily.

'No, it's not,' Ruth said, taking the earrings carefully away from her hot and dangerous little hands and replacing them on their velvet.

Venetia pouted and looked longingly at the earrings. 'OK, *please*,' she mocked.

'Pretty please,' Ruth said solemnly. James gasped, his horrified face warning Ruth to watch out for vengeance.

'Pretty please. Pretty please with knobs on,' Venetia conceded.

Ruth smiled. 'All right then, some time during the weekend I'll make you some, in time for when you go home.'

'Home? We *are* home,' Venetia crowed triumphantly. 'We're staying *here*. For *ever*. Mummy said. Didn't anybody tell you?'

Chapter Eighteen

'What do you think Venetia meant?' Ruth asked Toby as she tacked a poster for her jewellery to the garden gate. 'Do you think Abigail's buying somewhere to live on the island? What would she want to live here for? And anyway, what's for sale?'

Toby shrugged off the uncomfortable questions. 'Nothing that I know of. I suppose Willow might get rid of her place now she's moved in with Bernard, but can you honestly see Abigail living there?' He laughed, but only half-heartedly.

Ruth didn't laugh at all. She didn't want daily contact with Abigail's sharp-angled body, subtle bitchiness, the fierce yellow hair like gold-painted spikes on park railings. The island just wasn't like her, its residents were slower, gentler, rounder. No one's hair went upwards like that into such sophisticated shock (apart from Willow's after the drastic chopping, but even that was calming since the fates had taken pity on her). No one had shoes without mud on them, or clothes that would be in *next* month's magazines. 'She couldn't live there,' Ruth assured herself and Toby, 'wouldn't even think of it. She's probably got a garden shed bigger than that. *And*,' she added, 'I don't think Willow would start selling her place when she's only been living with Bernard a week. Even she would

266

realize that sticking a "For Sale" sign up this fast would terrify him, the idea that she really is a permanent fixture.' She thought for a moment and graciously conceded defeat to Willow with, 'Even though she obviously is one now. It's only Bernard who's going to need time to work it out.'

'The thing with Abigail,' Toby said, 'is that she makes Mum different. She makes her go sort of silly. I don't like it.'

'Mum might like it though,' Ruth argued, 'I expect Abigail reminds her of being young and irresponsible, before she had us and all the boring grown-up stuff to worry about.'

'She doesn't make Dad feel like that,' said Toby gloomily, 'he just goes round looking petrified and cross. He's not even going to be in for supper – I heard him telling Mum he had to see his agent, something to do with the next book. She didn't look as if she believed him.'

Ruth laughed, 'Well it *might* be true. I wish I was going with him. I don't want to eat with Abigail, she'll give me indigestion, glaring at me when I dare to put a potato into my bloated body.'

Toby said nothing. He could tell Ruth what he'd seen at the restaurant, make her as depressed and concerned as he had been feeling but it wouldn't change or solve anything. He knew other people's parents could be a lot less than perfect – perhaps the grown-up attitude would be to stop expecting his own to be different. That he hadn't been wrong in thinking the worst was only confirmed by Adrian's slippery absences. But somewhere in the back of Toby's mind a tiny seed of amusement was sprouting. It had to – he needed a bit of self-centred distancing at the moment. Soon he'd be going away but he was still young enough to need to picture home life continuing reasonably harmoniously without him. It just had to be there to come back and visit. His father was acting like a two-timing teenager, shiftily avoiding confrontation and sliding out of the way of trouble, looking for all the world as if he was living in fear of being caught out and told off. Toby decided he'd need time, maybe all the way to Giuliana's part of Italy, to decide whether it was cheering or disheartening to think that middle age didn't automatically bring with it immunity from getting tangled up in the consequences of bad behaviour.

Abigail was being extraordinarily helpful, Stella thought, as together they assembled the supper. It was as if, this time, it was Abigail who was administering the sympathy and help, and Stella who was in dire need of it. She wasn't sure, anymore, whether she was or not. On balance she thought it was more comfortable to decide she wasn't, not really. Adrian was just having a simple sulk and it would pass, though probably not until Abigail had left. Stella watched her confidently making her way round the kitchen, opening and shutting drawers and cupboards, searching for whatever implements she needed without feeling the need to ask where they were, chopping up vegetables and switching on the oven as if she'd always lived there. Stella, washing potatoes and watching, felt uneasy, taken over. When Venetia came in and asked if there was any apple juice, it was Abigail she went to and asked, and Abigail who immediately said, 'Of course, darling,' opening the fridge and pulling out the bottle for the child.

I'm just being picky, Stella decided, trying to feel more relaxed. Of course Venetia's going to ask her own mother. What's the point of inviting people to stay and then not expecting them to feel at home. Surely it's a sign of good hospitality. And after all, looking on the positive side, surely it was better to have Abigail's considerable cooking talents put to good use than to have to keep serving her spritzers while she lounged in the garden and Stella slaved alone and resentful in the kitchen. She blamed Adrian – if he wasn't in such a fraught mood she wouldn't be finding fault with everything. Poor Abigail, and poor everyone else at the moment, couldn't really do a thing right.

'It should be ready in about half an hour, I think,' Abigail said, opening a drawer and selecting cutlery. 'Another drink now, or would you rather wait?'

'I'll have one now,' Stella decided, heading for the fridge.

'No, let me, you just sit down and relax,' Abigail ordered, intercepting her at the fridge door. Stella wondered if she was imagining things, or did she really feel Abigail shoving her hand firmly off the door handle, as if she was a child who couldn't be trusted not to spill things?

Adrian sneaked up from Peggy's barge, feeling like a spy in a bad movie. He crept past the garden, along the path on the far side of the hedge. He flinched at every gravelly crunch, fully aware that when Bernard's art class tramped along it every Tuesday evening, each step, each whisper could be heard from just outside the kitchen door. That was the problem with being so close to the river. All around, every sound that was made could be picked up, seemingly for miles, like living in an echoing canyon. He would use that in his next book, he decided as he tip-toed furtively. He'd have a cheated husband find out the bitter truth from hearing his wife and her lover having raucous sex across half a mile of foaming estuary, perhaps somewhere in steamy Africa. They'd sound eerie and wild, like mate-seeking foxes at night in the island's wilderness. Creeping on, Adrian's heart almost stopped as he heard the kitchen door open. Through the dense cotoneaster he saw Abigail step out (wearing *gold* deck shoes, for heaven's sake) and start snipping at the pot of chives on the terrace. She looked very contented, very at home, he thought. She looked as if she had nothing at all on her mind beyond helping with the supper and having a relaxing weekend. It occurred to him he might be overdoing the avoidance tactics. What was the big deal about *him* compared with all the lovers Abigail had had in her time? Probably she gave no more thought to what they'd done under that willow tree than she did to her last session at the gym. They would both be in the same category to her, just part of her usual selection of therapeutic leisure activities. It was likely she thought no more intently about what they'd done than she did about her last leg wax.

All the same, and just in case, Adrian slid past the front of the house, crawling on all-fours past the front gate and finding himself at the sinewy feet of Ellen MacIver. She was carrying, inadequately covered by a flapping bin liner, a catering size box of pork and herb sausages and an expression of embarrassed confusion. For once he remembered something useful that he'd read: never explain, never apologize. He continued to crawl on past her as if it was a perfectly normal way of moving till he was safely past all possible viewpoints from his house and then stood up and greeted Ellen who was waiting to be told what was going on. 'Good evening,' he said, using the kind of exaggerated polite tone that goes well with the raising of a hat.

'What were you doing down there?' Ellen couldn't resist the question, 'If you don't mind me asking that is.'

Adrian treated her to a manic smile and she backed away slightly. 'I do mind,' he said, 'though I'll make you a deal: I won't tell everyone that you're planning full-scale catering for tomorrow when you know it's against the rules,' – he pointed at the box of sausages – 'if you don't mention that you've just seen me.'

Ellen smiled uncertainly, looking as if she was wondering how to mollify a mugger. She shifted the huge box as if there might just be somewhere around her body where she could hide it and then gave up the struggle, defeated. 'Oh, all right then, I won't say anything. I shall just go on wondering . . .' She wandered away towards her house, muttering quietly to herself and looking forward to telling Fergus.

Peggy and Ted made an early morning start, equipped with a supermarket trolley each – freshly purloined from the local store and with fully working wheels, not pulled out from those fatally twisted and half buried ones in the mud on the bottom of the river. By soon after eight they were waking and infuriating the other residents with the clattering of hard wheels on rough paving as they made their laborious journeys from barge to shore and across on the ferry to the van that Ted had hired. On their way they met early visitors who were already stepping carefully onto the ferry, eager to snap up Giuliana's best scarves or rummage through Willow's selection of imperfect bargains. Some simply wanted to whisk round the exhibits and move onto Sainsbury's before the crowds arrived, content that they'd at least have picked up something to talk about. Others took their inquisitive time, peering through splintered fences and uncurtained windows, hoping to see some of the goings-on that Mr Karesh the newsagent so luridly described, sniffing at the air for the sweet scent of cannabis and waiting to catch a resident wearing nothing but woad and a beatific smile.

Philip Porter took his time and arrived just after ten.

This way, he was sure he wouldn't arouse suspicion by being too eagerly early. He'd been ready to leave his home for some time before that, with his late mother's second best shopping bag containing a small camera and a pair of light leather gloves. He wouldn't look out of place snapping away like a tourist, he thought gleefully, but just in case anyone recognized him, he'd also got a Panama hat and a pair of gold-rimmed sunglasses. He felt a dashing excitement, actually setting foot onto the rickety ferry and fastidiously pulling on his gloves before attempting to turn the handle. Two elderly ladies joined him on the platform and looked at him doubtfully, as if they couldn't quite believe that he, so scrupulously dressed with the hat, his cricket club blazer and a neat maroon cravat, could actually organize the energy needed to make the ferry move. Philip winced as flakes of rust fell off the handle onto his gleaming shoes. The whole thing was falling to pieces, he thought. When they finally got their bridge they should name it after him out of sheer gratitude because surely it was only a matter of a very, very short time before the ferry collapsed and drowned someone – maybe that pretty young red-haired mother and her little girl. They'd be sorry then, wouldn't they, he thought with relish as he and the ferry reached the island shore and he stepped out onto its pagan land.

'Nice day for it,' Peggy greeted Philip as she waited by the landing stage with her loaded trolley.

'For what?' Philip Porter enquired, recognizing the rebel bargee and wary of what she might mean. She might think it was a nice day for shoving him back towards the way he'd just come, but without the means of the ferry. Something told him the residents wouldn't exactly be rushing to pull him out of the river.

'Moving house. Or boat,' she told him. 'Give me a hand with this lot,' she ordered, shoving the trolley towards the ferry and running over the front of his glassily polished shoe.

Philip squared his shoulders and obediently manhandled the trolley onto the ferry platform. It was precariously loaded with books, bin-bags full of what he assumed were soft furnishings, a stack of saucepans. Cutlery jingled in a basket at the bottom of the trolley.

'Performance art,' muttered one of the two old ladies knowingly, from where they lingered at a polite distance and watched intently. One of them cuddled her handbag close to her stomach as if afraid someone would ask her to open it and throw money into a hat.

'You're actually leaving then?' Philip Porter couldn't believe the luck of it. The old bag was going. He'd won, though without much of a fight. He'd been hoping to spend the day in the exciting pursuit of damning evidence – hygiene regulations abused, broken bye-laws – enough for an instant and dramatic eviction. Water bailiffs still existed, he was pretty sure of that, though whether they'd have been willing to come along with a removal order and tow away Peggy's barge with a hefty dredger or tug he wasn't sure. He could only hope. Now he felt curiously let down. Peggy's voluntary removal downgraded his efforts. Cheapened them. Ted Kramer must have said something, the right thing. The thing he'd just not thought of himself. It was tempting to tip the whole trolley into the cut and watch her cushions float downstream but he couldn't of course do that. It would count as litter and be quite against the grain.

'You're not ill, are you?' Stella asked Adrian as he lay inert and shallowly breathing on his side of the bed. She thought he very much resembled a cat lying low under a sofa in fear of a visit to the vet. 'It's not like you to stay in bed this late. I suppose you drank too much last night. I didn't hear you come in. You always creep about when you're pissed,' she said cheerfully, 'that way you think I won't notice. Once I saw you say "sshh" to your own reflection.'

Adrian groaned and wondered what to let her think. 'No, I'm OK,' he admitted, 'just, you know, post-book inertia, I suppose.'

'Oh *that*,' Stella said, climbing out of bed. 'We real people call it laziness.'

'You're being bossy again,' he grumbled from the depths of the duvet. 'Don't you have any sympathy?'

'Not when there's a lot to do,' she told him briskly. 'Ruth could need a bit of help today, selling her stuff. And there'll be people up and down the garden all day. It's a big day for her, she's never had to deal with real live face-to-face customers before. We might need to pick up the emotional pieces if she gets the sort who go round the summerhouse picking up and putting down and telling her how much they *don't* like everything.'

Adrian sat up and rubbed his eyes. 'You don't have much faith, do you? She might have sold the lot by eleven and spend the rest of the day counting her money and grinning at everyone.'

Stella opened the bathroom door, reached in and switched on the shower taps. 'Of course I hope she'll do well,' she told him, 'I suppose I just like to imagine the worst as a kind of insurance so that it doesn't creep up and surprise me. That way, the only surprises I *do* get are the nice ones.' With that she disappeared into the bathroom and started splashing about.

Adrian groaned, muttered, 'Bloody Pollyanna again,' and slid down under the duvet once more, wondering how soon he dare face the day and Abigail.

*   *   *

Abigail found the little doll under her pillow. She'd had a vaguely uncomfortable feeling all night that she wasn't the only item in the bed. It had one black-headed pin stuck right through where its heart should be and she knew immediately who'd put it there. She sighed and smiled to herself in the mirror. 'Ruth will like Sussex. Soon she'll be thanking me,' she said. She pulled the pin out from the doll's body with difficulty. It must have been baked in, she realized, wondering just how much damage its powers would have caused if she'd been inclined even the slightest bit towards superstition. She put the little doll in a drawer in the blue painted chest and closed it firmly. Venetia would love it, she knew, but somehow it didn't seem at all like a toy.

Willow floated around the gallery feeling important in a way she never had before, not even at her own exhibitions, or the first day she'd seen her work displayed in Liberty's window. Artistically, she felt she was Bernard's equal, that their work, arranged together like this, complemented each other's perfectly. She had been photographed with him, and being the opposite to Abigail in terms of superstitious leanings, felt that this somehow linked their souls. More importantly, they would appear together in the press, in art magazines and at least one (he promised) Sunday colour supplement. Willow dreamed forward to the next set of photos in which she would appear with Bernard. In them she planned to be wearing the antique Russian wedding robe she had kept wrapped in tissue paper and stored high above the damp level in her cabin, ever since the BBC costume auction that a psychic medium in Muswell Hill had told her she must attend. Thoughtfully, as she watched visitors nervously stroking her exhibits, she tugged at her straggly hair. When it grew this time it would be lustrous and golden, she decided. Not only had the man of her fantasies been lacking from her life for too long, but also a competent hairdresser.

Ruth was thrilled. She'd sold so much that the summerhouse was starting to look bare and it was still not quite lunchtime. 'You should have had a couple of boxes of spares under the table,' Melissa told her, sitting on the window ledge and eating a banana. Ruth, in black velvet to show off her finest silver pieces, thought Melissa's torn Levis lowered the tone and looked untidy, unprofessional. Presentation was so important.

'I'm not a factory,' she told her disdainfully, 'I'm an artist. If I make millions of the things I'll be into mass-production and that's not what people want. They want *unique*.'

Melissa pulled a distinctly unimpressed face, 'Well, you'll have to have more *unique* ideas then, won't you, if you want to get rich. Today's takings won't buy you a car.'

'They'd buy me a moped, second hand, easily,' Ruth retorted quickly. 'How many Saturdays behind some miserable dull shop counter would that take *you*?' she asked. She picked up one of the few remaining voo-doo dolls and threw it to Melissa. 'Here, stick some white pins in that. Perhaps you'll get lucky. Wish for something.'

Adrian thought it was safe to venture out some time close to lunch. Still exiled up in the bedroom, having had a slow bath and pretended he just didn't fancy breakfast, he could smell the barbecue in the MacIver's garden and decided that Ellen's sausages, with a roll and some onions, would make a very good brunch. Abigail and Stella would probably be safely out of the way in the boathouse gallery, drinking the wine that Bernard would be pouring into his choicest guests.

He sauntered out through the back door and went first to the summerhouse to see how Ruth was doing. He could hear footsteps from the path beside the house and the contented voices of those who'd bought something they liked from the MacIvers. 'A perfectly *sweet* mallard drake . . .' he heard an appreciative woman telling a friend, which he assumed referred to one of Fergus's paintings and not her plans for lunch. As he approached the summerhouse, nervous from Stella's morning conversation that Ruth might be in a blue sulk, nothing sold and her confidence shattered, the summerhouse door flew open and a selection of customers flew out in a bunch like racing pigeons from a loft at exercise time.

'*Well*,' an outraged beige-clad matron said in scarcely-hidden delight, 'what did you think of *that*?' Her companions, now level with Adrian, looked at him and sniggered. Oh God, he thought, quickening his step, they must have found a manuscript under a table or something and sneaked a shocking read. Thinking of what his *Maids of Dishonour* had been up to, he was surprised the women weren't in a collective dead faint. He ran to the door and flung it open. Inside, Ruth and Stella faced each other in fury over the black-clothed table. Melissa and Abigail sat together on the window ledge like an audience that wasn't sure how much participation was required.

'It's only *art*,' Ruth was shouting as Adrian went in.

'It's only *pornography*,' Stella yelled back. 'Just because it's painted doesn't mean it's not obscene. How *could* you? How many hours did he make you sit like that? I bet it was for a lot longer than it took for the work . . .'

'What's happening?' Adrian tried to make it sound like a perfectly normal enquiry. Ruth and Stella both glared at him and he looked away, meeting Abigail who gave him a broad and encouraging smile. This made him want to go straight out and get his sausages from Ellen's, but he didn't dare.

'It's Bernard,' Stella finally explained, 'I've just been up to the gallery and there's a painting of Ruth.'

Adrian could have laughed. 'Is that *all*?' he said. 'It sounded like World War Three when I came in.' He sat down next to Melissa on the ledge, joining the audience to see what would happen next.

'*All*?' Stella shouted, waving her arms. Adrian ducked. '*All*? Adrian you should just go out and see it. Down there in the gallery is a portrait of your daughter, naked as a newborn, legs splayed in a pose like something from one of your favourite magazines and all you say is "Is that *All*?"'

Adrian fidgeted uncomfortably, feeling the eyes of all the women turning on him in moral judgement. All except Abigail, he suddenly thought, she didn't go in for moral anything. 'Well, I haven't seen it, yet,' he shrugged. 'I mean, Bernard is fairly renowned and all that,' he said feebly, 'I expect it's perfectly above board . . .'

'No, it isn't,' Ruth said quietly. 'But it's my choice, I haven't been exploited or used. I wanted him to paint me, it felt like an honour. I wanted him to make love to me too,' she admitted, looking across at Abigail as if drawing courage. 'And he did,' she added simply, her brave face blazing with spots of pink colour.

'It's not that,' Stella said more quietly, 'it's just the pose. If he'd asked you to be photographed like that you'd have given him a sharp lecture on feminism. But you'd do it for a painting,' she sighed, puzzling to find a viable difference and wondering how much of a philistine she was for failing. The painting hadn't been on view the day before when she'd visited the gallery, she recalled. Perhaps even cowardly Bernard had thought it better to keep it away from the general neighbourly preview.

'It's just that she's your daughter,' Abigail contributed.

'Well yes, Abigail, I think that it probably is. But only partly. Thank you for reminding me of that,' Stella fumed.

'Why don't we just go and get some lunch at Ellen's and talk about this later?' Adrian suggested, feeling a change of venue and a degree of levity was called for. Stella glared but everyone else immediately headed for the door, causing a sudden crush. Abigail squeezed past him, and Adrian could feel Stella watching as she slid her breasts across the front of his sweatshirt. Involuntarily his hand came up to brush at the fabric as if she'd left a trail, sticky like a snail over carpet.

'I'll stay and do the selling,' Melissa told Ruth, looking relieved at the prospect of being left alone.

The MacIvers' garden was full of island residents who'd either sold out of stock or given up for the day. Empty bottles sat among the begonias and salvias. Venetia and James sat tormenting Ellen's aged tortoise, trying to get it to race between them for dandelion leaves. Toby was sprawled on the MacIver's lawn with his eyes closed, one hand on Giuliana's golden thigh and the other clutching a can of beer.

'He looks like he's gone to heaven,' Abigail commented to Stella. Stella felt like a child having difficulty coming out of a severe sulk. Perhaps she had over-reacted to the painting of Ruth. It wasn't that it was *recognizably* her. She wasn't feeling 'what will the neighbours say' about it at all.

'Giuliana's a beautiful girl,' she agreed. 'Well, *woman* really, isn't she?'

'Oh, she's not that much older than him,' Abigail commented, making the contrary Stella feel that she was being humoured.

Adrian headed quickly for the barbecue, collected food for all of them and went to join Toby and Giuliana. He had a basic parental certainty that they'd all feel better when they'd eaten something. And drunk something too, he decided, swiftly dashing into Ellen's kitchen and stealing a bottle of Chardonnay from the ice-filled coolbox under the table. Stella sat on the lawn next to her son and gazed out at the river. She could hear the gentle tinkle of Enzo's wind chimes. The afternoon should have been idyllic.

'It'll be much better when you're in Sussex,' Abigail suddenly announced to Stella as Adrian returned with the opened bottle. 'I'll give you the key now, shall I?' She fumbled in her bag and pulled out a bunch of keys, disconnecting the one for her car and handing all the others to Stella. 'I'm keeping the car,' she said with a grin, looking around at them all, 'I hope that's all right.'

'Why do I need the keys to your house?' Stella asked, mystified, and offering them back to Abigail.

Abigail laughed and pushed Stella's hand away again, 'To get in, of course! Take it, the whole place is yours, just like we said!'

'*Said*? Said what? When?' Stella trawled her memory to see if she'd agreed to house-sit or something, but nothing came to the surface. Perhaps Abigail had booked a sudden holiday for herself and the children.

'Oh, you remember,' Abigail was laughing, her hand on Adrian's arm, 'I asked you if you could live in my house and you said yes. So you can. It's simple.'

'I like it here,' Adrian said.

'But you're staying here of course, darling,'

'Darling?' Stella questioned, eyes widening. Something told her that Abigail wasn't using the word in the theatrical sense. Across the garden, Venetia was holding the tortoise too high. Tortoises were heavy things, she thought, it was going to be dropped, and hurt.

'*Yes*,' Abigail insisted. 'I would have thought it was no problem for people like you. Artists. Living here,' she waved her arm round, imperiously including the whole population of the island, 'swopping round, change of partners, all that. I told you ages ago I should have settled for what you'd got. And now I can. But *you*,' she pointed a spiky finger at Stella, 'you get what I've got. So it's all right, isn't it?'

'No,' Adrian and Stella spoke together. Stella looked at him sharply, trying, like someone who suspects they're being short-changed in a smart shop, to do some complicating adding up. However she added the one and one, it didn't come to three.

She resorted to straight questioning, the only possible way, 'Are you telling me that you and Adrian are having an affair?' she asked incredulously, lateral thinking taking her to the only possible, though unlikely conclusion.

'Yes,' Abigail confirmed.

'No,' Adrian denied.

'Well, which is it?' Stella sipped her wine, spilling some down her chin as her hand trembled. Toby got up quietly and wandered away. Stella watched him detachedly. He looked like just any man walking across a garden, avoiding some truth he'd rather not hear.

'He asked me to marry him,' Abigail explained, leaning forward in a confiding sort of way. For a second, still watching, Stella thought she meant Toby.

Adrian laughed suddenly, loud and raucous with relief. 'Oh *that*,' he yelled, '*that* was twenty years ago! I'm pretty sure I asked every woman I ever slept with to marry me in those days.' He turned to Stella and topped up her glass with wine, 'Gratitude, probably.'

'Sorry,' he then said, looking suddenly terribly

young and penitent, 'you didn't know I'd slept with Abigail, did you?'

Stella smiled coolly, 'I assumed you had,' she lied in an attempt to keep some kind of dignity. 'After all, she'd slept with everyone else, why leave you out? It would have been insulting.'

'But then there was the next time. It was just the same, same place, same sort of time of year, same everything really,' Abigail said, her eyes wide, marvelling at the coincidence. Stella thought she sounded as if she was describing a return visit to a monument. 'At Chameleon, you know, week before last,' Abigail prompted, looking to Adrian for confirmation.

'Oh fuck,' Adrian said, staring at the grass.

'Fuck's the word,' Stella agreed.

'Well not quite, not all round,' Abigail laughed mockingly, 'I mean, you didn't *quite* go to bed with that Simon you picked up at the hotel, did you, *Samantha*? I expect you will with the next one.'

'Who the hell's Samantha?' Adrian asked.

'Your oh-so-saintly wife, of course, who's always fancied a bit of the wild life on the sly, just like mine. And now she's got the chance. I'm beginning to think you two hardly know each other at all.'

Stella stood up, surprised that she still could. 'Look, I'm going home. To *my* home, the one down the lane. When you two have decided what you both want, do come and let me know.'

She walked out of the MacIvers' garden, passing Peggy and Ted on the way, pushing another overloaded trolley between them. A straggle of curious town visitors followed them, animatedly discussing art as a whole-life experience. Stella's feet, on the ground, felt like sponges full of water, heavy and hampered as they walked. At the gate, too shattered to go in and face possessions, furniture, sitting there just as if nothing had changed, she turned away and walked down the garden to Peggy's barge and clambered aboard. Ruth was there, down in the cabin surrounded by bin-liners and holding a duster. An unusual sight, Stella registered.

'This is all mine now,' Ruth explained, grinning hugely. 'Peggy's given me the barge. She says it would make a good studio and that we all need our own space. She says there's more than enough of it in Cornwall so she and Ted are going there to live.'

Stella smiled, 'That's lovely for her. And for you, of course. At least you won't have to go to Sussex.' She felt dangerously close to tears.

'God no, why? Who *does* have to go?'

Stella slumped down on the nearest bin bag and leaned on the wall, exhausted. 'Oh no one. Well Abigail, as soon as I can get her out of the house.' With or without your father, she added mentally. There was no point loading it all onto Ruth, she knew. Grown-ups' problems, to teenagers, were for magazine columns that weren't like 'Go Ask Alice'. They were something middle-aged and only slightly salacious in the back pages of sensible magazines, turned to in boredom in a supermarket queue.

Adrian drove to the airport, Abigail beside him, this bit of sorting out, for now, done. In the back of the car, Venetia and James jabbered excitedly about Concorde and their daddy. Abigail said nothing but sat looking contrite. 'It's all gone pear-shaped,' had been the last thing she'd said in the MacIvers' garden, which he'd assumed had been an admission of defeat. She hadn't uttered a word since. Even her hair was starting to droop. *She'd* never be pear-shaped, he was appalled to catch himself thinking, even now, as he drove her as fast as was legal out of the town. It had taken only three phone calls, he thought proudly, wondering where in his idle brain such organizational skills had been kept.

Just three phone calls and he'd found Martin, persuaded him to accept the return of his wife and children and booked their immediate flight to New York. He didn't trust Abigail to a taxi. She, in her strangely deluded state, might just have gone round the block a couple of times and come striding back in to claim him. Even now, and he glanced at her nervously, she might be under some mad impression that he was running away to the States with her. Martin would sort her out, he thought with optimism, as the car turned off the M4. That's what husbands were for. And after he'd checked Abigail and the children safely into the Concorde lounge, he'd go home to Stella ('Samantha' he thought with a tingle of excitement) and she could sort the two of *them* out. That was what wives who happened to be agony aunts were for, too.

The house was calm and empty now Adrian and Abigail had gone. Nothing of Abigail's remained at the house except a faint scent of perfume and the little cat curled up comfortably on its cushion in the kitchen. 'You can stay here if you like,' Stella told it, stroking its translucent ears. 'With me. Possibly even with *us* – we'll just have to see what happens.'

While she waited for Adrian to come back, Stella looked through the bag of problem post that had arrived that morning from *Get This!*, distracting herself with other people's problems. She wasn't too surprised when she picked the letter out and read its angst-filled confession about having a quick fling with 'my girlfriend's best friend'. Adrian had even used the same distinctive cream paper he used for his manuscripts and his hopeless lack of subtlety made her smile. The letter, just like the hundreds of similar ones she got, was full of too-late remorse, rueful regret. I should bloody well think so, Stella murmured, reaching across to the dresser for a pen. Next week's star letter, I think, she decided, beginning on the back of it to sketch out the reply she'd give.

'Well, for a start, she's not much of a friend, is she . . .' she wrote.

THE END

JUST FOR THE SUMMER
Judy Astley

'OH, WHAT A FIND! A LOVELY, FUNNY BOOK'
Sarah Harrison

Every July, the lucky owners of Cornish holiday homes set off for
their annual break. Loading their estate cars with dogs, cats, casefuls
of wine, difficult adolescents and rebellious toddlers, they close up
their desirable semis in smartish London suburbs – having turned off
the Aga and turned on the burglar alarm – and look forward to a
carefree, restful, somehow more *fulfilling* summer.

Clare is, this year, more than usually ready for her holiday. Her
teenage daughter, Miranda, has been behaving strangely; her
husband, Jack, is harbouring unsettling thoughts of a change in
lifestyle; her small children are being particularly tiresome; and she
herself is contemplating a bit of extra-marital adventure, possibly
with Eliot, the successful – although undeniably heavy-drinking and
overweight – author in the adjoining holiday property. Meanwhile
Andrew, the only son of elderly parents, is determined that this will
be the summer when he will seduce Jessica, Eliot's nubile daughter.
But Jessica spends her time in girl-talk with Miranda, while Milo, her
handsome brother with whom Andrew longs to be friends, seems
more interested in going sailing with the young blonde son of the
club commodore.

Unexpected disasters occur, revelations are made and, as the summer
ends, real life will never be quite the same again.

'A SHARP SOCIAL COMEDY . . . SALES ALONG VERY NICELY
AND FULFILS ITS EARLY PROMISE'
John Mortimer, *Mail on Sunday*

'WICKEDLY FUNNY . . . A THOROUGHLY ENTERTAINING ROMP'
Val Hennessy, *Daily Mail*

0 552 99564 9

BLACK SWAN

NO PLACE FOR A MAN
Judy Astley

Jess has just waved goodbye to her darling son, off backpacking to Oz. She's left with two teenage daughters and husband Matt – all of whom find themselves regularly featured in her popular and lighthearted newspaper newspaper column in which she conveys to her readers an enviably cheery muddle of family life.

Things become less rosy when Matt, after twenty years with the same firm, is made redundant. Only Jess sees the potential calamity in this. Matt is delighted with his new freedom and takes to hanging out at the local bar with others of the male barely-employable tendency, drinking and drifting and dreaming up hopeless schemes to make them all rich. Daughter no. 1, meanwhile, has taken up with a mysterious boy living in an abandoned car on the allotment, and her younger sister is over-burdened with a surfeit of secrets. For Jess, trying to hold everything together and missing her first-flown child, it becomes ever-harder to maintain the carefree façade for her readers. Of course she could just tell them the truth . . .

0 552 14764 8

BLACK SWAN

A SELECTED LIST OF FINE WRITING
AVAILABLE FROM BLACK SWAN

☐ 14721 4	TOM, DICK AND DEBBIE HARRY	*Jessica Adams*	£6.99
☐ 99822 2	A CLASS APART	*Diana Appleyard*	£6.99
☐ 99564 9	JUST FOR THE SUMMER	*Judy Astley*	£6.99
☐ 99565 7	PLEASANT VICES	*Judy Astley*	£6.99
☐ 99629 7	SEVEN FOR A SECRET	*Judy Astley*	£6.99
☐ 99766 8	EVERY GOOD GIRL	*Judy Astley*	£6.99
☐ 99768 4	THE RIGHT THING	*Judy Astley*	£6.99
☐ 99842 7	EXCESS BAGGAGE	*Judy Astley*	£6.99
☐ 14764 8	NO PLACE FOR A MAN	*Judy Astley*	£6.99
☐ 99619 X	HUMAN CROQUET	*Kate Atkinson*	£6.99
☐ 99854 0	LESSONS FOR A SUNDAY FATHER	*Claire Calman*	£5.99
☐ 99836 2	A HEART OF STONE	*Renate Dorrestein*	£6.99
☐ 99839 7	FROST AT MIDNIGHT	*Elizabeth Falconer*	£6.99
☐ 99910 5	TELLING LIDDY	*Anne Fine*	£6.99
☐ 99795 1	LIAR BIRDS	*Lucy Fitzgerald*	£5.99
☐ 99759 5	DOG DAYS, GLENN MILLER NIGHTS	*Laurie Graham*	£6.99
☐ 99801 X	THE SHORT HISTORY OF A PRINCE	*Jane Hamilton*	£6.99
☐ 99800 1	BLACKBERRY WINE	*Joanne Harris*	£6.99
☐ 99887 7	THE SECRET DREAMWORLD OF A SHOPAHOLIC	*Sophie Kinsella*	£5.99
☐ 99737 4	GOLDEN LADS AND GIRLS	*Angela Lambert*	£6.99
☐ 99697 1	FOUR WAYS TO BE A WOMAN	*Sue Reidy*	£5.99
☐ 99952 0	LIFE ISN'T ALL HA HA HEE HEE	*Meera Syal*	£6.99
☐ 99819 2	WHISTLING FOR THE ELEPHANTS	*Sandi Toksvig*	£6.99
☐ 99872 9	MARRYING THE MISTRESS	*Joanna Trollope*	£6.99
☐ 99720 X	THE SERPENTINE CAVE	*Jill Paton Walsh*	£6.99
☐ 99723 4	PART OF THE FURNITURE	*Mary Wesley*	£6.99
☐ 99834 6	COCKTAILS FOR THREE	*Madeleine Wickham*	£6.99